WICKED HO'

Bost<

Tess Summers

Seasons Press LLC

BLURB

The player doctor left behind more than a broken heart.

Dr. James Rudolf made Yvette Sinclair believe in fairy tales, and he was her Prince Charming. Then, out of the blue, he stopped taking her calls. Blocked them would be a more accurate descriptor.

Devastated, Yvette had no idea why the man she thought was *the one* had ghosted her. Even harder, she was three thousand miles away, so she couldn't just show up at his house and demand an explanation. Then her best friend started seeing him around Boston—a different beautiful woman on his arm each time. She felt like such a fool.

She was determined to move on and forget all about the playboy. Until two pink lines made that impossible.

THE PLAYBOY AND THE SWAT PRINCESS

BookHip.com/SNGBXD Sign up here to receive my weekly newsletter, and get your free book, exclusively for newsletter subscribers!

She's a badass SWAT rookie, and he's a playboy SWAT captain... who's taming who?

Maddie Monroe

Three things you should not do when you're a rookie, and the only female on the SDPD SWAT Team... 1) Take your hazing personally, 2) Let them see you sweat, and 3) Fall for your captain.

Especially, when your captain is the biggest playboy on the entire police force.

I've managed to follow rules one and two with no problem, but the third one I'm having a little more trouble with. Every time he smiles that sinful smile or folds his muscular arms when explaining a new technique or walks through the station full of swagger... All I can think about is how I'd like to give him my V-card, giftwrapped with a big red bow on it, which is such a bad idea because out of Rules One, Two, and Three, breaking the third one is a sure-fire way to get me kicked off the team and writing parking tickets for the rest of my career.

Apparently, my heart—and other body parts—didn't get the memo.

Craig Baxter

The first time I noticed Maddie Monroe, she was wet and covered in soapy suds as she washed SWAT's armored truck as part of her hazing ritual. I've been hard for her ever since.

I can't sleep with a subordinate—it would be career suicide, and I've worked too damn hard to get where I am today. Come to think of it, so has she, and she'd probably have a lot more to lose.

So, nope, not messing around with Maddie Monroe. There are plenty of women for me to choose from who don't work for me.

Apparently, my heart—and other body parts—didn't get the memo.

Can two hearts—and other body parts—overcome missed memos and find a way to be together without career-ending consequences?

Table of Contents

WICKED HOT BABY DADDY

PROLOGUE

Yvette

She took a deep breath as she smoothed her hair, then swiped away any imaginary wrinkles on her skirt, before knocking briefly and at her boss's open door.

"Mr. Burton?" Yvette willed herself not to fidget as she stood at the threshold.

He looked up from his computer, his reading glasses sitting on the bridge of his nose. "Ms. Sinclair, yes. Thanks for coming down."

Like I had a choice.

Yvette hated feeling like she was going before the principal. She worked damn hard and did a good job, she had no reason to be worried. And yet, she couldn't help wondering why the president of her resort's parent company had summoned her downtown.

Nigel was a good-looking man in his late forties/early fifties, and while he was a bit stuffy, she usually enjoyed their exchanges. He started with his usual pleasantries, inquiring about her family and her upcoming trip to visit her friend Hope in Boston.

Blah, blah, blah. Just get on with it, already.

He looked down at a piece of paper in his hand. "It says on your resume that you're fluent in Spanish..."

Why did he have her resume in front of him? She tried to remember if she'd embellished on it. It had been almost seven years since she submitted it, so she couldn't remember.

"That's true. I've lived in San Diego my whole life—we're seventeen miles from the border. My mother felt it only made sense to start me learning the language at a young age." Plus, it'd been a way to stick it to her father, who'd wanted his daughter to learn French. "I spent a semester of college in Acapulco."

"That's great news. The reason I asked you here is we're looking to make a management change in sixty days with the property in Puerto Vallarta. I'm wondering if you'd be interested in applying for the position?"

Um, live in paradise? Yes, please.

"Roger is leaving?"

"He's being reassigned."

Her tilted head must have conveyed her unspoken question because he supplied, "We feel his talents would be better served at another property. We believe the Puerto Vallarta hotel should be doing better than what it currently is."

Ouch. Roger was probably packing his bags for Kansas or New Mexico. Those were the hotels where careers went to die.

"How much better?"

The Mexico properties were some of the division's top performers.

"Seven percent more efficient."

She felt her eyes widen. "That's ambitious."

Nigel gave her his smile that Yvette was sure he thought was comforting, but it usually just came off as smarmy. "We have faith in you, Yvette. Otherwise, we wouldn't be asking you to consider it."

"I have to be honest, sir. I'm good, but unless Roger was skimming, I think the best I could do is two to three percent without compromising guest satisfaction."

Nigel was undeterred.

"I'll send you the latest financial report this afternoon. Look it over, come up with a proposal, then let's schedule another meeting when you get back from Boston."

"How soon after I get back?"

"You've got some time. I'm headed to Europe for a few drop-ins, so we can plan on the last week in July. That should give you enough time to look things over and come up with a plan."

Drop-ins. Translated: surprise inspections. Those sucked. Even though her staff had the advantage of being able to recognize Nigel since he was in the same city, it also meant he stopped in a lot more than the other properties. His appearance always sent her staff into a tizzy.

She stood and grabbed her satchel. "I will look the reports over. If I don't see you before you leave, I hope you enjoy your time in Europe; try not to make it all work and no play."

"You know me, Yvette."

Actually, she didn't, so she wasn't sure what he meant by that, but she laughed like she did, nonetheless, as she walked toward the door. "See you when you get back."

CHAPTER ONE

James

"There he is!" his brother, Zach, called when James walked toward the high-top bar table he was sitting at. "I wasn't sure if you were going to make it."

"Sorry, the surgery went longer than expected."

Sitting next to his brother was their good friend, Steven—head of the ER Department at Boston General where James worked. "Everything okay?" he asked.

"In the end, yes, but it was touch and go for a while. There was a lot more damage than Miles was expecting."

"Fuck Miles," Zach grumbled, causing Steven to burst out laughing. Miles began dating Zach's ex-girlfriend Bridget just after Zach broke up with her when she wanted a commitment. Miles swooped in, causing James's brother to have buyer's remorse.

"Are you ever going to let that go?" Steven asked as the waitress set two draft beers in front of the men. James gestured to her that he'd have one, too.

"Nope," Zach said as he took a swig of beer, then set his mug down on the napkin with a thud. "At least not until I find a Whitney of my own."

Steven had just started dating Whitney Hayes, who he met when she was opposing counsel to Zach in a case not long ago, and he was already head over heels for her.

"Here's a hint, you're probably not going to find her in the strip club."

"You don't know that. The girl on my lap last night was telling me all about how she was working her way through college." He grinned. "Just like the one last week."

James shook his head. "You keep saying you want a woman with substance to settle down with, but your actions indicate otherwise."

"I do want that. But no sense in turning into a monk until I find her. You should try it."

James chuckled. "Try what? Finding someone to settle down with?"

"Well, that, too—if that's what you want. But I was talking about not living like a monk."

"Fuck you, I date."

"Eating lunch in the hospital cafeteria with a coworker who just happens to be female doesn't constitute a date."

"No shit, Sherlock. I see women outside the hospital."

That made even Steven's eyebrows go up. "You do?"

Zach looked at him skeptically. "When's the last time you got laid?"

Shit. When was *the last time?*

Deflecting, he replied, "When's the last time you knew the *real* name of the girl you were banging? Not just her stage name?"

Zach pulled his neck back. "Why does that matter?"

The waitress handed James his beer, and he raised it at his brother before taking a pull. "Kind of goes with that substance thing you claim to be looking for."

"Once I find my Whitney, everything will fall into place."

Steven gave Zach the side eye. "Just make sure she's not *my* Whitney. Our friendship goes back a long way, but I will still beat your ass if you even think about it."

"Oh, I've already thought about it. You forget, I've known her a lot longer than you. I told you, it was a good thing she kept me on my toes in court, otherwise I'd have had a boner every time I went against her."

"Did you want to get punched in the face?"

Zach threw his hands up. "That was before you even met her. Now, she's strictly, *Steve's girl, Whitney*. No more underlying sexual tension between us."

James had met Whitney; he exchanged a look with Steve that seemed to convey that neither believed the sexual tension was mutual. Zach didn't seem like Whitney's type, while Zach didn't really have a type—other than two X chromosomes.

"Anyway…" his brother drawled. "Back to you. Will you have to wear the brown robes to work, or are they only for the monastery?"

James extended his middle finger against his beer mug as he took a drink, which only made Zach grin broader. "Now I know I'm right when that's your only comeback."

Zach wasn't the only one who wanted his own Whitney. Except in the meantime, James wasn't interested in the one-night hookup anymore. That had gotten old and he'd found his right hand and a porn channel were just as satisfying as rolling over, pulling off a condom, and going home. For the record, he always made sure she came first—it made it easier to finish and go.

He wanted someone he could wake up next to and have breakfast with. Repeatedly.

And Zach was wrong; he had been dating, just not having sex. Women from the hospital, setups from friends. Hell, he'd even tried online dating, but he'd yet to find one he felt a spark with. A connection. His Whitney.

He really was happy for Steven, but damn if he wasn't a little jealous, too. Even Steven's sister Hope—who'd just moved to Boston—seemed to have found someone. If the rumor mill were to be believed, anyway.

"So, are you both still on for the Cape on the Fourth?" Steven asked.

"Yeah," Zach and James replied in unison, followed by Zach asking, "Is it okay if I bring someone?"

Steve frowned. "Who?"

"Dunno, haven't decided yet." Zach grinned as he tossed some complimentary popcorn in his mouth.

"Whatever," Steven said with a shake of his head, then looked at James. "You bringin' someone, too?"

"Nope. Just me."

"I'm just giving you shit. *You're* welcome to bring someone if you want."

Zach snorted. "He'd need to find someone to bring first."

"Eat a dick. I'd rather come by myself than have to pay someone to be my guest."

"Gross. That would be prostitution, which is illegal in the state of Massachusetts."

"Luxury goods count."

"There's nothing wrong with spoiling a woman."

"Keep telling yourself that's what it is, dude."

Zach wasn't an idiot. He was one of the best attorneys in the city, and his salary reflected it. He had money to throw around on his "dates," and wasn't under any illusion it was more than transactional. James guessed it worked; they all understood the score. Zach got a trophy date—usually close to half his age—and his companion got expensive shoes, purses, and clothes, and oftentimes, a trip to an exotic locale.

Win-win, he guessed. Except it sounded exhausting.

But just because it wasn't for James, didn't mean he should begrudge his brother. Except then he didn't want to hear Zach bitch about wanting substance and settling down. He couldn't have it both ways. And by all accounts, he wasn't.

Then again, James wasn't either. Actually, he wasn't having it *any* way. Maybe Zach was onto something.

****

Yvette

"Are you still able to pick me up tomorrow?" she asked Hope over speakerphone as she packed her suitcase for her trip to Boston.

"Of course!"

"It's no problem to get a taxi."

"You will do no such thing. I am happy to fight bumper-to-bumper traffic so I can pick my best friend in the whole wide world up from the airport."

"It's not going to work," Yvette said as she folded a dress and put it in the luggage.

"What are you talking about?" her best friend asked in falsetto.

"Your feigned innocence isn't fooling anyone. I'm not moving to Boston."

"But you haven't even been here," Hope whined. "You might love it."

"My job is in San Diego," Yvette reminded her. *Maybe Mexico*, a voice in the back of her mind whispered.

"Your very own bed-and-breakfast could be right here in New England."

"And I already told you, I don't have the money for that."

"And *I* already told *you*, I do."

"For the umpteenth time, friends and money don't mix."

"All I'm asking is that you keep an open mind."

Yvette knew there was no point arguing, so she conceded with a sigh, "I'll keep an open mind."

She hadn't told her best friend about the Puerto Vallarta offer. That was probably better done in person—and when she was boarding her plane *back* to San Diego, so she didn't have to listen to all the terrible things Hope could think of about moving to a foreign country.

Maybe she wouldn't tell her at all until it was a done deal. Yvette hadn't even submitted her proposal to Nigel. If he hated it, it would be a moot point. And even if he loved it, there were still a lot of details to iron out. No sense riling Hope up for nothing.

"All right, hot cakes, I'll see you tomorrow. I can't wait to meet Dr. Dick, although I guess I probably shouldn't call him that to his face, huh? What's his real name again? Evan?"

"Absolutely, you should call him Dr. Dick."

"I'm not calling him Dr. Dick to his face."

"He'd probably love it because he'd think I had been talking about his cock instead of his personality."

"I'm not convinced you're not talking about his cock."

"Oh, the moniker applies in multiple ways."

Yvette smiled as she zipped up her bag. "I predict you're married by this time next year."

"You're insane. I only fuck jerks, I don't date them. And I'm certainly not marrying one. *Especially* Evan."

"Mmm, I hate to break it to you, babe, but from everything you've told me, you're dating the good doctor."

"Nope, just having filthy sex."

"If you say so."

Her friend could call it what she wanted, but she was dating the guy. Dinners, spending the weekend together... he even let her move her boxes into his basement storage and gave her the lock code to his house, for goodness' sake.

"Love you. I'll be waiting for you in baggage claim."

"You don't have to park. Just pick me up at the curb."

Hope tsked. "I'm not letting my best friend and future business partner wait by the curb."

"You're relentless."

"I know. See you tomorrow."

Yvette clicked off and sat on her bed to mentally run through her packing checklist to make sure she had everything she needed. They were spending the holiday weekend at Hope's brother Steven's beach house on Cape Cod, then the week after visiting different B and Bs throughout New England. There was no doubt in Yvette's mind that all the places they'd be staying at would also be for sale—that's how Hope operated. Her BFF wanted Yvette in Boston, and she knew Yvette's dream was to have her own bed-and-breakfast. In Hope's mind, being a silent partner in a B and B would achieve both goals.

Hope had more than enough money. She'd received a patent for a revolutionary prosthetic she'd developed in her parents' garage. After working with Armstrong Labs to make her prototype a reality, every hospital in the world tried to hire her. Boston General won out, in large part, because that's where her brother worked as the director of their ER.

The hospital paid her handsomely. And still, Hope lived with Steven free of charge; her brother had scoffed at the idea of his baby sister paying rent.

"I need someplace to put my money," Hope had said when she'd first floated the idea of a bed-and-breakfast partnership once she'd come back from her initial meeting with the hospital board. When the realization the two best friends were no longer going to be together every day became a reality.

"Have you thought about a retirement account?" Yvette had quipped, knowing perfectly well her friend had an investment account. They had both set one up on a Friday night in college after they'd completed an Econ assignment about compound interest.

"My retirement is fully funded, thank you. Now, I want to invest in my friendship. Besides, this is really just me being selfish on my part. I need my best friend nearby."

"Do you know how many businesses fail in their first three years? I'd be losing *your* money if it wasn't successful. That's too much pressure."

"Oh, but my darling, what if you fly?" Hope threw back a framed saying Yvette had kept on her desk all through college.

"You're not fighting fair."

"You say that like you'd expect something different."

"Good point."

"Look, just don't say *no* yet, okay?"

"Fine, but I am saying, *probably not.*"

"Fair enough. We'll talk after you've visited Boston next month—that's all I ask. Besides, you're going to meet Mr. Wonderful while you're there, I just know it, so you'll be on board."

"You're awfully confident," Yvette had said. She didn't even try to hide the skepticism in her tone.

"I can feel it. Something's going to happen to convince you to stay there. You meeting Mr. Wonderful and us finding the perfect B and B makes the most sense."

"I think maybe you're confusing your own Dr. Wonderful from the elevator with my Mr. Wonderful."

"Please. I said he was handsome, but he was hardly wonderful. More like Dr. Dick."

And the nickname Dr. Dick had been born.

Hopefully, Yvette would meet him during her visit. Hope kept insisting he was an asshole, probably in part because that was normally her type, but he'd sounded like anything but. She bet that scared the hell out of her friend.

Unlike Hope, Yvette was ready to find someone and settle down. Unfortunately, the men she'd met lately held no long-term potential.

How funny would it be if Hope was right and she met Mr. Wonderful while visiting Boston? Maybe it'd be like a Hallmark movie. Big city girl visits a quaint bed-and-breakfast and falls for the grumpy proprietor who doesn't want to sell but has to for some dramatic reason. She comes in and saves the day, and they live happily ever after.

Except, it'd be more like Hope and her money saving the day; although Yvette was damn good at what she did, so she had no doubt she could contribute, too.

Your life is not a G-rated Christmas movie, she reminded herself. Cringing as she tried to think back to the last time she'd had sex—the G-rating felt more appropriate these days. She said out loud, as if that would make it true, "Definitely not G-rated."

What she wouldn't give for an X-rating—or at least a questionable R, at least in the bedroom, but more importantly, it'd be nice to have someone she cared about to do those things with.

Maybe someday. Who knows, maybe her Mr. Wonderful was waiting for her in Mexico.

CHAPTER TWO

Yvette

She spotted Hope on the escalator as she made her way toward luggage claim and let out an excited yelp as she ran toward her.

Her friend's grin was as big as hers as they hugged; rocking back and forth while holding on to each other. Finally, they broke apart and Yvette looked Hope up and down. She was practically glowing.

"You look amazing. Having great sex regularly is definitely working for you."

Hope looked around as if to see if anyone had overheard Yvette, then smirked. "You should try it."

"I agree. I need to find my own dirty doctor."

"Maybe this week."

She decided she wouldn't let her BFF get her hopes up about Yvette moving to Boston. "That would be perfect. Some dirty sex, then I'm back to California after a week with no complications."

"You're so full of it. You're the biggest romantic I know. And my sister is Ava Sterling, so that's saying something."

"If I had Ava's love story, I'd be a hopeless romantic, too." Hope's sister had landed San Diego's most eligible—and probably wealthiest—bachelor, almost by accident.

"Maybe you can find your confirmed bachelor and convert him this week," Hope said with a sly smile.

"Come on. Even Ava had to work a few months on Travis."

"Actually, I think it was the other way around. He was the one who had to convince her to marry him after she got pregnant. So, that's all you need to do, find a confirmed bachelor to knock you up, the rest will fall into place."

Yvette spotted her suitcase on the carousel and tugged it off. "You shut your mouth, Hope Francine Ericson. I think you're the one who needs to convert Dr. Dick."

Her tall, blonde friend patted a spot on her upper arm where she got her birth control shot. "No babies for me for at least two more years, and when I do finally have one, it will not be with Dr. Dick. We can't stand each other when we have our clothes on."

They walked toward the sliding exit doors, and Yvette slowed. "Really? You seem like you're spending a lot of time with someone you can't stand. You can't possibly be screwing the whole time."

"It's not *that* much time together."

"That's not what it sounds like to me."

Hope frowned at her, then groaned. "Okay, fine, he's grown on me. I can tolerate being around him when he's not naked."

That made Yvette burst out laughing. Only Hope would be upset about liking the guy she was screwing regularly. "There's nothing wrong with liking him, you know."

"I can't like him. There's no future with him."

Hmm, she was gonna call bullshit—gently. Being Hope's best friend for eighteen years had taught Yvette a thing or two about how to handle her. She needed to ease her friend into recognizing she was full of it. Otherwise, she'd shut down.

"Why?"

"He and Steven hate each other. No one can know that I'm seeing him. Steve would be so hurt, and after everything he's done for me... I just couldn't betray him like that."

Yvette cocked her head. "But aren't you already doing that just by sleeping with Evan?"

Hope opened the Tesla's trunk and lifted one of the suitcases with a defeated sigh. "Yes. And I don't need to compound it by making him my boyfriend. Besides, he's not looking for anything other than sex anyway. He likes the idea of pulling one over on Steve by sleeping with his sister."

"This sounds complicated," she said as she set her carry-on suitcase next to the larger one.

Closing the trunk, Hope grumbled, "You have no idea."

"When do I get to meet him?"

"Probably this weekend. He's going to be at the Cape, too." Yvette must have raised her eyebrows in surprise because Hope continued, "Not *at my brother's*. His sister rented a house not far from there though."

"That's convenient," Yvette teased as she got in the passenger seat.

A soft smile escaped Hope's lips when she started the car. "Kind of."

"You are such a smitten kitten. It's adorable."

"Am not. He's just really good in bed."

"Yeah, okay. You're right. A good-looking, smart doctor who's good in bed would probably be a bad choice for a relationship."

"You forgot about the part where he hates my brother, and vice versa."

Yvette could see how that could be a deal breaker for someone like Hope, whose family was close-knit. Her BFF had grown up in a traditional household, where everyone loved and supported each other. Compared to her dysfunctional mess of a family, it was almost scary how idyllic Hope's family was whenever Yvette visited. They'd welcomed her with open arms; Frannie Ericson treated her like another daughter—including her whenever she took Hope dress shopping for school dances or back-to-school shopping.

Yvette hadn't grown up poor, but her mother chose to spend her paycheck on "other" things, like breast implants or designer clothes, in an attempt to find Yvette a new stepfather.

It wasn't that her father didn't provide for his daughter. He paid his court-ordered child support on time without fail, but her mother always liked to point out food and rent were expensive, so there wasn't much left over for extras when it came to things for Yvette. Pierre Sinclair would buy her nice things when he came to see her, but he'd moved back to France not long after divorcing Yvette's mother when Yvette was six, so his visits were annual, at best. And he decided early on that it wasn't worth the fight with her mom to bring Yvette to France for the summer. It wasn't until her mother remarried when Yvette was in eighth grade that she relented and let Yvette travel.

Her parents were the classic example of people who should never have gotten married simply because there was an unplanned baby on the way. And was why Yvette was diligent about taking her birth control—so that never happened to her.

Seeing her BFF's family, with two parents who not only loved their children, but each other, gave her hope that she could have a happy family of her own someday. And she wasn't settling for anything less.

A problem for another day.

"Do you know why Evan and Steve hate each other? Maybe there's a solution?"

"Steve says Evan is jealous that he got the ER Director position instead of him. Evan scoffs and says that is not the reason, so I really have no idea."

"Well, if anyone can solve this mystery, Daphne—it's you, Fred, and the rest of the Mystery Gang."

That made Hope laugh out loud as she pulled into traffic. "Except Lola is no Scooby Doo."

*

"The traffic was even worse than usual. I think everyone is trying to get out of town at once," Hope grumbled when they finally pulled into a gated parking lot next to a luxury high-rise.

"This is where Steven lives?"

"Technically, although he rarely is there. He and Lola spend most of their time at his girlfriend's brownstone."

"Sounds like he's getting serious."

Hope pulled into a covered spot and shut the car off. "I've never seen him smile more."

"Have you met her?"

"Yeah. She's great. Had I met her elsewhere, I would have thought she was the perfect woman to set my brother up."

"Does your mom know about her?"

"Yep. I threw him under the bus when my mom started asking if I was dating someone."

"Ruthless." Yvette lifted her carry-on out of the trunk then gestured to the bigger bag. "Will this be okay here overnight?"

"It should be fine," Hope replied as she closed the trunk. "It's his own fault. He threw me under the bus first, so I didn't even feel bad returning the favor."

Yvette got to meet Whitney later that night when she came with Steven to pick up Lola and head to the Cape. In the short time they talked, Yvette came to understand what Hope meant about her being perfect for Steven. She was witty and intelligent, and there was something about her that made you immediately like her.

Being nine years older than Yvette and Hope, Steve had already left for college when Yvette started hanging around the Ericson home, so she only saw him when he was home on break. He'd always seemed so intense, but being around Whitney, he was relaxed and smiling and obviously happy.

"We'll see you ladies tomorrow," Steve said with a duffel bag over his shoulder while Whitney held Lola's leash and the pup's overnight bag as they walked toward the front door.

"We'll try to get there in the morning," Hope replied.

"I don't have to worry about telling you two not to be too early," he said with a laugh.

Ah, he knew them well. Neither girl was an early riser— one of the many reasons they had been such great roommates in college.

"We might surprise you," Hope said with a mischievous grin.

Which led Yvette to think Evan would be at the Cape in the morning.

If the man could convert her friend into a morning person, there was no doubt in Yvette's mind that Hope was a goner.

She couldn't wait to meet this guy.

****

James

His brother Zach honked the horn of his Corvette when he pulled up to James's brick Tudor in Moss Hills.

"You ready?" his big brother yelled out the driver's side window when James walked out of the open garage door toward the red sports car and noticed a life-sized Barbie doll in Zach's passenger seat.

Guess I'm driving myself. Which was probably just as well—who knew when his sibling would want to leave their friend's beach house, and he had to work Sunday night.

"Yeah, just let me grab my bag."

"I'll text you the address, in case we get separated."

Translated: *In case I pull over to fuck my passenger.*

James gave a thumbs-up and grabbed his backpack from inside the door, then threw it in the passenger seat of his Porsche Taycan.

Zach backed out of the brick driveway, and James followed, making sure his garage door was all the way down before pulling away.

He was looking forward to some time at the beach with his friends this weekend. He hadn't been to the ocean once this summer, so this trip was long overdue. Granted, it'd be nice to have someone to snuggle with next to the bonfire, but he hadn't had time to ask anyone—not that there was really anyone worth asking. But there were bound to be single ladies at the beach on the holiday weekend, right?

James was an eligible bachelor that women usually went out of their way to try to meet. He was handsome and in shape, made a good living, and had all the trappings of a successful career: a nice house, fancy car, and an impressive portfolio. The problem was that none of the women he met were long-term material, and that's what he was looking for. They were either too focused on their careers or too flighty, too political, or not informed enough, too intense, or too superficial, too this or not enough that. He wasn't sure what he was looking for exactly, but it seemed like he'd know her when he found her.

Maybe he should just get laid in the meantime. It had been a while, and as much as he wanted someone with long-term potential, perhaps a fling wasn't such a bad idea after all. Too bad he was deciding this on the drive after he'd already packed. Condoms were *not* in his suitcase.

Maybe that was better. Packing Trojans would probably just jinx his chances.

CHAPTER THREE

James

He pulled into the driveway of Steven's Cape house right behind Zach. His brother had managed to keep it in his pants for the whole drive—or at least he hadn't had to pull over. Although when his weekend companion exited the car, James was surprised he'd been able to. She was hot. Granted, her fake boobs were way too big for her petite frame, and she was wearing high heels with shorts, but still, she was nice to look at.

James could hear her giggling before he even got out of the car, and she pawed at Zach's chest with feigned disdain at something he said. Her Louis Vuitton bag hanging from her forearm, no doubt, compliments of his brother.

He couldn't imagine she'd have much to contribute to the conversation this weekend, but as long as she looked good on Zach's arm and blew him, Zach would be okay with that.

They stood at Steven's front door, waiting for their host to answer. It was taking a while. They could hear dogs barking inside, and Steven's SUV was parked in the circular drive.

"He left the hospital last night around seven."

"We're probably interrupting Whitney time," Zach grumbled as he pressed on the bell longer.

"Jesus Christ, I'm coming! Hold your damn horses!" came a voice from inside.

Steve yanked open the door in shorts and a T-shirt—his hair sticking up. With a smirk, Zach grumbled, "'Bout time, fucker. I thought I was going to have to crawl through an open window."

"You would've been out of luck, then. The alarm company makes sure this place is locked up tight."

Steven fist-bumped Zach, then James.

James felt bad for disturbing his friend. Steve hardly ever got a chance to get away. "Sorry to wake you up. I thought I saw you leave the hospital early last night."

"I did. But then we went out to dinner and had to pick up the dogs, so we still got here late."

Zach introduced his companion—her fucking name really was Barbie—and she giggled when she took Steven's hand before walking through the threshold. The look Steven gave Zach seemed to convey the same thing James had thought when he first saw her. Zach simply shrugged as he looked around and said, "I hope we're the first ones here. I wanted to make sure to claim the best guest room."

"You know where it's at."

Zach took Barbie by the hand, and they exited down the hall.

James looked through the sliding glass door at the patio and the ocean. "I'll be happy with a pillow and a hammock."

"That's probably a good thing because we're expecting a full house."

"Oh yeah? Any single ladies?"

"Actually, yeah. My sister, for one."

"Hope? I met her the other day. She seems great; Parker has been on Cloud Nine since she started. But I thought she was dating Evan Lacroix?"

"*What?* No, I can promise you she's not dating Evan."

Oh yeah. Steve and Evan have been on the outs ever since Steven got promoted over Evan. But James had seen Evan and Hope on more than one occasion, and there was absolutely something going on.

Still, he didn't want to piss his host off. "I guess I heard wrong."

"You definitely heard wrong. They've been butting heads since her first day."

They've been butting something, but it wasn't heads.

"I guess the gossips got it wrong. Wouldn't be the first time."

"And I'm sure it won't be the last."

"Hellllllo?" a woman's voice called from the entry, causing the dogs he'd heard earlier to start to yip with excitement.

Steven laughed. "Speak of the devil." Then yelled, "In the living room!" before walking away.

"Hey, James. Good to see you!" Hope said with a cheerful grin as she walked into the living room. Standing next to her was a woman with light brown hair piled in a messy bun on top of her head. She was shorter than Hope by at least six inches, but her legs were tan and toned, along with the rest of her. But it was her smile that made James unable to look away from her pretty face as Hope introduced them. "This is my best friend from San Diego, Yvette Sinclair. Yvette, James Rudolf."

As he took her hand in his, the first thought that popped in his head was, *This is my future wife.*

Which was quickly followed by *What the fuck?*

But he couldn't stop staring, and when their eyes met, the zing of electricity that bolted through his body made him catch his breath.

A blush crept from her chest to her face, so she felt it also.

Two dogs came bounding through the door and headed straight toward Hope, who kneeled and met them with hugs and laughter.

Steven appeared, with leashes in hand, and said to the dogs, "All right, you two, let's go outside!"

"I can take them," James quickly offered. He didn't know why he'd just said that. Maybe to make Yvette think he was a good guy. It must have worked because she chimed in with a soft voice, "We can help."

"Thanks," Steven replied, then gestured to the women's luggage. "I'll put your bags in my office. You guys will have to sleep on the pullout in there. Zach already laid claim to one of the guest rooms, and we're putting Whitney's friend in the smaller guest room."

"I'm sleeping in the hammock," James offered.

"Oh, we can sleep on the patio loungers," Hope said, making James perk up. Even if it was just sharing the same patio, spending the night with Yvette sounded like a good night. He glanced over at her, and she gave him a shy smile, like maybe she was thinking the same thing.

Steven handed his sister the leashes and kissed her forehead, then disappeared when the doorbell rang again.

Hope looked at James like she was trying to figure something out, then handed one leash to him and the other to Yvette. "You can let them off lead once they're outside. They'll stay close, they just get the zoomies, so it's better to just let them run it out." She glanced at her phone. "I need to reply to this message. Go ahead, I'll catch up."

James fought the urge to reach for Yvette's hand as they stepped onto the beach and instead leaned down to unclasp the leash from Ralph, Steven's dog's collar. Yvette followed and unhooked Lola from hers, and the two pups sprinted off.

It was fucking adorable how much Steven's and Whitney's dogs already loved each other.

"Do you have any pets?" Yvette asked as she watched the dogs disappear from view around the corner of the house.

"Don't laugh, but I have two cats named Tom and Jerry. Tom is completely anti-social, and Jerry loves everyone. They're quite the duo."

"Who's taking care of them this weekend?"

The two dogs tore past them to do another lap around the house.

"I pay my neighbor girl to come over and feed them when I'm gone. But last time, she asked if it'd be okay if she just stayed in my guest room. She's in college but lives at home during the summer, so I think she likes the break away from her family, especially her younger siblings."

"Makes sense," she murmured.

"Do you have any brothers and sisters?"

"I have a younger half sister and brother, but they live in France with my father, so I hardly ever see them."

"So, nobody to follow you around while you were growing up?"

"Nope, just me and my mom."

"Well, as the kid who followed his oldest brother around everywhere," he grinned as Lola and Frank raced toward the water, "let me just say... you missed out."

There was her beautiful smile again. He was going to have to be witty and charming all weekend to keep seeing it.

James couldn't help staring at her, and she tucked her caramel-colored hair behind her ear and glanced down nervously as she said, "What?"

That brought him back to reality. "Nothing, I'm sorry. Just reminiscing about what a pain in the neck I must have been for Zach."

They walked toward the beach—the surf and the seagulls screeching echoed in the air.

"Zach's your brother?"

"Yeah. You'll meet him later; right now, he and his date are 'unpacking.'" He used his fingers to make air quotations around the word *unpacking*.

She smirked as she brushed away hair that had blown in her face. "Good for them, I guess."

James wouldn't mind *unpacking* with Yvette.

"Yeah, you'll probably think differently once you meet them."

Yvette cocked her head as if confused.

"Trust me; you'll understand," James said confidently.

Ralph dropped a blue rubber ball on Yvette's foot and backed up as she picked it up to examine it.

"Where did you find this?" she asked. The two pups stared intently at the ball and stutter-stepped every time she moved it an inch.

She tossed it along the wet sand and they were off.

"What about you?" he asked. "Do you have any pets back in San Diego?"

"No. My mother isn't an animal person, so I never had any growing up, and I'm too busy with work now to be a good pet owner."

"What do you?"

"I'm the GM for a boutique hotel in San Diego. As a subsidiary of Marrion International, we have properties all over the world."

"Very cool. Do you get to stay at all these great places for free?"

"Not free, but almost."

"Lucky you. I'd love to travel more; see the world."

"That was the goal when I started in the industry. But I've found as I've gotten promoted and can now actually afford to go, I no longer have the time."

"Catch-22. You either have the time but no money, or money but no time." He understood it well.

"It seems like there's got to be a happy medium, right? I mean, I want to have kids someday, but I don't know how that would even be possible with how much I work. And, if I get the job in Mexi—" She stopped short.

"You're moving to Mexico?"

Yvette looked around like she was making sure no one could overhear her. "It's a possibility—but don't say anything in front of Hope. She wants to go in as partners on a bed-and-breakfast in New England, so I'll be closer to her."

"I like the idea of that."

She tried to disguise her smile. "You do? Why?"

"So, I can take you to dinner whenever I want."

"And, what makes you think I'd be willing to go?"

He shrugged, as if the answer was obvious. "The way you blush every time I look at you."

****

Yvette

Even as she felt the color flush from her chest to her cheeks, she grumbled, "I do not."

He grinned as he placed a hand on her hip. "I wish I had a mirror; you're doing it right now."

"It's because I'm hot."

The corner of his mouth lifted. "Yeah, you are."

Yvette rolled her eyes, causing James's face to fall. "So, you wouldn't go out to dinner with me?"

"I don't know... You'd have to tell me more about you first."

"What do you want to know? I'm an open book."

"Have you ever been married?"

"No."

"Serious girlfriend?"

"Not since college."

She narrowed her eyes. "Why? What's wrong with you?"

"There's nothing wrong with me. My mom says I'm quite the catch."

That made her smile, despite trying to appear skeptical. Although obviously, it was just a façade. The man was gorgeous and clearly in good shape, not to mention smart. And, if one of the cars parked out front was his, more than likely successful. Even though he was probably only thirty-four—she'd done the quick math based on the clues he'd given her—he was starting to grey around the temples, which was her kryptonite.

"No, seriously. Why aren't you married or in a relationship?"

"I'm an anesthesiologist in one of the best—and busiest—hospitals in the country, which means I work *a lot*. I'd love to find someone to settle down with, I just don't have the time to find her right now, let alone devote any time to falling in love with her."

She could understand that.

"What about you?" he countered. "What's wrong with you? Why don't you have a husband or boyfriend?"

With her sandals dangling from her finger, she spun on the ball of her foot in the soft sand and jogged toward the surf, calling over her shoulder, "Who says I don't?"

CHAPTER FOUR

James

No, no, no. She couldn't be involved with someone else. That would be the cruelest joke of all.

He started after her, trying to keep his voice steady once he caught up with her.

"Are you really?"

He must not have disguised his dismay very well because she took one look at his face and burst out laughing.

"No, of course not. Same as you, I'm way too busy."

He felt his shoulders relax. "Well, we're both available this weekend..."

"What are you suggesting? That we hookup this weekend because we both happen to be single and available?"

Yes, exactly. Except he got the feeling he wouldn't be satisfied with just a weekend with her.

"No, of course not."

It was far more than their schedules matching up that weekend. Yes, she checked his boxes: beautiful, witty, smart, and ambitious, but there was just something about her. He'd been enchanted with her since the moment he laid eyes on her.

"But maybe we could get to know each other better, and see what happens," he continued.

"I wouldn't be opposed to that," she replied softly. "For the weekend. Obviously, this couldn't be anything more. We live on opposite coasts. Maybe even different countries, soon."

Or maybe she'd buy a bed-and-breakfast with her best friend in New England, and he could take her to dinner whenever he wanted.

****

Yvette

Had Hope known this sexy doctor was going to be here this weekend? Did she have something to do with it?

Yvette wouldn't be surprised if her best friend had orchestrated the whole thing. A handsome, smart, charming, successful man with an athletic build who happened to have grey streaks in his hair? What were the odds? Hope probably had him go to the salon and add the grey.

Her best friend appeared not long after James's brother Zach and Barbie came down to frolic in the surf. The girl was beautiful in a high-maintenance kind of way. Zach didn't seem to mind. Yvette suspected the strips of cloth barely covering her modelesque body might have something to do with that.

"Hey!" her BFF called. "Do you want to walk the dogs down to the fish market?"

Ralph dropped the ball on Yvette's foot, so she picked it up and tossed it for him. "The fish market? You want to buy fish? Why?"

"Well, not necessarily *buy* fish. More like... just walk around."

"At a fish market?" James asked. "Kind of a weird place to pick to want to walk around."

"It's famous. I wanted to show Yvette."

Yvette smelled bullshit. "Yeah, because living in San Diego my whole life, I've never been to a fish market."

James started laughing.

Hope looked at him with a scowl. "Well, if you'd rather stick around and help Zach and Barbie build sandcastles, by all means, suit yourself. I'm going to head down to the pier. You have fun."

Yvette looked down at her own body; she was in good shape, but she was far from the model that Barbie was.

"No, no. I'll go," Yvette said as she leashed Lola up.

"Me, too." James whistled for Ralph and put the lead on him when he appeared.

They walked along the sand, chatting about what Boston and San Diego had in common and how they were different. James made her laugh out loud more than once—he really was witty. But even as gorgeous as the man was with the ocean breeze rustling through his hair, walking in the sand was starting to wear Yvette out, and there was no market in sight, just endless beach.

"You didn't tell me it was this far of a walk," she grumbled.

"I didn't know, to be honest," Hope said sheepishly.

Ugh. The realization that they still had to walk back after they reached their destination hit her. "We probably can't get an Uber back with the dogs, either."

"I can walk the dogs back, and you ladies can get a ride," James offered, his hand going to the small of her back. She liked the feeling until she realized she was probably sweaty.

She turned so she was out of his grasp but looked up at him with a smile. "Don't be silly. We all came together; we'll go back together."

Fortunately, they crested a dune, and the market appeared.

A good-looking couple walked toward the pier, and James mumbled, "Well, well. Look who it is..." Then he glanced at Hope with a smirk before calling out, "Olivia! Evan!"

So, this is Evan. Yvette could see why Hope would like him. He was exactly her type: tall, broad shoulders, and pretty blue eyes. The woman with him was obviously pregnant, but as Yvette looked closer, she realized she was the feminine version of Evan.

"What's going on, James?"

The two men fist-bumped, and Lola tugged on her leash to get closer to Evan, her butt wiggling.

Evan reached down and scratched under her chin with familiarity. "Hey, pretty girl. How've you been?"

"We're here to celebrate the holiday at the beach. For some reason," James paused dramatically and looked in

Hope's direction, "Hope wanted to come down to the fish market. It's such a coincidence to run into you two."

"Isn't it though?" The pregnant woman said with feigned shock.

"It's a small world," Hope said with a nervous laugh.

"Yeah, that's it," James replied. "Small world. Nothing planned or anything."

Evan stood and put his hand on the pregnant woman's biceps. "Olivia, have you met Hope Ericson? She's with the prosthetics department at the hospital."

"No, but I hear your invention is revolutionary." Olivia smiled as she extended her hand. "Olivia Lacroix. So great to finally meet you."

"Same here," Hope said while shaking the woman's hand.

Evan stuck out his hand with a friendly smile. "And I'm sorry, I don't believe we've met. Evan Lacroix."

"Yvette Sinclair. Nice to meet you. I've heard a lot about you."

He didn't let go of her hand as he smirked at Hope. "Oh, you have, have you?"

"I told her how full of himself my mentor doctor is."

Olivia chuckled to her brother. "I like her."

Evan paid no attention to the insult. "Do you want to walk with us? We're going to get some cod. My niece—or nephew—needs some fish for her developing brain."

"Sure. If you don't mind," Hope said.

They walked along the pier, stopping at stands and inspecting fishermen's catches.

"Hope," Evan said loudly as he tugged on her friend's arm. "I wanted to clarify something about that patient we were discussing this week."

The two walked away together. James looked over where they were now standing at the railing and remarked, "Do they really think they're fooling anyone?"

"I don't think they do," Yvette replied. "But at least they can have plausible deniability. I think they're most worried about Steven finding out. At least I know Hope is."

"I'm flattered that they trust me enough to only quasi-pretend around me," Olivia said with a wistful smile as she looked over at her brother, enthralled with Yvette's BFF. "My lips are sealed around Steven."

Hope could say what she wanted about the two only being a fling, but watching them together, it was plain to see they were anything but.

The three left the lovers and walked further down the pier; James and Yvette stayed on the main boardwalk while Olivia went inside the market, leaving her alone again with the sexy anesthesiologist—not that she minded.

"Did you grow up in San Diego?"

"Yes, born and raised. Hope and I were best friends throughout middle and high school, then we were roommates in college at San Diego State. What about you? Are you originally from Boston?"

"No. I grew up in Chicago. Went to Northwestern for my undergrad, then University of Michigan for med school. When Zach got a job in Boston, I came for a visit. I'd known Steven for over ten years by then, and he recruited me to Boston General."

"Are you happy there?"

He paused while he considered her question.

"For the most part. Boston is a great city, I make a nice salary, and I have great friends."

"I'm sensing a *but*."

"Sometimes I just wish there was more to my life than work, ya know?"

"I understand that. And yet, if I get this job in Puerto Vallarta, I'm going to be working more than I do now because I'll live on the property and be available pretty much twenty-four seven."

"Oh, wow. You'll live at the resort? My first thought was, how cool. But I can imagine it would get old fast, not ever being able to get away from the job."

"Exactly, it's not like I can lounge by the pool on my days off and have my staff wait on me like a guest."

"And you have to live on the property?"

Yvette furrowed her brows. "I guess I never thought of it. It's considered one of the perks of the job, having free housing and all my meals provided."

"Makes sense you wouldn't live elsewhere then. Puerto Vallarta is a great city. Hopefully, you'll be able to explore it when you aren't working."

"I'm looking forward to that. I love the Mexican culture. I spent a semester in Acapulco when I was in college."

Olivia reappeared, holding a bag. "I have dinner."

"What did you get?" James asked.

"Cod. I'm going to a clambake tomorrow and I'm bummed that I'm not going to be able to partake."

"Oh, that's right. You can't have shellfish while you're pregnant," Yvette replied.

The pregnant woman sighed. "Nope. Just one more thing I'm not allowed for another five months. This kid better appreciate my sacrifices."

"He won't," James said with a chuckle.

"No, probably not."

"When are you due?" Yvette asked.

"The middle of December."

James asked, "Are you taking time off?"

"My allotted twelve weeks."

"Do you think you'll be able to go back that soon?" Yvette wondered out loud. "I know so many mothers who say they're going back, but when it comes time to leave their baby in daycare or with a nanny, they can't do it."

"I know, I have a lot of patients who do the same thing. Unfortunately, I can't afford to take any more time than that, since I only have about ten weeks of accumulated leave. By

December, I should have earned another few days, so hopefully, I'll only end up taking about ten days of unpaid leave. Fortunately, my mom will watch the baby three days a week, and then she can stay in the hospital's daycare the other two days."

"*She*? You're having a girl?"

Olivia shook her head. "I use pronouns interchangeably to keep people guessing."

"You don't know the sex, or you're not telling anyone?"

"Yes," the dark-haired woman cryptically replied with a smile as they all walked toward her brother.

"Did you two get that patient situation figured out?" Yvette called, fighting off a knowing grin.

Hope and Evan turned to look at them as they approached; Olivia held up her purchase.

"I guess we better get that home before it begins to stink," Evan said as he stepped toward them.

"We're having a bonfire tonight," Hope blurted out. "You two should swing by if you're not busy."

"Oh, shit," she heard James grumble under his breath.

Evan looked toward Olivia before slowly replying, "Yeah, we could probably do that. What time?"

"I'm assuming when it gets dark, around nine."

He looked at his sister. "Can you stay up that late, *mamacita*?"

"Yes, but I'm going to need a nap this afternoon."

"I better get this lady home then. Can you text me the address, so we don't show up at the wrong house?"

"No problem. See you tonight."

Evan leaned down, scratched both dogs behind the ears, then bumped fists with James before nodding at Yvette. "Nice to meet you, see you later tonight."

Yvette sighed wistfully as she watched them walk toward the parking lot. "They were smart and drove."

Hope hugged her around the shoulders. "Come on. I'll buy you some ice cream, then we'll make the trek back."

As they walked to the ice cream shop, James remarked, "You do realize the two of you aren't fooling anyone, right?"

She felt Hope's body stiffen, yet she airily replied, "Why, Dr. Rudolf, I have no idea what you mean."

James looked at them with a scowl, and Yvette gulped. Even his frown was sexy.

"Yeah, yeah. Just be careful tonight. I don't want your brother getting into a fistfight with Evan. We can't afford to be down two more ER doctors."

"I know. I'll be on my best behavior."

At least one of them would be. As Yvette looked at the sexy doctor scolding Hope, she wasn't so sure she wanted to be. When he looked at Yvette, his face softened into a smile so his dimples were on display. She decided being bad was the way to go.

CHAPTER FIVE

James

They sat on the ice cream shop's patio as they finished their ice cream cones. Yvette popped the last of hers in her mouth, threw her napkin away, then flopped back into the metal chair.

"I can't walk back. It's too far," she cried dramatically with her head thrown back. "You didn't tell me I'd have to walk a marathon—in the sand."

Even her whining was adorable. It made James want to tug her into his lap and kiss her pouty mouth.

"I know. I'm sorry," Hope replied. "But the ice cream had to have helped a little?"

Yvette pursed her lips. "A little. You still owe me, though," she said as she stood up and pushed in her chair.

Yvette refused to walk fast back to Steven's house. Instead, she purposefully strolled at a leisurely pace in the wet sand while Hope power-walked ahead. Once again, James had to resist the urge to grab Yvette's hand, while wondering what she'd do if he entwined his fingers in hers.

Hope finally paused and waited for them to catch up. Even as her friend waited, Yvette stubbornly didn't increase her pace.

"God, you're such a bougie bitch," Hope sputtered when they finally reached her.

"You say that like, one, this is something new, and two, it's a bad thing. I'm a bougie bitch and proud of it. And I don't know who you're trying to kid because you're even bougier than me."

"You think so?"

Yvette tapped her chin with her index finger. "Hmm, let's see. Owns a Tesla—that she paid cash for. Only wears designer labels with her designer purses and shoes. Goes to the salon every three weeks, gets a massage every other week... should I go on?"

"You forgot about the part where I'm generous with my friends."

"As much as I want to, if for no other reason than to see your reaction, I can't argue with that. You're incredibly generous."

"So are you." Hope looked at James. "She's smart, talented, beautiful, *and* generous."

Like he needed to be sold on how awesome she was.

"I believe you."

"Good. Now, can you get her to walk faster, please?"

"You can go ahead. I'll make sure she gets back safe."

James wouldn't mind some more alone time with her. Apparently, Yvette wasn't on board because she gave Hope a stern look. "I came all this way, Hope Francine Ericson. You can slow your roll and walk back with us."

Hope sighed dramatically. "Fine." The two women had him laughing the rest of the way back with their bickering. He knew it was done with love.

"Hey, brother. Where have you been?" Zach called from his beach chair when they finally reached Steven's house.

"We took the dogs for a walk, trying to wear them out."

Ralph and Lola noticed a stunning dark-haired woman sitting in a beach chair not far from where Zach and Barbie sat and tugged on their leashes with a whine. She appeared to be in her thirties, while a muscular, much-younger man frolicked in the surf in front of her.

The woman called, "Ralph! Lola! Come." And Hope and Yvette dropped the dogs' leads.

"You didn't do a very good job of wearing them out," Zach said with a grin as he watched the two dogs bound over to the woman. Hope followed behind.

James put his hand possessively on the small of Yvette's back, then turned toward Zach. "Have you met Yvette?"

His brother got out of his chair. "Not officially," he said with the grin he usually reserved for getting a woman's phone number.

James shot him a look that conveyed, *I will kick your ass. Back off.*

That didn't deter Zach in the least. Holding out his hand, he said, "Zach Rudolf. Oldest, sexiest, and richest of the Rudolf brothers."

"Well, at least he got the oldest part right."

Hope called to James, "Do we know what time the bonfire is tonight?"

"Probably at dusk."

James and Yvette walked to where Hope was chatting with the woman the dogs seemed enamored with. Zach was not far behind.

"This is Steven's neighbor, Zoe. I invited her and Rolando to the bonfire."

Zach extended his hand before anyone else could even respond. "It's a pleasure to meet you. I'm Zach."

The woman took his hand with a knowing smile. "Zoe Taylor." She gestured to the empty chair next to her. "Won't you sit down?"

Zoe looked at Zach, then at James. "I don't like making assumptions, but I'm going to guess you two are brothers."

"James Rudolf. And this is our friend from San Diego, Yvette."

Hope shot him a look when he said *our* friend. He simply smiled, then glanced over at Yvette. Her hair was coming out of her bun, and her cleavage had a sheen of sweat that he wanted to taste. Yeah, he considered her his friend, but he wanted a lot more than just her friendship. An image of her sweaty and naked underneath him popped in his head, and he pushed it away. Getting a boner would be hard to disguise in the shorts he had on.

Zoe had a certain air about her, assured yet friendly. She asked Yvette, "How do you like the Atlantic versus the Pacific?"

"It would be interesting to see the sun rise over the ocean rather than watching it sink into the horizon."

The women started talking about sunrises, and James had a sudden urge to watch the sun come up with her in his arms.

He zoned back in just as Yvette mentioned, "We're sleeping on the patio."

Zoe quirked her head. "You're sleeping on the patio?"

"All the bedrooms are taken," James supplied. "I called the hammock, and these ladies are on the loungers." But if he had his way, Yvette would be snuggled next to him tonight.

"Oh, that's nonsense when I have lovely unoccupied guest rooms."

Zach perked up. "Well, now I feel bad. Sending you guys next door. I should be the one to go."

Hope shook her head. "You and Barbie have already unpacked."

"Oh, yeah," he mumbled like he was embarrassed to admit in front of Zoe that he was sharing a room with the woman almost half his age.

Zoe gestured to where her date—also half her age—was playing in the surf with Zach's date. "It'd probably be better if they didn't sleep under the same roof."

A crooked grin formed on his brother's face. "You're probably right."

The two seemed like kindred spirits. Maybe Zoe was the "substance" Zach had been talking about. It was too bad neither seemed to date people their own age.

****

Yvette

"You and James seemed to be hitting it off." Hope smiled at Yvette through the mirror's reflection as she ran a brush through her hair.

Yvette sat on the edge of the tub in the guest bathroom. They'd come back to the house after getting everything situated for the bonfire to change into warmer clothes.

"Yeah. He seems great. Too good to be true."

Hope tilted her head. "What makes you say that?"

"I don't know. Rich. Successful. Smart. With greying temples? Come on. You had something to do with him being here, didn't you?"

Hope set the brush down on the counter and turned around.

"I swear to God, I had nothing to do with it. His brother is one of Steven's best friends. They all hang around together. He has a great reputation at the hospital as a very skilled anesthesiologist and a good guy, in general. Did I object when Steve told me he was coming? Not a chance. Did my wheels start turning when I saw you two together? Maybe. Am I thrilled that you guys seem to be hitting it off? You're damn right."

"We live three thousand miles apart."

Hope shrugged. "So, have fun this week. Get laid. You never know, he could be Dr. Right and you could decide to move here. In which case, you'll be glad we're looking at B and Bs this week."

Yvette pursed her lips, trying to disguise her smile. "You're relentless."

Hope turned back around to look in the mirror while she pulled her long blonde hair into a ponytail. "You know it, babe."

CHAPTER SIX

James

He was sitting in a camping chair next to the bonfire when he noticed Yvette walking toward the beach from Steven's house. She'd changed into yoga pants and a T-shirt with a sweatshirt tied around her waist, and she was laughing with Hope as they approached.

He couldn't take his eyes off her. The can of Modelo slipped from his grip, and he barely caught it before it dropped to the sand. Thankfully, it was almost empty.

She approached the group with a smile—the same smile that made him catch his breath when he first met her earlier today. When she caught him staring, she waved, and he gestured to the empty chair next to him.

Yvette held up one finger in the universal "wait one second" gesture and went over to the cooler, where she got caught up in a discussion with a group that included Steven and Whitney.

Evan and Olivia appeared. Evan carried a box of Summer Shandy and a six-pack of Sprite, and James tensed as the duo approached the cooler. He wasn't worried Steven and Evan would have an actual knock-down, drag-out fight—they managed to work together on a regular basis without even a raised voice, but there wasn't alcohol in the mix at the hospital, so it wouldn't surprise him if a punch got thrown.

James sprang to his feet and welcomed the new arrivals. "Hi, guys! Glad you could make it!" Then he guided Olivia to the green camping chair next to him. "You need to sit down, little mama."

She let out a deep sigh as she rubbed her lower back before sitting down. "You realize I'm never going to be able to get out of this thing on my own, right?"

That was the least of James's concerns. "There're plenty of people to help you with that. Don't you worry."

Zach appeared carrying two beers and offered the second to Zoe, who was sitting across the fire from James. Rolando and Barbie were deep in conversation to the right of Zoe, but instead of taking the empty chair next to his weekend date, his brother sat down next to Zoe.

After spending the afternoon engrossed in a conversation with Steven's beautiful neighbor, Zach had been incensed that the patio dwellers, as they'd come to collectively call themselves, were the ones staying at Zoe's and not him. Although James suspected his brother wouldn't be content in her guest room if she were in the master.

It was probably for the best since both Zach and Zoe were with other people this weekend.

As Zach handed the beautiful woman his second beer, James sarcastically offered, "No, I'm good, thanks." Zach barely glanced his way, too interested in talking to Zoe.

Yvette approached with a smirk and presented a beer as if she were Vanna White presenting a new puzzle.

"Your beer, sir,"

He made sure their fingers touched when he took it from her. There weren't any empty chairs, so he wanted to offer her his lap but opted for, "Thanks!" then grumbled loudly, "At least someone around here is considerate."

Again, Zach couldn't' give two shits about what his brother said. He was too enthralled in what Zoe had to say.

Interesting.

What alternate universe had James stumbled into where his brother was interested in having a conversation with a woman—fully clothed? He had to be in the Twilight Zone. Aiden, a recently single cardiologist who'd become grumpy post a very ugly divorce, was smiling next to Dakota, one of Whitney's friends. Dakota was a beautiful hippie chick and so polar opposite of Aiden's former wife, an uptight socialite. Hell, even Steven and Evan seemed to be getting along in this dimension.

James decided he didn't give a shit what universe he was in, as long as it included Yvette smiling at him like she was.

He jumped up and offered her his chair.

She waved him away. "I've got it," she said and turned toward the camping chairs still in their bags near the pile of wood that James, Aiden, and Zach had brought down earlier.

James was quicker than Yvette and pulled one from the stack, then set it up next to his chair.

He looked at Olivia, then at Yvette as he sat back down. "Surrounded by beautiful women, just like it should be," he said with a cocky grin as he picked up his drink from the chair's flimsy mesh cupholder.

Even though her lids were getting heavy, Olivia smiled.

Yvette rolled her eyes. "I'm sure the women you're surrounded with are usually fawning all over you."

Zach, who'd been blissfully busy in conversation with Zoe, snorted. Apparently, he hadn't been too wrapped in his discussion with the beautiful neighbor.

"The man's a monk. He wouldn't know it if a woman was throwing herself at him unless she was naked and grabbing his—" He paused and glanced at Zoe like he didn't want to say *cock* or *dick* in front of her. "Privates."

I'm going to kick his fucking ass.

Yvette didn't seem to notice his embarrassment, just gave him a soft smile. "Is that true?"

"Which part?"

She seemed surprised at his question. "All of it."

"Contrary to what my brother thinks, I am in tune with women and know when they're flirting with me. I just don't always reciprocate. Usually because they're a colleague, and I don't date people from work. And no, I'm not a monk, I'm just *selective* about who I spend my time with." He leaned closer and murmured, "Unlike my brother, who is indiscriminate about who he chooses to... *spend his time with.*"

She giggled. "I've kind of gotten that impression from him."

"What about me? What's your impression of me?"

Yvette glanced down shyly. "I don't know yet."

"You have to have at least had a first impression."

"First impression? You're very handsome."

He raised his eyebrows. "Annnnd?"

She shrugged, her voice going an octave higher. "I don't know? You're easy to talk to."

"That's it? I'm handsome and easy to talk to?"

"What else do you want?"

"How about, sexy? Dangerous? A man of mystery."

She laughed. "I'll give you sexy. But dangerous? A man of mystery? No, not in the least." The smile fell from her lips and she leaned over and whispered, "I'm glad. Dangerous and mysterious don't interest me."

"Not even a little?" he asked with a wink.

Yvette shook her head slowly while maintaining eye contact. "Not even a little."

"Well, if reliable and rich are your thing," he said with a chuckle. "Baby, you are in luck."

The corner of her mouth turned up. "Good to know."

He groaned internally. Why the fuck did he just say that? He might as well have thrown in boring and a snoozefest in bed.

"I mean, I can be spontaneous and exciting, too..."

The amusement was evident in her eyes as she nodded at him. James was trying entirely too hard now.

"Okay, I'm just going to shut up," he said with a self-deprecating smile.

She reached for his hand. All his senses woke up at her touch. "Aw, don't do that. I love talking to you."

Just then, Evan announced, "I need to get this mama-to-be home while she's still coherent enough to walk."

James glanced at Olivia, who'd just opened her eyes. She gave Evan a puppy dog look and held her hand out in the universal *help me up* gesture.

James jumped up to assist, and the two men got her up from her seat.

"I told you not to worry," he told her with a grin.

"Thanks. I appreciate it." She rubbed her pregnant belly and looked toward Steven's house. "I need to go to the bathroom before we head back."

"Let me show you where it is," Hope said, and she led the Lacroix siblings toward the lights of the beach house.

James watched them disappear into the night, then leaned down to murmur to Yvette, "You want to go for a walk on the beach?"

"I'd love to."

****

Yvette

James reached for her hand as they walked along the surf, and she noticed how comfortable she felt with him. Like holding his hand was the most natural thing in the world.

"What's your impression of New England so far?"

"It's nice. Charming. It feels like there's a lot of history here, ya know?"

"That's exactly what I thought when I first moved here."

"What about you? You must like it here; I'm sure there are a lot of places you could move to if you didn't."

"That's true. I'm sure I could get a job anywhere. But I like Boston General. Dr. Preston and Liam McDonnell are great to work for. Like I said earlier, I have a comfortable salary and great friends. Plus, my brother's here, and my parents have a vacation home in Vermont where they spend the summer so I can see them regularly. I can't complain. I have a great life."

That made her smile in the dark. She loved people who appreciated their good fortunes. "That's great."

"What about you?"

The question surprised her. "What do you mean?"

"Are you happy?"

"Um. I think so? I like my job, for the most part, and am ready for the next challenge. But I'll admit I've been lonely since Hope moved here. She's been my best friend since forever. My mom and I have gotten closer as I've gotten older, but she and Jerry, my stepdad, travel a lot, and my father and his wife, Juliette, live in France with my half-siblings, so I don't see them that often. There's nothing really keeping me in San Diego."

"So, you could move here without any hesitation..."

"Or take the job in Puerto Vallarta."

He adjusted their entwined hands and brought her knuckles to his lips. "Or become the owner of a New England bed-and-breakfast and let a handsome doctor take you to dinner every chance he got."

The moon was bright, and Yvette could see the intensity of his gaze. She had to admit; New England was starting to sound better and better.

"We'll see what we find next week."

"I guess it's in fate's hands," he murmured wistfully.

"I guess so."

****

James

He'd never wanted to kiss someone so badly. Then as if scripted in a bad romance movie, his ringtone for the hospital started going off as he leaned toward her.

If it were anyone else, he'd ignore it. But work wouldn't call him on his day off without a legitimate reason.

"Sorry," he said with an apologetic grin as he pulled his phone from his pocket. "It's the hospital, I need to take this."

"Of course," she replied graciously. "Do you need privacy?"

He answered the phone at the same time he shook his head at her and reached for her hand to keep her from walking away.

"James Rudolf."

The chief of staff, Parker Preston's, voice replied, "Have you left for the Cape yet?"

"I got here this morning."

"Dammit," his boss muttered.

"Everything okay?"

"Yeah, it's fine. We're a little short-staffed right now, and I was hoping to talk you into working this weekend. I'll make it worth your while to come back."

Normally, Parker offering to make it worth James's while would have enticed him to return to Boston and help out. The money would have been great, and being a single guy with no obligations afforded James the luxury of being able to leave on a whim—something Parker often used to his advantage.

James glanced at Yvette, who gave him a small smile as she swept her windblown hair from her face.

"Sorry, boss. I'm not available."

Parker chuckled. "Well, that's a first. Sounds like there's a story."

"Possibly." He didn't want to say too much in front of Yvette and freak her out.

"Good for you, James." There was a wistful tone in his boss's voice.

"I'll talk to you next week. Try not to work too much this weekend. It's the Fourth, for Chrissake."

Like that meant anything to Parker. The man practically lived at the hospital.

"Enjoy your holiday."

He glanced at Yvette again and couldn't help but smile.

"I plan on it."

He slipped the phone back into his pocket, his eyes never leaving Yvette. He'd just murmured, "Where were we?" when he heard Hope's voice exclaim, "There you guys are!"

He sighed as he watched her walk toward them in the wet sand. Even though the glow of the bonfire and the lights from Steven's house were visible from where they were standing, he'd thought they'd walked far enough away. Apparently not.

"Here we are," James replied, not even trying to disguise his annoyance.

"Sorry to bother you guys, but things are starting to wind down. I think Zoe wants to get us situated in her guestrooms, so we need to grab our stuff."

He couldn't catch a break.

When they walked back to the beach in front of Steven's, Barbie was sitting on Zach's lap, and Rolando was doting on Zoe again. None of them acted like the situation was anything but ideal.

James, Yvette, and Hope grabbed their bags from the front closet and reappeared at the bonfire. Only then did he notice Zach give Zoe a wistful smile when Rolando reached for her hand. The beautiful woman thanked Steven and Whitney for a lovely evening and said good night to Zach, Barbie, Aiden, and Dakota.

"Are you guys ready?" she asked, gesturing to her house.

James waved his hand in front of him. "After you."

His brother watched them go, then turned his attention back to Barbie at the same time Rolando grabbed Zoe's ass.

James almost felt bad for Zach and Zoe. It was obvious there was chemistry between them. Maybe they'd do something about it in the future when they both could.

CHAPTER SEVEN

Yvette

"I'm sorry you have to share a bed," Zoe said when she opened the guest room that Hope and Yvette would be sleeping in.

"It's no problem," Yvette replied as she set her bag down on the bench at the foot of the bed. The bed was a king—plenty big enough for the two women not to bother each other. Besides, Yvette would be surprised if Hope even slept there tonight.

Zoe opened the door across the hall and smiled at James. "And this is your room."

Their hostess did a quick rundown of where the bathroom and towels were, then gave a quick tutorial on how the TV remotes worked. They stood in the kitchen, and she said, "I'm on the other side of the house, upstairs, so don't worry about making noise, it won't bother me a bit. I won't set the alarm tonight so feel free to go on the deck, or..." She glanced at Hope with a smirk. "Wherever. *Mi casa es su casa.*"

The trio murmured their thanks and Zoe quickly disappeared.

James sat at the round table in front of a large window overlooking the dark ocean and counted the cards in the deck he'd found on Zoe's kitchen desk. Hope glanced at her phone and shifted her weight while Yvette moved to the chair opposite James.

"I'm going to go back to Steven's for a while."

Yvette nodded as James handed her the deck. With a smirk, she riffled the cards like a pro and murmured, "Sure, you are. Tell him we said hi."

"We won't wait up," James added with his own grin.

Hope rolled her eyes. "You guys think you're so smart."

"It's not like we need to be in Mensa to figure out where you're going."

Hope pressed her lips together to disguise her smile. Yvette liked seeing her BFF this happy. Evan seemed to be good for her.

"Have fun. I'll talk to you in the morning."

Her friend purposefully looked back and forth between James and Yvette. "You too." Then she spun on the ball of her foot, sing-songing over her shoulder, "Don't stay up all night."

The sliding glass door clicked shut, and Yvette looked at James as she shuffled the cards from one hand into the other. "So. What are we playing?

****

James

It was probably too juvenile to suggest strip poker. Still, the corner of his mouth quirked up at the idea—giving him and his horny thoughts away.

She raised an eyebrow. "So... gin rummy?"

"How about blackjack?"

"Blackjack?"

"I'll even let you be dealer."

She narrowed her eyes at him. "What are the stakes?"

He shrugged, trying to act blasé. "I win, you have to kiss me."

She seemed to mull it over and finally said, "And what if *I* win?"

He grinned. "I have to kiss you."

She didn't respond, so he laughed and tried to play it off like he was kidding. "What do you want?"

"Um..." She tucked her hair behind her ear and shifted in her seat, not looking at him when she murmured, "What you said works."

His heart was doing a happy dance while his dick started to stir. Again. This time he didn't even give it an internal lecture to settle the fuck down.

Yvette set the deck in front of him and handed him a red cut card. He slid it in the middle of the cards, and she palmed the deck to deal the cards.

The first two they each got were face down, while she dispensed the last two face up. A king of hearts for him, while she was showing a seven of diamonds.

James lifted the corner of the bottom card with his thumb—a ten of diamonds. With a grin, he turned the card over, revealing his twenty. "I'll stay."

She flipped her hole card, revealing a five of clubs. "Dealer has twelve."

He wondered if she'd be aggressive or timid when she kissed him and couldn't decide which he'd prefer. He gave himself an internal shake. He didn't care as long as her body was pressed against his when their lips met.

Yvette dealt the next card. An ace of spades.

"Thirteen," she said out loud.

She moved to flip the next card, and in his head, he chanted, "Face card!" Then his brain chided him. *Who the fuck cares?* It wasn't like he was really "losing" if she beat him. He was too competitive for his own good.

A two of clubs.

"Fifteen..."

"Oh, for fuck's sake," he grumbled.

She grinned at his impatience and lifted the next card from the deck, holding it in front of her to look at it before slowly and deliberately laying it on the table.

Her voice was barely a whisper when she looked at him and declared, "Twenty-one."

"You win."

Losing never seemed so appealing.

Without a moment's hesitation, he cupped the back of her head, then ever-so-slowly leaned in and gently tugged her bottom lip between his. Her lips were soft, and she smelled like flowers.

He felt her body relax, and when he deepened the kiss, she let out a little noise that was a cross between a whimper and a sigh that went straight to his cock.

James pulled her toward him, and she went willingly into his lap—never breaking their kiss as her arms snaked around his neck.

He dragged his lips to her neck, where he murmured against her skin, "Damn, I've been wanting to do this all day!"

With her fingers in his hair, she tilted her neck to give him better access and panted. "So why didn't you?"

He chuckled at her response while his hands roamed up her sides, under her shirt. "I wasn't sure if that'd earn me a slap."

"And here I thought you weren't interested because I was being too obvious."

That made him pause, and he lifted his head to look at her. "You weren't being too obvious. And even if you were, why would that make me not interested?"

"Oh, come on. You know... guys like the chase."

He nuzzled the hollow of her neck. "Mmm, the chase can be fun." He slipped his hand under her bra and rolled her nipples between his fingers. "But I prefer what happens once you've been caught."

****

Yvette

Oh my.

His cock pressed against her ass felt impressive, and he seemed to know pleasure points in her body that even she wasn't aware of.

Yvette wanted to yank her top and bra off her body to allow him easier access, but when she lifted the hem of her shirt, he pulled his hand away from her nipple and stilled her wrist. She let out a frustrated whimper. The ache between her legs only intensified when he pulled her top from her chest to leer unapologetically at her boobs under her bra.

"Perfect," he murmured before tracing his tongue along the exposed skin.

His hard dick told her he wanted her, but he didn't seem to be in a hurry to get her naked. Instead, he took his time, kissing and nipping her exposed flesh, but made no move to remove any of her garments.

She reached down and squeezed his cock over his shorts. "I think we'd be more comfortable in your room."

The lust in his eyes made her feel like a goddess. Without a word, he swiftly stood, holding her in a bridal carry, and made his way to his bedroom.

James shut the door with his heel and took deliberate steps to the bed, depositing her gently on the edge then kneeling between her legs. He drew circles over the black yoga pants on her inner thighs and looked up at her.

"Let me know now if we're not on the same page."

She smirked. "About what?"

James raised his eyebrows in warning. "About getting naked."

"Oh that..." She giggled. "If by *on the same page* you mean that we should get naked. Yes, we are."

"Good to know."

Without preamble, he pulled her yoga pants down her legs, tossed them aside, leaned closer to her drenched panties, and took a deep breath in, as if smelling her.

"Did you just sniff me?"

He did it again and looked up at her with a grin. "Yep, and you fucking smell delicious." Sliding his thumbs under her waistband, he inched her panties down. "I wonder if you'll taste as good as you smell." When he'd gotten her underwear off, he spread her legs to accommodate his broad shoulders and moved his mouth close enough that she could feel his breath on her wet center. "Let's find out, shall we?"

Yvette tightened her abs in anticipation of his tongue, but instead of licking her slit, he gently kissed and sucked her left inner thigh while his hands held her legs apart, immobilizing her.

It was a wonderfully tortuous tease like he'd done in the kitchen.

He grazed her clit with his nose, his breath hot against her folds as he switched to her right thigh. Again, he leisurely explored an erogenous zone she didn't know she had.

She wanted to cry out and beg him to touch her pussy, but she knew he'd get there—eventually. And she knew by the time he did, she'd fall over the edge in record time. So, she lay on the bed with her legs shamelessly spread and let him touch her in the most wonderful places.

She felt like Aphrodite being worshipped by Adonis. Normally, when she was with a lover who was going down on her, she felt self-conscious and never allowed herself to let go—usually because she knew the guy was only doing it so she'd reciprocate or that he felt some sort of obligation to perform.

But with James, it was like she was the one doing him a favor by allowing him between her legs and that if she'd let him, he'd stay there all night because he wanted to.

What a wonderful, empowering sensation.

When he finally ran his tongue down her seam, she arched her back, grabbed a handful of comforter, and let out a long moan of, "Oh yes!"

Yvette's body temperature rose as the beginning of her orgasm slowly crept from her toes.

"James, god that feels so good," she moaned when his tongue circled her clit, and he slid a finger inside her pussy. "Oh my god, just like that!"

She felt his smile and wantonly lifted her hips to grind against his mouth.

"That's it, baby. Let me taste your cum."

Chanting, "Yes! Don't stop!" Please don't stop!" Yvette fell off the cliff into orgasmland. She'd fight anyone who argued *that* wasn't the happiest place on earth.

****

James

He chastely kissed her knee and watched her reverently as she came down from her climax. Watching her come had been the hottest thing he'd ever seen, and his dick was leaking with how badly he wanted her.

With a soft smile, she ran her fingers through his hair. "Wow. That was incredible."

He'd never had any complaints, but his ego appreciated her approval.

"You are so fucking sexy. I could eat you all night."

Her hand went to her stomach, and she chuckled.

"What? It's true. You're amazing." To prove it, he swiped his tongue through her folds, causing her to jump, push his head away, and try to close her legs.

"I believe you!"

He felt satisfied he'd made his point and lay on the bed next to her, slipping his arm around her waist.

She rolled to face him and caressed his jawline. "Being the object of your desire is such a turn-on."

He did, without a doubt, desire her. She was his dream girl.

"I fucking you want you so badly, but..."

Her eyebrows lifted. "But?"

"I don't have a condom. I wasn't planning on meeting anyone this weekend."

Yvette slithered down his body so she was eye level with his fly and palmed his hard dick in her hand over his clothes. "We don't need a condom for what I have in mind."

"I'm clean... just so you know."

Unbuttoning his shorts, then slowly pulling the zipper down, she murmured, "Good to know. I am, too."

His cock was throbbing so hard, he swore he could feel his heartbeat in it. She pulled his shorts off to reveal his grey boxer briefs; they had a dark spot from where his dick had leaked while he'd made her come.

She stroked the outline of his length over the cotton, and he thought he was going to burst.

"I feel like I need to preemptively apologize in case I shoot my wad without warning. You're fucking hot, and it's been a while."

"Apology preemptively accepted," she said with a smirk as she shimmied his boxers down. His cock bounced when it sprang free.

Yvette took an audible intake of breath, then murmured, "Oh my," as she fisted his shaft and moved her hand up and down. "You have a beautiful cock."

"Thanks? No one's ever called it beautiful before."

She swirled her tongue around the helmet, and he closed his eyes with a groan.

"Oh, but it is," she said, pulling him into her throat.

"Fuuuuck!" he snarled as he weaved his fingers into her hair.

She moaned then slurped off his shaft, leaving it nice and slippery. Jerking on his cock, she lowered her mouth to his balls and took one in her mouth, swirling her tongue along the sensitive skin.

"Yvette, baby." He moaned as he tightened his hold on her hair.

Releasing him with a *pop*, she smiled up at him then pulled the other ball into her mouth while one hand still worked his dick in a slow, steady rhythm.

James closed his eyes because if he kept watching her, he was going to blow his load. He couldn't help but open his eyes when he felt her lips tugging on his sac.

She lowered her tongue to his taint, and he let out a long, low moan. "Oh fuck, baby. You are a dirty, dirty girl." He quickly added, "And I fucking love it," so she knew he meant it as a compliment.

The tip of her tongue ran up his balls and shaft, and she took him deep in her throat and held him there. The head of his dick pulsed in her neck a beat before she slowly slurped off him with her hand dragging behind her mouth to give him just the right amount of pressure. Then she repeated the process in reverse. Her hand ran down his shaft, followed by her mouth until he was deep in her throat.

She did this over and over... sensuous enough to make him crazy, but not enough to make him come.

Then, she sucked as she pulled off him. Increasing the tempo, she took him shallower in her mouth and worked his shaft from the base, her mouth and hand meeting in the middle.

It was fucking nirvana.

He whispered, "Baby, I'm going to come," when his balls began to tighten.

She ignored his warning and kept working his dick over.

James tugged on her hair. "Yvette..."

Their eyes met and a smile formed on her face while she kept going. It was so fucking hot.

He moaned louder, and he closed his eyes as he erupted with a long, "Fuuuuck!"

She didn't stop until he'd emptied his balls and was suddenly sensitive.

"Okay! Okay!" he yelped as she continued stroking.

Sitting up, she gave him a siren's smile. "Not nice, is it?"

"Lesson learned. I'll never do that to you again."

"Stay right there, I'll get you a towel."

James took a deep, contented breath as he looked up at the ceiling. Moments later, she was wiping his stomach. "Sorry, I'm a spitter..."

Spit, swallow; he couldn't have cared less.

"Whatever you are, it's amazing."

She tossed the towel toward the bathroom, and he pulled the covers back, turned to his side, and gestured for her to snuggle in next to him, then stopped.

"I'm sorry, no. You can't sleep in here."

Her mouth formed a little *O*, and she looked around the floor as if looking for her clothes. "Yeah, okay. No problem."

He leaned over and grabbed her wrist with a grin. "I didn't finish. You can't sleep in here with your shirt and bra on. This is a clothes-free zone, miss."

Yvette looked pointedly at his T-shirt with a hand on her hip and her eyebrows raised.

James reached behind his neck and pulled the offending material over his head, so he was completely naked. "Better?"

She looked him up and down as he stretched out on the bed and purred, "Much."

He put his hands behind his head and crossed his ankles. "Your turn."

With a seductive glint in her eye, she lifted the hem of her T-shirt above her navel and paused. James was entranced by her narrow waist, flared hips, muscular legs, and beautiful waxed pussy. When he'd pulled her panties off earlier and found her smooth, his dick almost punched through his zipper.

Slowly, she pulled it over her head, leaving her in nothing but a sports bra.

Looking down at her cleavage, she let out an embarrassed laugh. "I'm afraid there's really no seductive way to take this off."

He was itching to touch her. "I don't care, just get it off and get your naked body over here."

She turned her back to him and removed the bra. When she turned around, she was nude.

"Perfect," he muttered as he stared at her perky tits and pink, pebbled nipples. "So. Fucking. Perfect."

Tucking her hair behind her ear with a shy smile, she climbed into bed next to him, and James quickly pulled her flush to his body so they were spooning.

Her skin felt like electric satin, silky soft, yet it made him feel like a current was running through his body when he touched her.

His dick, which had never completely gone soft, was hard as he pressed it against her ass.

"You know..." she murmured while playing with the hair on his arms. "I'm on the pill. And since we're both clean..."

That was all the invitation he needed.

He flipped her onto her back and enveloped her body with his, burying his face in her neck. "I think it's going to be a long night."

With her arms around his neck, her hips moved in circles around his cock in invitation as she whispered, "Maybe we'll get to see the sunrise."

He pushed his cock into her wet heat, and they both moaned at the intrusion.

"Fuck your tight pussy until dawn? That sounds perfect."

CHAPTER EIGHT

Yvette

She lay in post-orgasmic bliss in his arms. She'd lost track of how many times he'd made her come last night.

I'm going to be sore tomorrow.

With her eyes closed and a dreamy smile on her face, she mumbled out loud, "Totally worth it."

James kissed her temple. "What is?"

"How sore I'm going to be later."

He squeezed her waist then dragged his index finger along her hipbone and down the crease of her thigh. "I can kiss it and make it better."

"You're insatiable!"

He drew his arms back around her waist and kissed below her ear. "Only for you."

"I've created a monster," she grumbled as she burrowed closer to him, only to be met with him removing their warm covers.

"Come on, baby. Let's go watch the sunrise."

"Nooooo. I want to sleep in James's love cocoon."

That made him chuckle, and he sat up. "We'll take a blanket. I promise the cocoon is portable. You wanted to watch the sun come up."

She let out a deep sigh then sat up. "Fine, but we're sleeping until noon."

"That works for me."

Yvette leaned down to pick up her shirt but he tsked.

She pressed the fabric against her chest. "We can't go outside naked!"

"We won't be naked; we'll be wrapped in a blanket."

"What if someone comes outside with us?"

"Who? Zoe and Rolando? Hope?"

Okay, probably not Hope; she'd give him that. Her best friend notoriously slept late even now that she had an important job in the hospital's prosthetics lab. She had it written into her contract: no meetings before ten.

"It's possible. We don't know if Zoe is an early riser."

"Fine," he grumbled. "Panties and bra *only*."

Yvette watched him put on his boxer briefs, then he pulled the comforter from the bed and held out his hand. "Come on."

They got situated on a lounger, Yvette in between James's legs with her back to his front. The chilly morning air originally woke her up when they walked onto the deck, but back in James's embrace, his warm skin lulled her back into a sleepy state.

They didn't speak when the tip of the sun appeared on the horizon, ushering in a new day. The orange ball rising slowly but surely felt like Providence, and the day suddenly felt like it was full of possibilities.

Movement on the beach caught her eye, and she saw Hope and Evan walking toward Zoe's beach house. Hope stopped, said something to him, then continued the rest of the way by herself.

"Good morning," Hope said as she walked up the deck steps. "I hope you guys didn't sleep out here. That'd kind of defeat the purpose of staying at Zoe's."

"No, we just wanted to watch the sunrise."

"It is beautiful," Hope said as she walked toward the door, not even giving the dawn's majestic light another glance. "I think it's going to be a great day, that I will enjoy later, because I'm going back to bed. Enjoy your sunrise, morning people. You freaks."

"Night," the two called in unison.

"She is *not* a morning person," James observed with a chuckle.

"You have no idea."

"Why do you think she got up so early then?"

"I think we both know the answer. So, she can give the illusion she was here all night and not with Evan."

The fact that she was willing to get up at dawn so she could spend the night with Evan said a lot about how much her friend felt about the man.

"That sucks that they have to sneak around. They're both single adults, for fuck's sake."

"Yeah, but it's complicated. Hope is really close with her family; she wouldn't want her brother upset with her."

"I'm close with my brother, so I get it. Although I don't know if I'd go so far as to let him dictate who I can date."

"I don't think they intended on anything other than a hookup."

He kissed her temple. "Funny how things sneak up on you when you least expect them."

Indeed.

****

James

They woke up in time to shower together before lunch. They soaped each other's bodies, and he rinsed, lathered, and repeated her breasts a few times before turning his attention to her hair. But he took to heart her quip about being sore and didn't initiate anything else. And neither did she, he noted.

After a quick lunch, they went down to the beach to play volleyball. Being on opposing teams made it easier for him to flirt with her.

He made sure to wink at her before his serve. She didn't disappoint with her response, blowing him a kiss from the other side of the net. All the while, the rest of their teams groaned and told them to get a room.

"They already did," Hope called. "You should have seen them this morning... all snuggled up together on the deck, watching the sunrise."

"What were you doing up so early, Hope?" he teased.

Her eyes got big, and she looked around. Zoe laughed from the sidelines as she poured what looked like sangria from a pitcher. "Relax, I saw Steven and Whitney leave a while ago."

"I have no idea what you're talking about," Hope replied, then pointed at James ominously and mouthed, "You're lucky."

He blatantly looked at Yvette. "I agree." His sweet girl looked away with an embarrassed smile. She couldn't be more adorable if she tried.

The volleyball game was the only time he was separated from her the entire day. It was tolerable because James had a first-row seat to her jumping around in her bathing suit.

He and his team—which consisted of Evan, Rolando, and Barbie, easily beat Yvette, Hope, Zach, and Aiden's team. Something that Hope had a hard time swallowing, so, of course, Evan and James had to keep talking about it.

Yvette pulled him away toward the surf. "This is for both your and Evan's sake."

"Aw, Evie, you're no fun."

"Actually, my assistant is Eve."

"So, what do your friend's call you?"

"Yvette," she deadpanned, then admitted, "Although sometimes Hope calls me 'Vette."

"No." He shook his head. "That's too much like the car. I'll think of something."

An hour later, while they were at the beach with the rest of the partygoers, Katy Perry's song came on. He wrapped his arm around her waist and swayed them to the beat as he nuzzled her hair.

"I have my very own California girl, right here."

And her nickname, California girl, was born. But what he needed was to make her a Boston girl—permanently.

CHAPTER NINE

James

The dazzling display of fireworks was nothing compared to the beautiful woman snuggled next to him on a blanket. Her eyes danced in wonderment every time there was a new burst of color in the sky. James would much rather watch her than the show.

Yvette nudged him with her shoulder. "You're missing the finale!"

Reluctantly, he took his gaze from her face to view the end of the show, ever cognizant of her body next to his.

"That was great," she said as she broke out in applause with the rest of the beachgoers.

"Not bad for a little island."

"Are they always this good?"

"I wouldn't know. This is the first time I've been here for fireworks."

"You'll have to come out to San Diego next year, They put on an amazing display."

"It's a date."

They'd both been carefully avoiding the elephant in the room, even though it hung over them like a heavy fog.

Finally, she leaned against him and sighed. "I can't believe it's our last night."

He couldn't either. He was scheduled at the hospital tomorrow night, but he didn't know how he was going to leave her.

"When do you go back to California?"

"On Thursday."

"And how long are you looking at bed-and-breakfasts this week?"

"We're supposed to come back to Boston on Wednesday."

"That works out perfect. I'm scheduled Sunday night through Wednesday morning, then I'm off all day Wednesday and Thursday."

Yvette cocked her head. "Is that true?"

James grinned. "It is now." He kissed her lips softly. "And we still have tonight. Let's make the most of our time together."

****

Yvette

Tears streamed down her face as she kissed James in the open driver's door of his fancy sports car late Sunday morning.

Everyone else had left, but James had stayed until the last minute he could before having to leave so he could get a nap in before his overnight hospital shift.

"It's not fair," she said as he brushed her tears away with his thumbs.

"It's only for a few days. We'll see each other on Wednesday. Let's plan on dinner and you staying over at my place. I'll drive you to the airport on Thursday."

The idea of getting on a plane to San Diego made her chest physically ache.

"Okay." Yvette nodded dumbly and took a step back. She knew he needed to get on the road.

James stepped forward and kissed her again, pulling her tight against his body like he didn't want to let her go. Finally, he broke the kiss and whispered, "I'll text you," before getting in his Porsche.

He started the car and rolled down his window. Yvette cupped his cheek and leaned in for one last kiss.

She was the first to pull away. Tears filled her eyes again. "Drive safely."

"I will."

Slowly, he pulled out of the drive. Yvette stood watching until his car was out of sight, then walked to where Hope was loading the car.

Her BFF hugged her around her shoulders. "You okay?"

"Geography is a stupid whore."

"You know, there's an easy fix for that."

"Your diabolical plan is coming together."

Hope clapped her hands in front of her and jumped up and down. "Yay! Let's go look at some bed-and-breakfasts!"

Chapter Ten

Yvette

She went inside and washed her face before she and Hope said goodbye to Steven and Whitney, then they got on the road.

"The first place isn't far—maybe twenty-five minutes," Hope said as she called up the mapping software on the dashboard.

"But we're not staying there."

"No, we've got reservations at another inn. I'll be honest, the realtor didn't sound very enthusiastic about either place, but since we have some time, I thought we should at least check them out."

Yvette found herself disappointed that the two inns they were looking at didn't have much potential.

Woah. Where did that come from? She couldn't go into partnership with Hope; she was just doing this little B and B tour to placate her friend. Right?

Ten minutes into the ride, Yvette's phone dinged with a text.

James: I miss you already. You sure you can't just come stay with me for the rest of the week?

Yvette giggled when she read it, then replied. **Don't you have to work?**

James: I'll call in sick.

"What did he say?" Hope glanced at her, then back at the road. "You're smiling like a lovestruck teenager."

"Nothing. He's just teasing, saying I should stay at his place this week instead of visiting these B and Bs."

"Ask him how I'm supposed to get you to move here if you do that."

Yvette shook her head and reiterated, "He was just joking."

"Ask him anyway."

Yvette: Hope wants to know how she's supposed to get me to move here if I'm at your place instead of looking at B and Bs.

He responded a few minutes later.

James: She and Evan can go look at them and you can video chat with her from my bed.

She snorted. "He says you and Evan can go, then video chat me."

"That's actually not a bad idea if we strike out this week. Evan and I can go, then I'll video call you."

Yvette hadn't told her friend about Mexico yet. Instead, she'd been trying to figure out a way to get Nigel to give her a hotel in New England. Surely someone living in cold country would be interested in going to Mexico.

Over the next few days, they wound up visiting two and staying at three different inns. Yvette was more disappointed than she expected when none proved to be anything either woman wanted to invest their time, energy, or money in.

James worked a lot, but he texted Yvette every day, often multiple times. His messages were the high point of her day.

She and Hope got in the car just after noon on Wednesday to head back to Boston. "We'll keep looking," Hope said when she put the car into drive.

Yvette knew she didn't have that much time before she had to give Nigel an answer. They were supposed to meet the last week of the month when he got back from Europe.

"Maybe you and Evan can keep looking. Are you going to see him tonight?"

"I don't think so. Things are getting too serious with us; I need to cool things off."

"Why is serious a bad thing? Especially at our age."

Hope came up with five different excuses why, but Yvette knew what it boiled down to was her friend was scared. She'd never had a man challenge her intellectually, emotionally, and sexually like Evan did. But Yvette also knew better than to argue with Hope. That wasn't the way to get through to her friend. However, Yvette didn't want Hope to think she agreed with her either, so she said, "I think you're wrong, and you're just scared." Then looked at the window and mumbled, "But what do I know? I've only been your best friend for eighteen years."

As expected, Hope ignored her comments and exclaimed cheerfully, "So, where are you and James going for dinner? Do you know?"

"No idea."

Her phone buzzed, and she instinctively smiled.

James: I got home earlier than I expected this morning, so I've already slept and am just putzing around until you get here. Not trying to rush you. I'm just letting you know I'm here when you're ready.

Yvette: You don't strike me as much of a putzer.

James: Oh, I can putz with the best of them, baby.

A picture of him puttering around the house popped into her head. It was such a domesticated image, and she realized that she wanted that for herself. And for her friend, too.

Yvette: Where are we going to dinner?

James: I thought I'd cook for you.

More domesticated bliss.

She should get the thoughts out of her head. She was going back to San Diego and possibly to Mexico. The chance of this becoming anything was slim, at best.

Still, she was going to let herself daydream. At least until she got on the plane tomorrow. Then she'd worry about reality.

CHAPTER ELEVEN

James

He gave his house a once-over, trying to picture it from Yvette's point of view. Her opinion of his home mattered to him for some reason.

He knew his place was nice. A five-bedroom, six-bath red-brick Tudor in the upscale neighborhood of Moss Hills. He had more room than he knew what to do with, especially after he had the basement finished and increased the square footage by a third.

His furnishings were expensive but tasteful, and the design elements weren't cluttered. He'd told his interior designer he didn't want to come across as pretentious, and he didn't want his housekeeper to have to dust a lot of crap. She was already charging him a premium for having to deal with the cat hair from Tom and Jerry.

Tom wrapped himself around James's ankle and meowed loudly. His damn cat was so adorable, James would have paid any amount of money his cleaning lady charged.

He leaned down and picked up the furball to nuzzle him for three seconds—about all Tom would allow before biting him. Jerry, Tom's cohort, was much more social. James knew the minute Yvette came in the house, Tom would scatter, and Jerry would appear from wherever he was currently lounging.

His security cameras alerted him to a car pulling into the drive, and James stepped out of the front door to greet Yvette and Hope as they got out of the Tesla. Yvette looked gorgeous in a red tank top that showcased her trim waist and toned arms. Her white jean shorts created a sexy contrast to her tan legs, and the nude sandals revealed her adorably candy-apple-colored toes. Her hair was pulled back in a high ponytail, and the only makeup she had on was lip gloss and mascara, making the freckles across her nose and cheeks obvious. She was the girl-next-door personified and his fucking wet dream.

"Wow," Hope said as she looked up his front walk. "This is beautiful. I had been considering a brownstone, but this is making me have second thoughts."

"I love the neighborhood. Come on in, I'll show you around."

She shook her head and walked to the trunk of her car. "I can't stay. I need to get to the lab. They're having problems and apparently..." She rolled her eyes as she lifted the trunk and hefted a suitcase out. "I'm the only person who can fix things."

At the same time, Yvette reached for a smaller, matching piece.

James grabbed the handle of the larger bag Hope had set down and reached for Yvette's as well.

"I can get it," Yvette protested. "They have wheels, you know."

He didn't release his hold on her bags. "Yes, but that's not how my mother raised me."

Hope smirked, and the resemblance to her brother was undeniable. "And they say chivalry is dead."

"Not on my watch."

Yvette's eyes filled with tears, and for a second, James thought she was about to cry because he'd taken her bag. Then he realized Hope was standing in front of her with a matching sad look.

Hope pulled her in for a hug, not letting go as she murmured, "I had so much fun this week."

Yvette sniffled. "Me, too."

The two rocked in an embrace. "When are you coming back?"

"I don't know..."

It'd be soon if James had his way.

"I'll make sure my realtor keeps her eye out for anything new on the market."

James felt his shoulders droop. They must not have been successful in their bed-and-breakfast quest. He knew they'd struck out the first two days, but he was hopeful about the one they'd stayed at last night. Unfortunately, he hadn't had a chance to talk to her about it since he'd worked all night.

When the two women pulled apart, they were both crying.

"I love you."

"I love you, too."

With a sigh, Hope walked to the driver's door of the Tesla. "Call me before you leave." Then she looked at James. "Thanks for taking her to the airport tomorrow."

"Of course." He wasn't going to say it was his pleasure because putting her on a plane was the furthest thing from pleasurable that he could think of.

Hope gave one more wave and got in her car. James put an arm around Yvette's shoulders and hugged her into him as they watched Hope back out of the drive.

"You okay?"

"Yeah, I'm just horrible with goodbyes. As you discovered last Sunday."

"Not sure if you noticed, but I didn't like saying goodbye last Sunday any more than you did."

She looked at him with a small smile. "I did notice that."

He nodded toward the house. "Come on. Let me show you my place."

Yvette snatched the handle of the smaller rolling case before he could, so he grabbed her free hand with his and walked her up the sidewalk to his front door. He felt it in his gut—she belonged there, with him.

They stepped inside and he immediately put his arms around her waist. Then, looking down at her, he gave her a soft smile.

"Hi, baby. I missed you," he said, then captured her mouth with his.

Her lips were soft and tasted like her bubblegum lip gloss; the smell of her lotion filled his nose. She felt familiar and right in his arms. When she darted her tongue in his mouth, their tongues began to tangle. He let out a moan and squeezed her tighter.

"Fuck, I'm so glad you're here," he said with his eyes closed and his forehead against hers.

"Me, too."

He wanted to drop to the floor and make love to her right in the foyer but didn't want her to think he was only interested in sex. He relaxed his hold on her and stepped back, reaching for her hand again.

"Let me show you around."

****

Yvette

"James, your home is stunning."

After their quick make-out session in his entrance that ended as quickly as it started, he took her on a tour—starting in the basement.

The first thing she noticed when they came down the stairs was the beautiful cherry wood bar in the corner. The rest of the huge room was open space, furnished with a grey leather sectional that seated at least twelve, two matching love seats, and two recliners. The biggest TV she'd ever seen graced one wall, and the back of the room housed a half-bath, arcade game classics, and pinball machines. There was also a guest room with a full bath.

"I'm guessing you're the designated host for all the major sporting events," she teased as she ran her hand along the back of the sofa. A black cat with white paws jumped up on the back and stared at her.

James picked up the cat and rubbed its head absentmindedly. "Yeah, the area behind the bar has a full kitchen, so I usually get the honors. Plus, I'm single, so it's not like I have a wife who will say no."

"Why would she? This place was made for entertaining."

He grinned. "Wait till you see the rest of the house."

He wasn't lying. The flow of the floorplan was perfect. From the family room, gourmet kitchen, beautiful formal dining room with a recessed ceiling, and formal living room, Yvette could easily envision large parties being held in the house, guests milling about the rooms. There were two bedrooms on the main floor, down a hall away from the living area.

The upper floor housed his office and an elegant master suite, complete with a sitting area that led to a balcony overlooking his lush backyard.

She stepped onto the terrace and took in the green grass, pool, barbecue area, and half basketball court.

"Your backyard is its own party space, too. Do you use your pool very often?"

"I do. I have a gym that's connected to the yard, so after working out, I usually get some laps in or sit in the spa."

She looked at the trees and flowers. "It's magnificent. The entire place."

He put his hands in his pockets and leaned against the doorjamb as he said sheepishly, "It's kind of big for just one person. I guess I bought it with my future family in mind."

Her heart squeezed. Why did the thought of being part of that equation seem so appealing?

He reached for her hand with a wink. "Let me show you the rest of the bedroom."

CHAPTER TWELVE

James

He circled his arms around her waist and looked down at her.

"Have I mentioned I missed you?"

She beamed back at him with her arms on his back. "You might have said something about that."

"Are you hungry?"

Please say no...

Running her fingertips up and down his spine, she whispered, "Yes, but not for food."

The corner of his mouth quirked up. "What a coincidence."

James kissed her gently, and just like in the foyer, she initiated deepening the kiss. He didn't plan on stopping this time; his bed was a much better alternative to the wooden floor of the entrance.

He felt her hands slide under his shirt and his dick got harder with the touch of her skin on his.

"Take this off," she whispered against his mouth as she lifted the fabric.

The shirt was gone in record time, and he raised the hem of her red tank top. Yvette lifted her arms, and he pulled the shirt off her, letting out a groan when she was left in nothing but a red satin bra and her shorts.

"You are so sexy."

She ran her hands along his chest. "So are you."

With her hands touching him like that, he felt ten feet tall and bulletproof.

James reached for the waistband of her shorts. "You should probably take these off, too."

She didn't raise any objections when he unbuttoned her denim, and even shimmied her hips to help as he pulled them off.

She stood before him in red satin matching underwear and bra.

"Fuck me," he murmured as he took her in from head to toe.

She looked down as if embarrassed.

"It's, um..."

He interrupted her as he skimmed his hands down her sides and rested on her hips. "It's fucking hot as hell, is what it is."

She gave him a siren's smile as she reached for the button on his jeans. "Tit for tat."

He didn't need any more prompting. Taking a step back, he undid the button and zipper, then shucked the material to his ankles and stepped out of the jeans.

"Better?"

She gave him an appraising look. "Mmm, much."

She let out a little shriek when he lifted her into his arms, pulled the covers down, and deposited her in the middle of the bed. He quickly joined her, hovering over her body, his weight on his forearms as he looked in her eyes that were the color of his coffee in the mornings after he'd added cream.

"Are you going to stare at me all afternoon or are you going to kiss me?" she teased.

He nipped her lips in reprimand, then slid down her body, so he was eye-level with her voluptuous tits. Tracing his finger along the outline of her bra, she arched her back and pressed against his hand. James pulled the satin down so both boobs were exposed to his probing hands and mouth.

He wasted no time pulling her right nipple into his mouth and running his tongue along the hardened peak. She let out a gasp when he bit down gently and dug her finger in his hair, holding his mouth to her chest.

With his left hand, he squeezed her right boob while grazing his thumb along the stiff point.

His tongue traced a line along her skin to her left nipple, where he suckled as she arched up. He could smell her arousal. It matched his wicked hard cock, and he couldn't wait to slide inside her.

He took advantage of her bent back and reached behind to undo her bra. The straps slid down to her elbows, and he peeled the garment away from her body and deposited it on the floor next to the bed.

Her freed tits were so beautiful, he couldn't help squeezing them together so he could alternate between them, sucking and biting her nipples.

With his hands still holding her boobs, James moved his mouth down her ribs until he reached her navel. He kissed along her flat stomach and moved his hands to the bed on either side of her to adjust his frame so his chest was nestled between her thighs.

There was a visible dark spot on the red satin, and his ego loved that he could make her soak her panties. She fucking smelled delicious, and he took a deep breath in to inhale her scent.

"You weirdo."

"I'm not even sorry. I love the way you smell."

Without warning, he mouthed her pussy over her panties, and she let out a little gasp and bucked her hips up. James held an arm across her middle to pin her in place as he teased her through the fabric until she begged, "Please, James."

He lifted his head to look at her face. Her eyes were closed, her mouth open, and her brows were drawn. "Please what, baby?"

"Please take off my panties."

She lifted her hips while he tugged her underwear off. Using both hands, he pulled her nether lips apart to peer at her glistening center. He dove in, exploring her folds with his tongue as he screwed two digits inside her tight channel.

Lapping at her clit, he slowly finger fucked her in a nice, steady rhythm. He sucked her pearl between his lips and increased the tempo with his fingers until he felt every fiber in her body tighten. He could barely fuck her, she was clenched so tight. James flicked her clit rapidly with his tongue, and she shuddered and lurched under him while crying out, "Oh my god, yes!"

"That's it, baby, come on my tongue."

He didn't relent until she put her hands on his head and squeezed. He took that to mean, *stop.*

She lay with her hand on her stomach, panting, and he crawled beside her with a cocky grin.

"Your tongue is magic," she whispered breathlessly.

He flipped her over onto her stomach, a pillow under her hips. With her legs pressed together, James slid his cock into her slick pussy,

"My cock is pretty good, too," he growled in her ear.

****

Yvette

The angle of his dick, along with the friction of the pillow and probably her heightened state, had her coming again at the same time James found his release.

Feeling his seed flood her womb as he grunted like a caveman appealed to her most basic desires. Having him wrap his arms tightly around her while he regained his breathing made her feel safe and protected.

"You are addicting," he uttered in her ear before rolling off and disappearing into the bathroom. He returned with a hand towel, but before wiping between her legs, he ran a finger along her seam then inside her.

"Seeing my cum in your pussy does something to me."

She looked back and saw he was hard again.

He smacked her ass and barked, "Lift your hips up. On your hands and knees."

Yvette did as instructed, then clutched the bedsheets tight when he began to rut her like a beast. The idea of him *having* to have her right then was such a turn-on, as was knowing he was using his cum and her juices as lubricant. He smacked her ass again, repeatedly, as he told her to take it.

It was the hottest thing ever, and when he gripped her hips and jackhammered into her, her body broke out into goose bumps from head to toe before she cried out in ecstasy.

Her orgasm must have pushed him to his own climax because he grunted ferally, then held her hips tight against him as he came deep inside her.

James lay his body on her back, his forehead between her shoulder blades, and his hands around her middle as he panted for breath.

She didn't dare move from her tabletop position.

Finally, he lifted his head and kissed her shoulder. "That was amazing, baby," he said, then swiped between her legs with the towel.

Yvette had a feeling his cum would be leaking out of her pussy for days, and oddly, she found the thought erotically appealing.

Something to remember him by, she mused with an internal sigh.

Tomorrow would be here before she knew it, and who knew what would happen once she returned to San Diego.

CHAPTER THIRTEEN

Yvette

She clicked End Call and fell back on her bed. Was it possible to be in love with James already?

She'd never been in love before. Maybe a few crushes here and there throughout her twenty-nine years, but she'd never felt like this before.

They'd only spent a week physically together, but oh, what a week it had been. And the sex... They got naked the first night they'd met, and she'd *never* done that. Not even in college.

And now, he was all she could think about. They'd talked for hours every night since she left Boston. But unfortunately, San Diego was three time zones away, so he was staying up a lot later than she was in order to be on the phone with her.

No, it was too soon. But she fell asleep once again with a smile on her face.

*

"Boston definitely agreed with you," her assistant Eve said when she brought in the week's occupancy reports. "You haven't stopped smiling for three weeks, since you got back."

Yvette pressed her lips together to try to disguise her happiness. However, she couldn't stop the smile if she wanted to.

"No, it's just our numbers have been that good."

"Mm-hmm. That's it. Funny, our numbers were just as good before you went to Boston, and they didn't make you this giddy. Are you sure it doesn't have anything to do with the sender of this bouquet?" Eve gestured to the gorgeous arrangement of flowers sitting on Yvette's desk.

"Maaaaaybe."

"Well, for what it's worth. He sounds pretty great."

"He is pretty great."

He was so great, in fact, that Yvette had found herself looking at the Boston job listings on Marrion International's website instead of focusing on the Mexico property like she should have.

Hope still hadn't found any B and Bs. Maybe Yvette could just transfer with her current company.

You're getting ahead of yourself. It was crazy; they hadn't even known each other a full month.

But it felt like she'd known him her whole life.

And the way James had been talking about their future, he felt the same way.

"Don't forget your meeting with Nigel this morning. I bet he wants to give you a big fat bonus."

Their numbers had been the best in the boutique hotel division of Marrion International. Of course, nothing compared to the mega-resorts the conglomerate also owned, but that would be comparing apples to oranges.

Although Yvette wouldn't say no to a big, fat bonus—she knew he had scheduled the meeting to talk about the Mexico job. She hadn't told her assistant about it yet. No need to upset her until she knew for sure.

The idea of moving to Puerto Vallarta now felt like a lead weight in her stomach. She wasn't sure how she could float the idea of getting a transfer to New England if she turned down the Mexico property. That is, if it was even offered to her.

"You should probably get going, you know how traffic is this time of day," Eve gently reminded her.

As she drove across town, she found herself secretly hoping that Nigel hated the proposal she'd sent. Then, in her "disappointment" at not getting the job, she could bring up New England.

Of course, she couldn't be that lucky.

"This is exactly what we were looking for," Nigel declared as he sat at his desk, flipping through the pages of the report she'd sent over.

Why couldn't she just be a slacker? Why did she have to take such pride in her work?

Yvette sat ramrod straight in the chair opposite her boss's desk chair with her hands on her knees.

"Nigel... I have to be honest. I'm not sure I want to move out of the country..."

He cut her off. "Before you make a decision, why don't you go and look at the property? Take some time to explore the city; walk on the beach."

She knew he thought she wouldn't be able to say no once she spent some time there. A month ago, that would have probably been true. Now her idea of paradise was in James Rudolf's arms.

Still, it would be in her best interest to at least pretend she gave it a shot. That would make it easier to ask for a transfer to Boston. Should she decide she wanted to do that.

"Yes, of course. You're right. I should go tour the hotel."

"Great. Diana booked you on the nine p.m. flight tonight and reserved you a suite for the weekend. The staff is expecting you, so you won't be able to go in anonymous, but this way you'll be able to talk to the employees and maybe some vendors, explore the grounds without restrictions, and get some honest guest opinions as you chat them up. You should have enough time to take in some of the culture of the city. As you know, experiencing things in person is completely different than reading about them on a spreadsheet or report. Take it all in and see what you think. We'll talk next week when you get back."

All she could think was *Puerto Vallarta isn't Boston*. Still, she knew she needed to play the game. So it looked like she was packing her bags and hopping a flight tonight.

James was on-call that night, so she'd have to talk to him tomorrow after she'd arrived in Mexico to tell him about her impromptu trip. She'd woken him up once before and had felt awful, so she always waited now until she heard from him first.

Hopefully, her cell phone plan worked in Mexico.

*

Yvette hadn't been able to reach James the entire weekend. She'd even tried from her makeshift office phone, but he must have thought her call was spam because it had been immediately rejected.

But her phone had worked. Eve had reached her in tears when Yvette arrived at the Puerto Vallarta airport and asked if she could crash at her place since her asshole boyfriend had locked her out of their apartment—again.

"Of course, you can stay at my place. You still have a key, right?"

Once Yvette was wheels down in San Diego, she turned her phone on and tried to reach James again, even willing to risk waking him up. Not talking to him for three days had been torture. She was more convinced than ever that she might be in love with him.

The phone didn't even ring, it just went to a fast busy signal, like the call had been dropped.

She tried again with the same result.

While they taxied to the gate, she typed out a paragraphs-long text to explain why she'd been MIA over the weekend and hit send.

Her phone buzzed immediately. **User not available.**

What the fuck did that mean?

She double-checked the number where she'd sent the text. It was the right one.

Had he gotten a new number?

Yvette pulled up her email and did a quick scan to see if he'd sent anything. He hadn't, so she opened a new email to him. Reiterating what she'd just tried to tell him in a text, she hit send.

Within seconds, she got the dreaded mailer daemon.

What was going on? Was he mad that he hadn't been able to get a hold of her over the weekend? This seemed a bit extreme—even if he was.

She dialed Hope's number as she walked down the jetway to the airport.

"Hi!" her friend answered enthusiastically. "I was just getting ready to call you! My realtor sent me an email about a new bed-and-breakfast that just went on the market."

Had this news come last week, Yvette might have felt more enthusiastic.

"I'm just getting back from Mexico. They want me to run their boutique hotel in Puerto Vallarta."

"I'm conflicted. I'm super excited and happy that you're being given a great opportunity that you deserve, I'm sad because I really want you to move here. I thought for sure James was going to convince you to."

"I haven't accepted the position yet. But speaking of James. Have you talked to him lately?"

"No, not since last week. I saw him this afternoon in passing in the cafeteria. Why?"

"Well, I think..." She took a deep breath; the idea of him doing what she was about to say out loud was still so foreign to her. "He might have ghosted me."

"What? No way. Totally not his style."

That's what Yvette would have thought, too, if it didn't appear that's exactly what he'd done.

"I don't know..." She told Hope about her texts and calls being rejected, and her email returned.

"That's super weird. Let me do some recon and I'll get back to you."

Yvette allowed herself to hold out hope that everything was just a mistake. Like, he lost his phone and all his contacts. Or maybe he was hacked and had everything electronically wiped out. What a nightmare that would be to go through. He'd probably been dealing with his banks and credit card companies all week. Poor guy.

He'd call her soon with an explanation and apologize profusely.

Her confidence waned as the week wore on. The only response she got from Hope when she'd ask for an update was, "Still working on it." Yvette somehow managed to put off giving Nigel a definite answer.

Friday night, she got a call around nine o'clock from Hope. It was midnight on the East Coast.

"You're calling awfully late," she said from under the blanket on her couch.

Her BFF sighed. "I went to the Animal Rescue gala tonight."

"That sounds fun. Did you adopt a new dog?"

"No. But I saw a big pig that I wouldn't mind butchering. He sat at our table."

Yvette had a feeling she knew who Hope was talking about but cautiously said, "Oh?"

"Oh, honey. I'm so sorry. James was there, and his date was the matching set to Zach's date. You remember Barbie? The girl he brought with him to the Cape."

It felt like her stomach dropped to her feet. Zach had brought a stripper—an actual stripper—with him to Steven's beach house over the Fourth.

"So, he really did ghost me," she whispered as the tears rolled down her cheeks.

"You're better off without him, babe. Now you can take that job in Mexico with no second thoughts. He's not worth another second of your time."

Oh, if only that'd been the case.

Yvette spent the rest of the weekend in a ball. Alternating between sobs of despair, feeling like she'd lost the love of her life and the will to live, to tears of frustration, wondering how she could have been so easily duped.

She called in sick on Monday, unable to find the energy to care about getting out of bed, let alone occupancy rates and guest requests.

Eve showed up at her apartment Monday after work with ice cream and chicken soup.

"I didn't know which you needed," she said, holding up both containers. "You didn't sound as sick as much as you did depressed, so I thought I'd cover my bases and bring both—just in case."

After a night with ice cream, rom-coms, and a pep talk from Eve and Hope—via video chat—she got up the following morning, put on her best power suit, and walked into Nigel's office to accept the Puerto Vallarta job.

Only to be sent home three weeks later by Mike Bejarano himself, the president of Marrion International; the only thing to show for her time in Mexico was a raise they were letting her keep and a new cat. And an extra three days paid off when he told her to "take your time packing—Nigel isn't expecting you back until Monday."

Since she didn't have much to pack—she hadn't moved her things yet—it didn't take her long. The most time-consuming thing was finding a store that sold a pet carrier to take on the plane. She was wheels up the next day.

She needed to find a new place to live. Once she'd accepted the Puerto Vallarta job, Nigel wanted her there immediately, so she gave her landlord notice via email, intending to fly back to box her things and ship them. She had a week left on her lease. Unfortunately, they'd already rented her place, so staying wasn't an option. It was just as well, a new place would give her a fresh start. She'd thought Mexico would be the answer, but in the three weeks she'd been there, they'd had fifteen weddings. Fifteen sets of happy couples so in love, she'd wanted to barf. At least the San Diego property catered more to families and business travelers, and she wouldn't have to be surrounded with that shit.

Yvette tried calling Hope several times over the next few days, but her friend didn't pick up. Although Yvette wasn't that upset about being fired from the Puerto Vallarta gig, she found herself sleeping a lot instead of packing. Between James and her job, she'd been put the through the wringer this last month. She deserved to let her body rest before she got up Monday and went back to her old job with her tail between her legs.

Fortunately, she hadn't burned any bridges on her way out. She knew better than that, so it wouldn't be that bad to return.

Saturday morning, she texted Hope's sister, Ava, about help finding a new place. Ava was a realtor, even though she had a PhD in chemistry, or something like that, and was married to one of the wealthiest attorneys in the county, if not the state. Hope said Ava was going to sell houses until their youngest started school, and then she was going to find something in her field of study.

Instead of texting back, Ava called her.

"Hey, honey! I would let you stay at the beach house, but we're letting Sloane Davidson stay there. He just got out of the hospital and Travis thought being at the ocean would be good for his mental health."

Yvette knew about Sloane—all of San Diego did. He'd been part of a convoy that had been hit by IEDs in Afghanistan. He'd survived, but many of his fellow soldiers didn't. Yvette could only imagine what he was going through both mentally and physically.

"That's really cool of you to let Sloane stay at your place."

"It's the least we could do. You know Travis is all about helping veterans."

That was an understatement. He'd been the title sponsor of The Wounded Warrior Project's ball every year for at least a decade. Frannie Ericson, Hope and Ava's mom, had been a volunteer for as long.

"But that's not what I meant when I asked for your help. I was thinking more of a professional capacity."

"Oh, I can definitely do that. Are you thinking about renting or buying?"

"I'm not really sure. I mean, I don't know if I could afford to buy anything. I know San Diego's real estate market is pricey."

"So is the rent," Ava countered. "Let's meet for lunch and go over some numbers. I've got time today if you're available?"

CHAPTER FOURTEEN

Yvette

Ava breezed into the café, looking like a million bucks in her cream-colored pants, baby blue silk shirt, and sensible cream pumps that still managed to look sexy on the blonde. Like her mother, Frannie, Ava's accessories were on-point. The aquamarine jewelry set was understated but elegant. She was tiny, especially compared to her siblings, and looked as beautiful as ever. You'd never know she'd popped out three babies in five years.

The beach house that Sloane was staying in had been a push present from her husband when she gave birth to their second child. Her third push present had been Travis's vasectomy and a week-long stay for her and ten of her closest friends, sisters, and Mom to Canyon Ranch in Tucson, Arizona. According to Hope, Yvette had been one friend away from making the cut. It had sounded like an amazing time.

Yvette waved at her to get her attention, and she walked over to the booth Yvette was at.

"You look fantastic!" Ava cooed as she slid into the vinyl seat across from her.

"So do you."

The waitress came to take their drink order, and Ava looked at Yvette. "I come here a lot, so I already know what I want. Did you have a chance to look over the menu?"

She had, so they ordered, and the server disappeared.

"I'm confused," Ava said, furrowing her meticulously groomed brows. "I thought you'd moved to Mexico?"

"I'm back. It didn't work out."

Ava studied her, probably trying to decide how much to pry. She'd been like Yvette's older sister, too, when Yvette was growing up, so the woman knew she had a lot of leeway with her.

"Are you looking for a new job?"

"Not right now. I think I just need to settle into a new place, then worry about changing jobs."

"So, you didn't get fired..."

"No, they didn't want that nightmare."

Ava raised her eyebrows and put her hands under her chin. "Ooh, do tell."

The server brought their drinks while Yvette explained the situation. When she was finished, Ava nodded her head, like she was thinking. "Make sure you get something in writing from Bejarano singing your praises—now, before you even go back to work. I'm surprised you'd want to go back after that."

"It's not ideal, and I know my time there is limited. But it's been a stressful month, I just need to get my bearings before making another change."

The server brought their food—a Cobb salad for Ava and a juicy cheeseburger for Yvette. Yvette took one sniff of her lunch and bolted for the restroom, barely making it to the stall in time before she lost her breakfast.

What the hell was that about? Had she picked up a dormant bug in Mexico?

After rinsing her mouth and splashing her face, she returned to the booth.

"Gosh, I'm sorry about that. I'm not sure what happened."

Her cheeseburger had disappeared.

"I ordered you something more bland," Ava said with a smile. "How you have been feeling, otherwise?"

She sighed. "Oh, you know. Other than just being tired and depressed, I'm fine."

"Yeah, Hope said you just went through a bad breakup. Are you seeing anyone new?"

"No, I haven't really had time to even think about it."

Ava chewed her salad slowly, then took a drink of her iced tea. "So, when was your last period?"

Yvette bit the inside of her mouth as she thought about it. "Um... right before I went to Boston."

"Which was, what, two months ago?"

"I guess. Why?"

"Well, there might be a reason you haven't had a period and are throwing up when you smell certain foods."

"I'm on the pill. I never miss one."

Ava shrugged. "So was I when I got pregnant with Alexander."

"What are you suggesting?"

"That you stop by the drugstore on your way home and buy a test."

She stared at Ava as she processed the woman's words.

Pregnant? Wouldn't that just be the ultimate *fuck you* from the universe.

CHAPTER FIFTEEN

Yvette

The two pink lines looked an awful lot like a middle finger.

Three days later, she was headed to Boston in her weighed down Honda Civic filled with everything she could fit in the trunk and back seat and her new cat in the passenger seat. She still had no idea when, or even if, she was going to tell James. She guessed she had three thousand miles to figure it out.

Maybe them breaking up before she found out she was pregnant had been a gift from the universe. She'd already come to view the little peanut growing inside her as a blessing. Maybe the universe had her back after all.

CHAPTER SIXTEEN

James

He pulled the yellow paper gown from the front of his scrubs, peeled the purple rubber gloves off, then wadded it all in a ball and threw it in the trash on his way out the double doors of the surgery suite. Leaning against the wall in the hallway for a moment, James blew out a deep breath while he pinched the bridge of his nose. That had been one long-ass brain surgery.

"Nice work in there, Dr. Rudolf," Amy Tees, the neurosurgeon who'd just performed the operation, called as she walked out of the OR and past him.

As the anesthesiologist, his role was important, but it was complementary to the surgery that was taking place. He'd seen thousands of different procedures in his career and worked with hundreds of doctors. Boston General's staff was top-notch.

"You, too, Amy. You did a great job."

The other doctor walked backward as she replied humbly, "We'll see how the patient does when she wakes up." Then she turned back around to head toward the waiting room to apprise an anxious family of their loved one's status.

He was glad he didn't have that role—especially when bad news was being delivered. Losing a patient was always a blow to the staff, but James couldn't imagine having to be the one to break it to a family.

"I need a shower and a drink," he said to no one in particular as he pushed off the wall and made his way to the locker room.

Evan Lacroix, was standing in front of an open locker when James walked in.

"How'd it go?" Evan asked when James pulled off his head cap.

"It went great. If I ever need brain surgery, I want Amy Tees to be the one to do it."

"That's what I've heard." Evan stood in front of his locker with his hand on the door but hesitated to close it like he was debating about something. Finally, he shut it and said, "You want to go for a drink?"

The invitation came as a surprise, but it wasn't unwelcome. Evan was now living with Hope Ericson, the little sister of one of his good friends, Steven Ericson, so the two men had started running in the same circles. They'd even spent the Fourth of July together in Cape Cod. The weekend his life was upended, never to be put right again—thanks to Hope's best friend.

"Yeah, that sounds good. I just need to grab a shower."

"Great. I'll be at Maloney's."

"Give me fifteen minutes, I'll be there."

As James showered and dressed, he wondered what prompted the invite from Evan. They were both going to Steven's wedding on New Year's Eve at the Dragonfly Inn later this month; maybe he wanted to talk about a bachelor party.

James chuckled at the thought of Evan attending Steven's bachelor party. The two men had been friends, then had had some sort of falling out. Steven had not been happy to learn his little sister was in love with his nemesis and fellow ER doctor. Fortunately, the two seemed to have patched things up—which was good, considering how close Steven and Hope were.

At one point, James had thought he and Evan would have to start hanging out more since he'd fallen in love with his girlfriend's BFF, and the two couples would spend time together.

That turned out not to be the case.

Fuck falling in love.

Now, when James dated, it was shallow and meaningless. The strippers his brother, Zach, set him up with were not relationship material, so there was zero chance of falling in love and having his heart wrecked again.

Before he'd met Yvette, he'd foolishly thought he wanted to meet someone and settle down. Then the girl whose brown hair with the streaks of blonde when the sun was shining on it, and a smattering of freckles across her nose after she spent the day playing on the beach, turned his world upside down. The thought of ever repeating that pain made his chest physically ache.

So, nope, never again.

He was all about superficial female companionship now. Maybe he'd even find someone at Maloney's to go home with tonight.

Evan was sitting at the bar when he walked in. The bartender leaning forward to display her cleavage seemed a lot more interested than just getting a big tip as she chatted the handsome ER doctor up. James knew the girl didn't stand a chance—he'd seen how Evan and Hope looked at each other.

He felt a pang in his stomach when he thought about how close he'd come to having that same thing. Now, he was considering taking a stranger home for the night to fill the void.

James sat on the barstool next to Evan, and the man turned his attention away from the cutie on the other side of the bar to cheerfully greet him. "You made it!"

"Of course. Although, I'll be honest, I was surprised you asked me."

"Yeah, about that." Evan took a pull of his beer before continuing. "You know Steven and Whitney are getting married New Year's Eve..."

So, this is about the bachelor party.

The bartender's bright smile started to wane at Evan's lack of interest. James winked at her and gestured to his friend's draft to indicate he'd have the same, and the woman disappeared.

"Yeah, they rented out an entire bed-and-breakfast not far from Steven's place on the Cape."

Evan looked around before replying. "You realize it's Hope's bed-and-breakfast, right?"

James pulled his neck back in surprise. "Hope's? I thought she was only interested in a B and B so she could go into partnership with Yvette."

Evan nodded his head slowly, letting James put the pieces together without saying anything else.

"So, Yvette…"

James felt light-headed as his stomach dropped to his toes. Yvette was *living* less than ninety minutes from him? The last he knew, she'd gotten the promotion in Puerto Vallarta.

Oh, and she had a boyfriend.

James wondered if the boyfriend had moved to Massachusetts with her.

"Look, man." Evan gulped his beer, clearly uneasy at having the conversation with James. "I need your word that you didn't hear this from me. Hope would have my balls if she thought I'd told you anything. All I'm saying, is you might want to check out the place *before* the wedding—like, maybe even this weekend, and you should probably register under an alias. And, definitely, do *not* take a date."

Fuck that. If Yvette was there, that's exactly what he was going to do.

His expression must have given him away because Evan gripped his forearm, brows knitted, and his tone anxious. "I'm telling you, as a friend. You need to go alone."

Evan had been at the Cape the weekend that James met and fell in love with Yvette. But James doubted he knew how she'd ripped his heart from his chest through his ass.

"She fucking broke my heart, man."

Evan didn't seem to care because his tone was insistent. "Listen to me. You need to go, but you will be sorry if you bring someone with you."

"What aren't you telling me?"

The other man shook his head and glanced away. He was beginning to regret telling James anything. "I can't say anything else. Just go to the bed-and-breakfast. By yourself, or at the very least, not with a woman. The sooner, the better."

James had no interest in seeing Yvette again. He'd blocked her for a reason, and it wasn't so he could go out of his way to run into her again. He'd learned his lesson with that tactic.

"I don't think that's a good idea. It's going to be hard enough to see her at the wedding."

"She's not going to the wedding."

James cocked his head. "She's not?"

"Nope."

"Why not?"

Evan shook his head, indicating he wasn't going to answer, and instead, finished the last of his beer then reached for his wallet, but James held up his hand. "I got it."

"Thanks." Evan slid off the barstool and pulled his leather jacket on. "Remember, we did not have this conversation, and if you say otherwise, I'll deny it, then key your Porsche."

James smiled and brought his beer to his lips but paused before taking a sip when he noticed Evan hadn't turned to leave.

"The Dragonfly Inn. Trust me."

"I'll think about it."

After Evan left, that's *all* he could think about. With no desire to find someone to hook up with, he went home alone and stared at the ceiling all night long.

Yvette was living in Massachusetts.

Had she tried to contact him? He wouldn't know, he'd blocked her number and her email. The only way she'd be able to reach him would be if she showed up in person, and any grand notions of that were dashed when he'd learned she'd moved to Mexico. The only other option would be through an intermediary. And Hope hadn't made it a secret how she felt about James these days. Like *he* was the bad guy for bringing a date when they were at the same event. Granted, if he knew Hope was going to be somewhere he was, he'd always been careful to show up with the most provocative woman available, knowing it'd get back to Yvette.

Or at least he'd hoped it would.

But now Yvette was here—in the same state. He could get in his car and be looking at her in person in less than ninety minutes.

Why would I want to do that? She'd ruined any dreams he'd had about living happily ever after—with anyone.

Still, he had to admit he was curious about what Evan wasn't telling him. That must have been the reason he found himself on the phone the next morning making a reservation for the beginning of the following week when he had two days off in a row. He used a fictitious name like Evan had suggested. *James Randolph* was close enough to his real name that he'd have plausible deniability it'd been on purpose.

Thank God it hadn't been her who'd answered the phone; he probably would have just hung up if it had been. If it had been her, James wasn't sure if she'd even recognize his voice although, she should, given how much time they'd spent talking to each other after she'd gone back to San Diego. They were on the phone for hours every chance they got, talking about everything and nothing, just like they'd had when they'd been together in July.

James remembered the two of them wrapped in a blanket on the deck after they'd made love for the first time the night before. They'd watched the sunrise while they shared their hopes and dreams for the future. That had been some romantic movie shit, and he'd fallen for her—hard.

He'd been such a fool.

If nothing else, maybe he'd get a chance during his stay at the Dragonfly Inn to let her know what a bitch he thought she was.

And he was bringing a date because, fuck her.

CHAPTER SEVENTEEN

Yvette

"If I have to pee one more time in the next hour, I'm going to scream," she said out loud as she got up from her desk and walked through the inn's lobby yet again on her way to the bathroom.

Still, she couldn't help but smile as she looked around at the Victorian bed-and-breakfast. The walnut wooden staircase, matching wainscoting, and tall ceiling with the intricate cornice—was beautiful. Perfect. And all hers. Well, half of it, anyway. It had been Yvette's dream to own a B and B, and it had come true, at the ripe old age of twenty-nine, thanks to the financial backing of her best friend.

She rubbed her ever-expanding belly—the cause of her constant urge to pee and the reason her walk was starting to become a waddle. The little girl growing inside her was unplanned, a shock actually, but if she hadn't come along, Yvette would still be running herself ragged in San Diego trying to get the next promotion instead of running her own bed-and-breakfast.

Finding out she was pregnant had been a blessing. After the Mexico fiasco, which she still had zero regrets about and would do again if the situation presented itself, rather than take her old job back, Yvette quit on the spot when she found out she was pregnant. Then immediately called Hope to take her up on her offer to be a silent partner in a B and B.

They were in escrow on the property within days of her arrival at Boston Logan. The timing was serendipitous considering they hadn't been able to find anything two months prior when she'd visited over the Fourth. And made a baby.

"Are you going to tell him he's going to be a father?" Hope had asked one night while they were eating dinner in Steven's vacant condo. He was letting Yvette stay there while she waited to close on their business venture.

"Tell who?"

Hope shot her a look. "Gee, I wonder."

"Maybe in eighteen years."

"If you can keep this a secret for eighteen years while living here, you should probably consider a job with the CIA."

Her stomach dipped, and it wasn't due to morning sickness this time.

"I know he'll find out eventually. It's inevitable. But I'm not ready to deal with it right now."

Hope dragged a French fry through the blob of ketchup on her plate. "Oh, so you're just waiting until you're ready."

"Exactly." Yvette knew where her friend was going with this but refused to acknowledge it. It was easier to play dumb these days.

"And when is that going to be?"

"I told you." A small smirk escaped her lips as she leaned over and dipped a fry in Hope's ketchup. "In eighteen years."

"Well, that might be easier said than done when we're hosting Steven's wedding at the B and B, and James will probably be a groomsman."

"I'll just some back to the city sooner than we talked about."

As Yvette's due date approached, the two friends had decided that it would be smarter for her to stay at Steven's condo rather than risk being snowed in at the bed-and-breakfast.

"*Three months* early?"

"Fine. Then just over New Year's."

"So, that's going to be your life? Spending the holidays alone because you can't risk running into James or anyone associated with him?"

"No. Just until the baby gets here. If I go to a party, no one will have to know I have a child who's with a sitter."

"Have you considered I'm going to want my goddaughter at important events in my life? Like birthdays, weddings, going to the Cape in the summers? Things that her daddy is also going to be at."

The queasy feeling intensified.

She closed her eyes tight and winced. "Well, her daddy ghosted me, so even if I wanted to, I couldn't just call him and let him know. Luckily, I don't want to."

Hope gripped the top of Yvette's hand. "I get it. This sucks. He's not who you thought. But he's still your baby's daddy. At least you know you're going to have a beautiful kid."

That was true. James was a gorgeous man. She'd been tongue-tied at just how good-looking he was the first time she'd met him. His dark brown hair was starting to grey, and his eyes sometimes seemed to match the color. Other times they appeared as blue as the ocean. She hoped their child looked more like him than her.

"Are you going to be okay if the ultrasound shows I'm having a boy?"

"You're having a girl," Hope said authoritatively.

"And you know this... How?"

"I had a dream that you and I were at the beach and there was a little girl building a sandcastle with us."

"Oh, how can I argue with *you had a dream?*"

"You can't," Hope replied with a grin.

The same grin she had as she'd held Yvette's hand when the sonogram revealed she was right—Yvette was having a girl.

"I told you!" she'd declared triumphantly. "Now I can really start shopping!"

Which meant Amazon deliveries now arrived almost daily to the Dragonfly. Yvette heard the jingle of the bell over the front door while she was in the bathroom and looked at her watch. It was right about the time the Prime driver showed up.

Yvette walked out of the bathroom and almost tripped over the grey cat she'd rescued from the resort in Puerto Vallarta.

"Jalisco!" she scolded as she bent over to scoop up the feline and nuzzle his soft fur against her skin. "I'm not going to be able to see you over my belly pretty soon, let alone bend over to pick you up."

Jalisco purred loudly in her arms as she walked toward the lobby.

"Here's the owner, now," Taylor, the recent college grad Yvette and Hope had hired to help run things, called loudly from the front desk when Yvette came into view. She put on her best *hospitable proprietor* smile to greet her guest.

Yvette turned to face the person Taylor was talking to and felt the blood rush to her feet. There stood James, looking as sexy as ever in his grey Henley and faded Levi's that fit him just right. He sported a pair of brown boots instead of the flip-flops that he'd worn in the summertime when they were together. He really was gorgeous. Then her stare traveled to his arm—or rather, *who* was hanging on his arm. The woman was perfect—not a long blonde hair out of place as her manicured hand clung to James's biceps. She also was wearing jeans and brown boots; only hers were over her jeans and came to her knee. Her brown cable knit sweater was tight, showcasing a beautiful set of boobs. She looked up at James with a fake pout on her perfectly made-up face. They were a model couple.

The thought hit her that that woman could be her child's stepmother. The lobby started to spin, and the last thing Yvette remembered was releasing Jalisco before everything went black.

CHAPTER EIGHTEEN

James

"Yvette!" Taylor, the girl on the other side of the desk who'd been helping him check-in, screeched when Yvette knocked a lamp over as she began to sway.

James reached her just in time. The familiar scent of her shampoo hit him as he held her limp body in his arms. He had an overwhelming desire to sit on the couch and hold her against him, but he opted for setting her down on the cushions and kneeling beside her.

Was he an asshole for the ego boost he felt that just her seeing him had that effect on her? Probably.

His date and Taylor rushed over. The hotel employee's tone was frantic when she asked, "Is she okay?"

James touched the pulse on Yvette's neck; it was strong but slow.

"She's okay. She fainted. Can you get her a cool rag?"

His date, Brandi—probably not her real name— observed, "She's really pale."

James looked down at Yvette's pretty face. It was the same one that had been standing beside him in his daydreams when he'd envisioned his future.

He didn't allow himself to daydream anymore.

Her brown hair was shorter than the last time he'd seen her—and darker. He'd remembered how it had looked almost blonde when they were on the beach, then by the light of the moon, seemed to have silver threads.

James stared at her lips. How he spent three days kissing them every chance he could flooded his memory. He could still hear the little noises she'd make when they made out in the sand. A picture of how beautiful she was when he'd made her come undone in his bed popped in his memory.

She fucking broke your heart, his brain reminded him.

But staring at her, he realized it'd been worth it.

"That's normal. Her cheeks will regain their color when she starts to wake up."

Taylor reappeared with a damp towel and handed it to him. "Poor thing. She'd just gotten over her morning sickness, now this."

"Oh my god," Brandi replied. "Exactly why I'm never getting pregnant."

Which was exactly why he dated her. There was no envisioning children or a future with her.

Wait.

Pregnant?

James let his eyes wander down Yvette's body, stopping at her full breasts peeking out of the mauve-colored peasant top she had on. They were bigger than he remembered. His gaze traveled further south, and that's when he noticed her round belly. It had been disguised in the flowy material when she was standing up, but there was no disguising it now.

Yvette was pregnant.

A knot formed in his stomach. Her boyfriend had gotten her pregnant. It should have been James.

He gave himself an internal shake. *No, you mean you lucked out it wasn't you.*

Wait—could he be the father?

"How far along is she?" His tone was urgent when he asked Taylor as she pushed buttons on her phone.

She glanced up at him as she lifted her shoulders. "I dunno. She's due the end of March, so I guess work backward from there."

He fell back on his ass with a *plunk* after doing the quick math. Almost six months along. Making her conception right around when they'd been together.

Holy shit, am I going to be a dad?

****

Yvette

She felt something cool on her forehead at the same time she heard a deep voice saying, "You don't need to call her. I'm a doctor, she's going to be fine."

Taylor, known for her spunk, didn't back down. "Well, she's my boss, and I was given explicit instructions to call her if anything happened."

The deep voice was much closer to her than Taylor's, and she heard him mutter, "Dammit."

A higher voice cooed, "She's just doing her job, Jamie."

Yvette slowly opened her eyes. She was lying on the couch in the lobby with a pillow propped under her knees, and yep, James was still there. He was the one blotting her forehead with the cold cloth.

And the beautiful woman was still next to him.

"Wh—what happened?"

"You fainted," he said with that same smile that had made her weak in the knees when she first met him. Damn dimples.

"Oh," was all Yvette could think to say.

"Have you eaten today?"

"I had a bagel for breakfast and some juice."

He made a show of looking at his watch. "It's two o'clock. In your condition, you should be eating every few hours and drinking plenty of water."

"Oh, she drinks plenty of water," Taylor chimed in from behind the desk.

Thanks for noticing my bathroom habits.

"It was a late breakfast," Yvette said defensively as she sat up on her elbows in an attempt to get up. Only to be met by James pressing on her shoulder for her to lie back.

"You need to rest here for a little while."

No, what she needed was to get some distance from him. "I'm okay, really."

"No, you're not. You're going to lie here until you've eaten, and I say you can get up."

"It's kind of hard to eat lying down," she sassed.

"Oh, Jamie," the beautiful blonde woman purred. "She's not one of your patients. If she says she feels okay, you should let her be."

"Yeah, *Jamie*. I'm fine."

"Goddammit, Yvette. You just fainted. That's not good for our—" He stopped and corrected himself. "The baby."

Fuck fuck fuck. He'd figured it out.

Of course, he had. It didn't take a rocket scientist. She supposed she could deny it, say the baby was someone else's. But Yvette suspected he wouldn't just take her word for it and demand a DNA test.

He interrupted her thoughts. "You're going to sit here and eat something, then let me examine you before you get up again."

"You're an anesthesiologist," she pointed out. "Not an ob-gyn."

"I went to medical school."

Touché.

His companion tugged on his arm. "I'm sure she doesn't want you hovering over her."

James didn't even look at the other woman. Instead, he scanned Yvette from head to toe, then looked her in the eye when he replied, "Too bad."

CHAPTER NINETEEN

James

Holy shit. I'm going to be a dad.

Yvette was having his baby. He'd baited her when he said, *our baby*, wondering if she'd correct him and tell him that her boyfriend was the father.

She hadn't.

He couldn't stop staring at her belly in wonderment. It took everything in him not to massage her bump, kiss it, and coo an introduction to his child through her skin.

Instead, he helped her sit up, then stayed at her side as he made sure she ate every bite of the sandwich and fruit that had been brought out to her on a bed tray.

"Here, you need to drink this," he said as he handed her the aluminum water bottle the staff had included on the tray.

She gave him a confused look when she took a drink. He couldn't blame her; he was just as confused. He'd come here intending to tell her off and rub the hot chick he was with in her face. Now, he learned he was going to be a dad, and he wanted nothing more than to take care of her.

The annoying whine of Brandi wanting him to pay attention to her was already old.

Hope burst through the door a little over an hour after Taylor texted her. She took one look at James sitting next to her BFF and gasped in surprise. Then she noticed Brandi, her eyes flashed, and she shot him a murderous look before turning her ire toward Evan, who'd walked in behind her.

"We'll talk about this later," she warned ominously. Her face softened, and she lifted Yvette's elbow to help her from the couch. "Come on, honey. Let's take you to your apartment."

"I fucking told you to come alone," Evan grumbled, clasping James's shoulder a little too hard before coming around and sitting in the spot Yvette had occupied. He looked pointedly at Brandi pouting in a chair while flipping through a magazine, then nodded toward his fiancée, who was dutifully walking beside James's baby mama. "Now, I'm on her shitlist. Thanks for that."

James had asked Brandi specifically because, out of all the women he was currently dating, she was the most obnoxious about flaunting her *assets* and fawning all over him. Talk about your all-time backfires.

"I'm sorry," he replied in a low voice. "You should have just told me instead of sending me in here blind with nothing but a cryptic message."

"Maybe. But I did tell you not to bring anyone."

"Had I known... I wouldn't have."

The two men watched Hope with one arm around her friend's waist as the two disappeared down a hallway.

"So, what now?" Evan asked at the same time Brandi huffed, "Can we *finally* go to our room?"

He looked over at the sexy woman he now had zero interest in—not that he'd ever really had that much interest in her other than passing time. Murmuring to Evan, he asked, "How much do you think an Uber is from here?"

"A lot. Good thing you're rich."

Good thing indeed.

*****

Yvette

"I would ask, how are you holding up, but given the circumstances..." Hope said as she closed Yvette's apartment door behind them.

"Yeah, fainting at the sight of James with his girlfriend didn't really put me in a power position."

"For what it's worth, I don't think she's his girlfriend. He seems to be playing the field."

"So, you've said."

"It brought me no pleasure telling you, but I thought you should know."

"I know it didn't. And I'm glad you did, even though it was painful to hear."

It'd hurt to find out he was just a player, especially after all the nights they'd spent on FaceTime, talking about their hopes and dreams for the future and how it seemed they'd wanted the same thing. But it explained why he'd blown her off. He hadn't wanted any of that.

She continued, "But the hurt eventually turned into anger, which helped me move on. Well, until I found out about..." Yvette gestured to her baby bump.

Hope reached over to rub Yvette's belly affectionately. "Everything happens for a reason."

"Yeah, well, I want to know what's the reason he's here?"

"I suspect Evan and his big mouth. I'm sorry."

"I thought you weren't going to tell him?"

Hope walked toward the kitchenette and opened the refrigerator. Pulling out a bottle of apple juice, she said, "Yvette, he's clueless about a lot of things, but even he would have figured out at Christmas that you're pregnant. Besides, I had to explain why you were planning on moving back to Boston for a month in March. Being worried about a freak snowstorm and unable to get out didn't make much sense if you were okay with being here until February."

Yvette let out a big sigh as she sunk back on the couch cushion. "I know. And I know I put you in a terrible position asking you not to tell anyone—especially Evan and your brother."

Hope put ice in two glasses and carefully poured from the bottle. "Well, now that the cat's out of the bag, what are you going to do?"

"I have no idea. Obviously, he and I need to talk, but I don't want to upset his girlfriend. Maybe I should get an attorney involved and just communicate that way."

Her BFF put the glasses on the coffee table in front of them and sat down next to her.

"I'd wait until you've at least tried talking to him first. He might view having an attorney contact him as antagonistic. Other than him being a man whore lately, which I've been told by more than one person is completely out of character for him, he's a good guy. His reputation at the hospital is stellar. I think he'll be reasonable and agreeable to your demands."

Yvette dropped to the throw pillows on the side of her. "That's just it, I don't have any demands. I'd planned on doing this alone, remember?"

Hope reached over and rubbed Yvette's arm. "You were never doing this alone."

She sat up with a sigh. "You know what I mean."

"I do. But I also think deep down, you knew he'd find out eventually."

"Yeah, when she was like sixteen!"

Hope shot her a look. "Come on. If you really wanted that you would've stayed in California where there would be almost zero chance of running into him."

Was that true? Had she come to Boston with the intention of co-parenting with James?

Yvette shook her head. "That's not it. I moved here to be closer to you, and to be able to run the bed-and-breakfast so I wouldn't have to worry about being away from her."

"Knowing that James lived here." Hope's voice got quieter as she reached over to squeeze her friend's hand. "There was no way you were going to deny her access to her father like your mom did to you."

Yvette pulled away and stood up. "That was different, I knew my dad. He and my mom were married until I was six."

"Doesn't matter; you remember what it was like not being able to see him. And you never forgave Nora for it."

Even though Yvette didn't have a single memory of her parents getting along, her mother had been bitter about the divorce. Her bitterness eventually turned to spite.

Yvette's first memory of the sniping was when her mother enrolled her in Spanish lessons in the third grade, instead of French like her father had asked, citing, "We live so close to the border. She'll need Spanish more than she'll ever need French."

Yvette had only been privy to her mom's side of the conversation, but even as a child, she recognized it had been a nasty thing to do. So, when she got older, she studied French on her own with the help of software her father sent. So, now she was fluent in English and Spanish and proficient in French. Enough that she could understand conversations and read menus when she was able to spend her summers and every other holiday with her dad and his new family as a teenager, once her mother married Jerry and mellowed out. Well, as mellow as Nora Sinclaire-Cox could be.

Her father was thrilled to learn he was going to be a *pépère*. Surprisingly, her mother was also excited about the prospect of becoming a "glamma."

Yvette had been sitting at her mom's kitchen island and fought an eye roll when her mom dropped that little moniker idea. "She's not going to call you that, Mom."

Nora sighed. "Fine. Anything but grandma."

"How about *nana*?" It seemed fitting since Nora had insisted Yvette take Spanish all those years.

"Nana Nora," her mom said it aloud a few times like she was trying it out. "I like it."

So her sweet princess was going to have a *nana* and a *pépère*. And, apparently now, a daddy and his family.

Yvette knew it was the right thing to do, but she was still pissed at James for ghosting her.

"Logically, I know he needs to be a part of her life. But emotionally, I'm still licking my wounds."

"Sort of like Nora."

"That's a low blow, Hope Francine Ericson. I thought you were on my side."

"I am, honest. But I've known all along that you would eventually tell him. It's not in your nature to be spiteful—especially when it comes to our princess. And now that James knows, you need to figure out what it is you want from him going forward. But figure it out *before* you talk to him—that way you're the one dictating the terms."

Yvette closed her eyes and rubbed her temples. The last few hours had been a lot to process.

"Let me think about it. Right now, I need a nap."

CHAPTER TWENTY

James

Brandi had not been happy to be shuffled into an Uber, but James concocted some lame story about Evan and Hope needing his full attention while they persuaded their friend that she needed to take it easy during her pregnancy. Evan had conveniently chimed in at the appropriate times to make it more convincing, and reluctantly, his companion found herself in the back of the car service with her suitcase in the trunk.

"Call me when you get back into town," were her parting words.

"I definitely will," he said before closing the door and tapping the roof.

"You fucking liar," Evan chuckled as they watched the car drive off.

"I know. I'm an asshole."

And now, Hope was standing in front of him in the hotel's living room, reiterating the same thing.

He and Evan had been eating a late lunch and talking about work, Steven and Whitney's upcoming wedding, and pretty much anything else other than the elephant in the room when Hope stormed in.

Both men jumped to their feet.

"How is she?" James anxiously asked, while Evan more sheepishly said at the same time, "Everything okay?"

She looked dismissively at Evan, then held her hand up in a *talk to the hand* gesture. "I can't even talk to you right now." She pointed her finger directly at James. "And you. What the hell were you thinking, showing up here unannounced—with a fucking hooker?"

"Technically, she's a stripper."

Hope's venomous look told him she didn't give a shit about technicalities, so he proceeded with caution. "I had no idea Yvette was pregnant."

The sassy blonde raised her eyebrows at him. The scowl on her face seemed to be permanent today.

James put a hand over his heart. "Swear to God, I had no idea. None. I just knew she was here, that's all."

"So, what... you thought you'd show up with a 'stripper' and rub it in her face? Because ghosting her for no reason wasn't enough?"

That got his hackles up.

"Oh, there was a reason. And Yvette knows damn well what it was."

"I'm here to tell you, as her best friend for over half our lives and the godmother to her baby girl, that no, she has no idea."

Baby girl.

"A daughter?" he whispered as he stumbled backward to his seat on the couch.

Hope must have realized the blow she'd just delivered because her shoulders sagged as she nodded and sat down in the chair opposite him. "She's due the end of March."

A thought occurred to him. Maybe he wasn't the father. The man at her condo had said they'd gotten back together and had warned James to back off, but who knows when they'd broken up. James knew sperm could live inside a woman for up to five days. Had she been with him before coming to Boston?

"Why didn't she tell me?"

"Why would she?"

Hope's words felt like a kick in the gut. Maybe his fears were founded. Although, she'd have to have done a DNA test to rule James out as the father...

Fuck! He couldn't quell the sense of panic and feeling of helplessness.

Then Hope continued, "After the way you treated her. You *blocked* her number and email, James. That was a pretty blatant *fuck off*."

He cast his line, praying Hope would take the bait.

"It seems like she could have a found a way to get in touch with me about something like this. Hell, even if it was just through her attorney for child support."

"She doesn't want your money, James. Even though I told her she should take you to the cleaners."

Bingo! That was what he'd needed to hear.

"What does she want then? Because there's no way I'm walking away from her or our daughter."

No fucking way.

CHAPTER TWENTY-ONE

Yvette

She was disoriented when she woke up from a deep sleep and found it dark outside. She didn't know if it was five in the morning or the afternoon.

This little girl growing inside her was sapping all her energy these days.

Still in her clothes, she put her feet in the cushy slippers by her bed and padded out to the apartment's kitchenette in search of something to eat. Thank God she could keep food down these days.

Finding nothing appealing in her tiny pantry, Yvette ran a brush through her hair and headed toward the main kitchen. The staff was great about always setting aside a plate for her along with some snacks for later.

The middle of December wasn't exactly the high season in Massachusetts. The leaves had already fallen, so the color tours had come to an end. Thanksgiving was over, which meant there was a lull before the Christmas bookings. She'd spent the last few weeks catching up on the paperwork and advertising she'd been putting off but still had more to do.

The low din from the TV, along with spirited conversation, drew her attention into the living room. There she found Hope, Evan, and James sitting around the coffee table. A Scrabble board was set up between them.

James was the first to notice her and leaped from his place on the couch, coming over to where she was standing in the doorway.

With no hesitation, he put his arm around her as if he had every right to and guided her to the sofa.

"How are you feeling?" he asked as he gently rubbed circles on her hip.

What the hell? She should have stopped him, but she didn't. It felt too nice being next to him.

"Hungry."

Hope jumped up from where she'd been sitting on the floor. "What can I get to tide you over until dinner's ready? The kitchen staff is prepping some meals, then I'm sending everyone home for a few days, since it's just going to be us here. We don't have any reservations until Friday."

Yvette didn't know how Isaac was going to feel about that. Her lumberjack-looking handyman was crushing hard on Taylor. He'd be disappointed to go a few days without being able to flirt with the pretty girl behind the front desk. Yvette doubted her lobby area had ever been so well-maintained before, he certainly spent enough time there. Not that Taylor seemed to mind. She was all smiles and hair twirling whenever Isaac was around.

Kind of like Yvette had been around James.

Then he ghosted me. After *he knocked me up.*

In all fairness, the ghosting wasn't because she was pregnant. He hadn't known about the baby when he stopped responding to her texts and blocked her number.

Fortunately, neither did she. She'd felt stupid and duped, but she'd had no idea she was pregnant.

"Sit down," James urged, then situated himself next to her. His attentiveness was almost endearing. She'd probably appreciate it more if it weren't for the fact that he was a user and a liar.

She gestured at the space between them, or rather, the lack of space. "Can you, um, give me a little room?"

He almost looked hurt. *Good.*

"Oh, yeah," he mumbled as he scooted over. "No problem."

Evan coughed into his hand like he was trying to hide the smirk on his face. "I'm going to go help Hope find you a snack."

The ER doctor disappeared, leaving just her and James to sit in awkward silence.

The quiet made her uncomfortable, so she was desperate to break it. She glanced down at the gameboard on the coffee table. "Who's winning?"

"That is up for debate. Hope had just played a word that I was arguing is not a word when you walked in."

That made her smile. "Yeah, you've gotta watch Hope. She likes to invent words when she plays."

"I'm learning that."

Once again, they sat, not speaking. Then finally, he uttered, "Were you ever going to tell me?"

Yvette blew out a breath at his loaded question.

"I don't know. Probably? Eventually. Maybe when she got older and wanted to know about her dad."

She snuck a glance at him and saw his jaw was set like he was clenching it.

His tone was sharp when he replied, "So it wouldn't have mattered if I'd missed out on important things, like her first smile or her first words, or her first steps."

Yeah, the guilt probably would have bothered her, but she had her righteous anger to counter it. That might have been why she flippantly remarked, "You're still more than likely going to miss all those things since you live in Boston, and she'll live here."

His shoulders slumped, almost as if in defeat. "Yeah, I guess so."

She appreciated that he hadn't been crass enough to ask for a DNA test. But, of course, there was zero percent chance this baby was anyone else's, not that he necessarily knew that.

Yvette knew they would have to get this co-parenting thing figured out, so she offered an olive branch. "I can always send you video. I'm sure I'm going to be constantly filming everything she does."

He gave a weak smile. "That'd be great."

She couldn't help but add with a smirk, "You'll have to unblock me first, though."

****

James

No. Hell no. No videos. No schedules or custody arrangements. He wanted his baby to live in his house. And he wanted his baby mama there too. In his bed.

He suddenly didn't give a shit that she had a boyfriend, other than if he was still in the picture. And if that were the case, James would make sure he wasn't for long.

Like he should have done in the first damn place, but his ego hadn't let him.

He took out his phone and went to the secret folder where he'd stored her number. It took a series of steps to get there—he'd done that on purpose so he wouldn't be tempted to reach out to her, but once her name popped up, he simply clicked a button.

"There. Now you can reach me anytime, day or night."

"You should probably unblock me from email, too."

He'd forgotten the lengths he'd gone to in an attempt to forget about her. Not that any of them had worked.

He clicked on his email app. Unblocking her there was a much easier process.

"You can now reach me however you want, whenever you want," he said as he slipped the phone back into his pocket.

She gave him a contrived smile. "Lucky me."

He turned his body to face her. "Look, I—"

"I've got delicious and nutritious snacks!" Hope announced as she came in with a tray of food. Evan entered behind her with another tray holding a pitcher of what looked like lemonade and four glasses.

James needed something stronger than lemonade.

"There had better be something yummy on that tray or you can turn around and try again," Yvette said as she eyed the plates of veggies.

"There's pita bread and hummus, and—"

"You know I can't have hummus." Yvette sat back against the cushions as if exasperated.

Hope opened a TV tray and set the snacks down. "Alice made this hummus especially for you. It doesn't have tahini."

Yvette sat up, clutching her hand to her chest. "She did that for me?"

Annnnd now she was crying.

James reached for her automatically. "Are you okay?"

"No, I'm not!" she sobbed into a napkin Hope had handed her.

He tried to put his arm around her to pull her against his chest, but she shrugged him off.

"Don't."

He looked helplessly up at Hope, who only shrugged. Then, with a knowing smile, she slightly mussed Yvette's hair. "Oh, mama. Those pregnancy hormones are a bitch. You went from hangry to emotional in one point six seconds flat. A new record."

Yvette started laughing through her tears. "I'm a mess."

"You've had a big day," Hope said as she plated the snacks. "Being hungry doesn't help. Here." She thrust the plate into Yvette's hands. "This should tide you over. Dinner will be ready in about forty-five minutes."

He couldn't help but smile when she sniffled as she took the plate with a grateful, but sheepish, "Thanks."

Hope looked at him with disdain. "I only serve the pregnant and the elderly, so you're on your own if you want anything. But there's plenty."

"You don't serve your guests?" James asked as he stood and walked toward the TV tray with the snacks.

"Guests that I like."

He looked back at her. "Ouch."

Hope didn't let up. "You better not be here on a Groupon or have used a discount code either."

"Nope." He took a bite of a baby carrot. "I paid the rack rate. And apparently, I'm not even getting staff services during my stay."

"I'll still provide you service," Yvette said softly.

Yeah, but not the kind of service he had in mind.

He shook his head. "I'll be fine. I'm a big boy and can make my own bed and cook my own breakfast."

Staring at the plate in her lap, she asked, "What about your... girlfriend? I'm sure she will have something to say about that. This is, after all, a bed-and-breakfast."

He sat back down next to her with a thud. "First off, she's not my girlfriend, and secondly, I sent her home in an Uber."

That made her look up.

"I'm sorry. I hope your stay wasn't ruined because of me."

He huffed a laugh. "You're not sorry. But neither am I." Reaching over to affectionately squeeze her knee, he continued, "I'm going to have a daughter, I couldn't be happier." Then he leaned against the armrest of the sofa and gave her a teasing smile. "I mean, I guess there are better ways I could have found out, but still..."

She had the decency to look guilty. At least that's what he thought she was feeling as she pushed the same baby carrot through the dollop of ranch dressing on her plate over and over without looking at him. Then she murmured, "You must not have gotten my text." And popped the whole thing in her mouth with a smug smile, her eyebrows raised in a challenge.

He couldn't help but grin.

Well played, little mama. Well played.

Chapter Twenty-Two

Yvette

Well, that had been less painful than she thought it would be. Granted, they still had a lot of things to iron out, but the initial bomb wasn't bad.

Before today, Yvette had played out a few scenarios in her head about telling James, but they all involved their daughter already being born and older. She hadn't come up with anything about while she was still carrying their baby. Maybe that's why seeing him earlier had been such a shock.

She'd seen a "James Randolph" on the guest list, which made her do a double take, but after confirming it was *Randolph* and not *Rudolf*, she didn't think about it again.

She turned to him while the four were sitting at the dinner table. "Did you purposefully use a fake name when you made your reservation?"

His quick glance at Evan gave her the answer before he said, "I might have misspelled my last name."

"So, you'd be the one with the element of surprise?"

"A lot of good that did me," he mumbled as he took a bite of his mashed potatoes.

"Why would you do that?"

"I was worried you'd see my name and not be here."

"You brought your girlfriend," Yvette pointed out. "Why would you care?"

Evan started coughing as if he were choking, and Hope patted his back while harshly whispering in his ear. Judging by the way the whisper sounded more like a hiss, her BFF was bawling him out.

James looked at his colleague's red face. When he was convinced there was no threat to Evan's life other than from Hope, he stabbed a piece of steak with his fork while she stared at him, waiting for an answer.

Finally, he shrugged. "I dunno. To make you jealous?"

That didn't make any sense. Why would he want her to be jealous when he was the one who blew her off in the first place?

"Why would—"

James cut off her. "It was a mistake. I'm sorry."

Yvette had two choices. She could push for a better answer and risk an argument, or worse, him shutting down, or she could accept his apology, back off, and try again later.

It'd been a long day, and she didn't feel like a confrontation right now, so she chose the latter.

The entire table seemed to be walking on eggshells as they made small talk the rest of the meal. When they'd finished eating, the other three raced to see who could clear the dishes away first. No one wanted to be stuck sitting at the table with her any longer. For once, Yvette didn't care that people were waiting on her. She was tired and didn't have the energy to help, even if she'd wanted to.

"Is there dessert?" she asked with a hopeful tone once all the plates were cleared.

"Would I let you down, my sweets craving friend?" Hope asked with a smile.

"I'm hoping not."

"Alice made cheesecake with strawberry topping."

"That's exactly what I was craving."

"What else do you have cravings for?" James asked as he sat back down next to her.

"Hmm..." Yvette thought. "Cliché as it is, pickles and ice cream, although not together. Sometimes, something will just hit me out of the blue. Like last week, it was fried chicken—at four o'clock in the morning. Obviously, that craving wasn't satisfied until later when Isaac made a run to Popeye's for me."

He scowled. "Is Isaac your boyfriend?"

She felt her eyes narrow and lips purse at such a ridiculous question.

"Isaac is our handyman," Hope interjected as she walked in with two plates of cheesecake. She set Yvette's down in front of her first before putting the other plate in front of James and walking back to the kitchen.

"And I'm pretty sure he wants to be Taylor's boyfriend," Yvette said as she took a bite. Closing her eyes, she moaned with her mouth full. "Oh my God, this is so good."

She opened her eyes to find James staring at her like he wanted to devour her instead of his dessert.

Yvette swallowed hard and glanced away. In an effort to change the mood, she called out loudly to Hope in the kitchen, "We need to give Alice a raise."

"We need to start turning a profit first," Hope stated matter-of-factly as she backed out of the swinging kitchen door with two more plates.

Oh yeah, a profit. Yvette used to be all about that when she was with Marrion International. You'd think she'd be more focused on that now that she was an owner.

She looked down and mumbled, "I know. I was just being facetious."

"Oh damn!" When she looked up, James was slowly pulling the fork tines from his mouth. "Facetious schmeesish. If Alice was the one who made this cheesecake, then she deserves a raise and a statue built in her honor."

That made her laugh out loud. "Since when are you into sweets? I distinctly remember you being *meh* about the ice cream we had on the pier last summer."

The corner of his mouth pulled up. "And I remember you being enthusiastic about it for the both of us."

Gesturing to her round belly, she replied, "She's only made my sweet tooth worse."

"She's going to be like her mama."

He touched her stomach with a soft smile, and Yvette caught her breath. His touch was as electric as the first time they shook hands in Steven's living room on Cape Cod after being introduced.

Oh, no. No. No. No. There weren't going to be any fireworks between them again. No chemistry. No instant attraction. She learned her lesson about where that would get her.

It's just the pregnancy hormones, she reasoned. They'd been making her exceptionally horny—she'd even had to replace BOB's batteries.

"Hopefully, she'll get her daddy's dimples."

Why did I just say that?

She knew damn well why. Those stupid dents in his cheeks had once made her knees weak. She could only imagine how adorable their daughter would be with them.

But no more! She was now impervious to James's dimples and everything else about his stupidly handsome face.

Impervious!

So, why hadn't she moved away from his touch?

****

James

The four of them watched the latest romantic comedy on Netflix in the living room, although Hope and Evan were whispering rather than watching it from their place on the loveseat.

After Yvette shushed them for the third time, they disappeared. Not long after, James felt her hair brush against his chin as she leaned against him. *That's a good sign, right?*

Then he heard her snoring and realized she'd fallen asleep. She probably didn't even know what she'd done.

Still, he maneuvered his body so he was lying on the couch behind her with his back as close to the cushion as he could get, and he gently moved her into a position, so he was spooning her, one hand on her belly.

He closed his eyes and let out a deep breath. The familiar scent of her hair and skin filled his nostrils, and he brushed his lips against her hair. It was the first time in months that he'd felt content.

Never in a million years did he think on the drive there that he'd be drifting off to sleep on the couch with his little family in his arms. But here he was, and he couldn't imagine anything sweeter.

Except maybe holding her in my arms in a bed, he thought after he woke up once the movie had ended and found his arm tingling.

But James wouldn't have moved her for all the money in the world. No way was he risking her leaving his embrace. He needed to feel her body next to his. Holding her made him feel whole. He hadn't realized how damaged he'd been until he realized he could finally breathe again.

He could handle a numb arm.

Thankfully, she turned over so that she was now facing him, and he could adjust his position. Once again, he drifted off to sleep, feeling lighter than he'd felt in a long time. Probably since the last time he'd fallen asleep holding her. There wasn't a doubt in his mind, she belonged next to him. Her and their baby. And he wasn't going to stop until he made that a reality.

*

James woke with a start. The space on the couch where Yvette had been lying next to him was empty and cold. Instead of her body heat, there was now a blanket covering him.

Someone had shut the TV off, but there was a dim light on in the hall, so he could also see the vacant place next to him as well as feel it.

He swung his feet to the floor and made a half-hearted attempt at folding the blanket before placing it next to the armrest and making his way toward the light in the hall.

Yvette's apartment door was out of the way of his room, and yet he found himself standing in front of it. He hesitated with his hand hovering over the knob. He had intended to see if it was unlocked. If it was, he'd planned on slipping into bed with her and resuming their spooning position. She'd felt so good in his arms—he wanted that feeling back.

If she wanted to be in your arms, she wouldn't have gotten up, the little voice in his head reminded him.

With a frown, he pulled his hand away from the knob and took a step back. He gave her door one last look, then walked toward his room.

James needed to fix things between them. He wasn't sure how and knew it was going to take a lot of work, maybe even a miracle. But the fact that he had a little girl growing in Yvette's belly made him believe miracles did happen.

He had his work cut out for him, but he was up to challenge. And there was no time like the present.

CHAPTER TWENTY-THREE

Yvette

Blurry-eyed, she followed the delicious smell coming from the inn's kitchen that had pulled her from her slumber. Pregnancy had her more sensitive to scents. Which, when she was dealing with morning sickness, wasn't a good thing. More often than not, a smell that she would have considered innocuous pre-pregnancy would send her running toward the bathroom. Thankfully, the morning sickness seemed to have subsided.

Apparently, fainting was now her thing.

Which she almost did when she walked into the kitchen that morning, but for an entirely different reason than yesterday.

At the stove stood a shirtless James with a Red Sox ball cap on backward, dressed only in blue and wine-colored plaid pajama bottoms and the complimentary slippers the inn provided guests, flipping pancakes in one pan before attending to another pan filled with what appeared to be eggs.

It was the sexiest sight she'd ever seen.

That's just the hormones talking, she assured herself when she remembered how he'd broken her heart. The same conversation she'd had with herself last night when she wanted to continue lying in his arms on the couch. Fortunately, their little girl had decided to use her bladder as a pillow, and she had to get up. She'd debated about going back and snuggling next to him. She wasn't proud about it, but she'd liked how it'd felt.

The gods had been looking out for her because when she did return, he'd sprawled out on the couch. That made her decision easier, and she pulled a blanket over him and went to bed.

She did *not* brush his bangs from his forehead while staring at his beautiful sleeping face. Or kiss his cheek.

And if she had, she must have been sleepwalking. That was her story, and she was sticking to it.

James called out from his place at the stove, "What do you want in your omelet?"

"Peppers, mushrooms, and cheese," Hope's voice replied.

Only then did Yvette notice Hope and Evan sitting in the breakfast nook by the window drinking coffee. Evan had a plate in front of him that was half-empty. A fresh blanket of snow had fallen last night, making the scenery outside a beautiful winter wonderland.

James caught a glance of her in the doorway, and his face lit up.

"Good morning, beautiful. Are you hungry?"

Yvette snorted as she shuffled to the chair next to Hope and opposite Evan. "Beautiful, yeah right."

She had flannel pajamas on underneath her fuzzy robe and slippers, and, knowing there were no guests at the hotel

Wicked Hot Baby Daddy

today, she hadn't bothered to do anything but brush her teeth. She was sure her bedhead was in full effect but didn't have the energy to care yet. She'd shower and change after breakfast.

James appeared with a plate of steaming food and set it in front of Hope, then looked at Yvette.

"Well, I think you're beautiful."

Hope leaned over and rubbed Yvette's belly. "Me, too. You have a glow."

She scowled. "If I'm glowing, it's from hunger."

James took her cue. "What can I get you?"

"A shirt for you, to start."

A cocky grin formed on his face.

Lest he think she said that because she thought he was too attractive, which he was, damn him, she followed up with, "I'm pretty sure you're violating the health code. I don't want to lose our A plus rating. We've worked too hard for that."

The grin didn't leave his stupid, handsome face, it only got bigger. "Soooo, you're worried about a surprise health inspection—in the middle of December—after we got six inches of snow last night?"

"It could happen."

He rubbed his chin while he nodded thoughtfully, still smirking. "Sure. Sure. Makes sense. I'll go put a shirt on. Be right back for your order."

Hope stared at her plate while she carefully cut her breakfast into bite-sized pieces, the slightest smile escaping her lips. Evan was suddenly interested in his phone.

"What?" Yvette said defensively.

"Nothing," Hope said, not looking up as she took a bite. Yvette noted how good her friend's breakfast looked, and her mouth watered a little.

She folded her arms and leaned back in her chair. "You can say it. That's what friends are supposed to do."

Hope finally looked up, and with an incredulous laugh, said, "Health code violation? That's what you went with?"

"I was on the spot! I couldn't think with him standing there without a shirt on, with his stupid six-pack abs, and his stupid arm muscles, making a stupid delicious breakfast."

"You think my muscles are stupid?" James asked as he walked in, pulling a navy-blue T-shirt over his head then put his Red Sox hat back on.

"Yes." She closed her eyes. "I mean, no. We weren't talking about *your* muscles."

He cocked his head as he leaned on the kitchen island, amusement written all over his face while he listened to her dig herself deeper. "Huh. Whose muscles were you talking about?"

Yvette must have looked like a deer in the headlights, because Hope chimed in, "Oh, some guy on one of those cooking shows, you know."

James's grin seemed to have morphed into a perma-one. Still, he let her off the hook with, "I never watch those shows. That one sounds interesting though."

"It is," Yvette said defiantly.

"What can I make you for breakfast?"

She was too hungry to be proud and refuse his offer. "Pancakes sound really good."

He pushed off the island and reached for a green bowl with batter drips on the side. "Pancakes coming right up. Evan, you want anything else?"

Hope's boyfriend looked up from his phone that he'd smartly kept his nose buried in. "I wouldn't say no to another pancake or two."

"You got it."

Yvette stole a glance at her baby daddy maneuvering around the kitchen with ease. He hummed a little tune as he poured ingredients into the bowl. Then, stirring them with a whisk, he gave her a wink when he caught her watching him. She hastily looked away, embarrassed at being busted.

It was perfectly natural that wink had made her lady parts tingle, she reassured herself. She had pregnancy hormones and hadn't had another man's attention since James's last summer. It would have happened regardless of who was standing in front of the stove if he'd winked at her like that.

And had dimples like that.

And an ass like that.

And had done deliciously wicked things to her body before.

"I'll be right back!" She jumped up and headed to the bathroom, where she knew she'd be safe.

"Pregnant woman bladder," she heard Hope explain as Yvette rushed out of the room.

Locking the door, she leaned against the wood, feeling like a coward. But it was either that or climb the guy like a tree.

And *that* wasn't happening. Not again. Not ever.

****

James

He wasn't bullshitting her when she'd walked in the kitchen—she was beautiful. With the sleep still in her eyes and her messy hair, he wanted to turn the burners off, take her in his arms, and wish her a proper good morning.

Obviously, they weren't on the same page.

Yet.

He set her and Evan's plates down, then went back to the counter for his omelet and pancakes and situated himself between Evan and Yvette at the round table overlooking acres of now-barren trees. He imagined they were incredible only a month ago, before their orange, yellow, and red leaves fell.

The fresh snow covering the ground had its own beauty, too. He could picture being snuggled up on the couch in front of the fire with Yvette, drinking hot chocolate as their daughter slept peacefully in a carrier.

Or, when she got older, the three of them making a snowman together. James stealing kisses from Yvette as their little girl played in the snow. Or teaching his daughter to ski. Swim. Throw a baseball. Everything his dad had taught him and Zach.

He wanted that life with Yvette and their children. Yes, plural. Because he wasn't stopping with just one with this beautiful woman.

Now to convince her of that.

He was willing to play the long game. He understood she wasn't going to let him back into her life without a fight, especially if she was back together with that douchebag from her apartment.

James knew the fact that she was carrying *his* baby was an advantage no other man had, and he planned on using that fully.

Hope and Yvette were talking about how many reservations they currently had and plotting strategy on how to increase occupancy during the winter months when Evan's phone rang.

Wiping his mouth with a napkin, he looked at the screen and quickly answered it.

"Olivia! Everything okay?"

He frowned as his sister talked on the other end.

James worked with both the Lacroix siblings at the hospital and knew Olivia was pregnant and ready to pop at any time.

Evan stood suddenly, his chair skidding back as he pushed away from the table.

"I'm on my way."

Hope looked at her boyfriend with raised eyebrows as he pocketed his phone.

"Olivia's in labor. She was snowed in and had to have the kid who plows her driveway take her to the hospital. They're headed there now."

Hope looked nervously at Yvette. "Are you going to be okay here?"

James fought to keep his ire down. *Fuck yeah, she'll be okay.* He was insulted at the insinuation she wouldn't be.

"I'll take good care of her."

"She's not to be left alone, James. You need to make sure someone is here before you head back to Boston."

"Um, right here!" Yvette snapped her fingers between them. "I'm just pregnant, not an invalid. I don't need a babysitter. I can take care of myself."

Hope passed him a look that he read loud and clear. *You leave her alone, you're a dead man.*

He subtly nodded to let her know he got the message.

"I know you are, but you also know I'm a nervous Nelly when it comes to my goddaughter. So just appease me, and let James dote on you until Taylor or Isaac come back to work or Friday. Or until I get back, whichever comes sooner."

Yvette's downturned mouth suggested she'd rather eat worms, but she grumbled, "Fine."

"When do you have to be back to the hospital?" Hope asked him as she pushed in her chair.

"I'm scheduled for Friday, but I have a lot of PTO that I have no problem using."

Although, he should save some for when the baby comes.

First things first. He'd take FMLA unpaid if he needed to, he could afford it. Right now, spending time with Yvette was the most important thing.

"Great. The inn staff is due back Friday morning before our weekend guests arrive, so try to play nice until then."

"Not a problem. I'll take good care of her. I promise."

Yvette shot him a look that let him know exactly what she thought of that idea, but she didn't say anything until they reached the front door.

"Give Olivia a hug from me. And drive safely!" She looked pointedly at Evan. "Going in the ditch will probably make it longer for you to get there."

"I know. I've been driving in this weather ever since I got my license. I understand speed is not my friend. We'll be careful."

Hope hugged Yvette then looked at James with raised eyebrows and a stern expression.

He raised his hands in surrender. "I promise!"

"Hmph, you better," was all the blonde dynamo said before walking out the door.

Evan grinned and smacked James's biceps. "Talk to you later."

James lifted his chin in acknowledgment. "Give Olivia my best. Let us know how she's doing."

"Will do."

The two stood in the doorway, still in their pajamas, quietly watching until the taillights on Evan's Mercedes were out of sight before stepping back inside.

He closed and locked the door and looked down at his little baby mama-to-be. She crossed her arms in front of her body and rubbed her biceps as if soothing herself while she looked up at him with an uncomfortable smile.

He hated that she was uneasy around him.

Grabbing her hand, he jerked his head toward the living room. "Come on. You need to get off your feet."

Yvette stopped in her tracks but didn't let go of his hand.

"I'll reiterate what I said in the kitchen. I'm pregnant, not an invalid."

He felt the corners of his mouth turn up as he tugged her forward. Her stubbornness was endearing.

"I know you're perfectly capable of taking care of yourself. But is it so bad to let someone else do it? I was going to suggest we stay in our pajamas all day and lie around watching movies and playing games."

She seemed to be considering it, so he attempted to sweeten the pot by leaning down and murmuring, "I'll rub your feet and let you pick the first movie."

"You have to make snacks and cocoa, too."

"You drive a hard bargain, California girl."

CHAPTER TWENTY-FOUR

Yvette

California girl. James had called her that last summer after he'd tried to shorten her name to Eve, and she'd told him that was her assistant's name.

It hadn't exactly been *baby* or *sugar* or some other term of endearment, but with the affection in his voice every time he called her it, it might as well have been.

She wasn't going to let him call her that again.

"I'm not a California girl anymore." Using her best Boston accent, she concluded, "I'm a wicked *smaht* Boston girl now."

He chuckled. "I don't think it works like that. You can take the girl out of California, but you can't take the California out of the girl."

There were those dimples again. And seriously, with the T-shirt that hugged his muscles like that? He might as well take the dang thing off.

No. No. No. That would be bad.

She sighed with a frown. He couldn't just be indiscriminately charming like this. Not with her hormones out of control and their close proximity for the next few days. This was so not fair.

He must have taken her silence as disapproval because he bent his knees to look her in the eye with a soft smile as he reached for her wrists. "Okay, how about this? You're a wicked *smaht*, wicked *pissa*, California girl?"

"Excuse me? Pisser?"

He chuckled. "It means awesome. But how about wicked *haht* instead?

Despite her best effort, his exaggerated Boston accent, coupled with his new descriptor of her, elicited a smile.

"I'll think about it," she said as she pulled from his grasp and walked toward the couch. Plunking down, she turned and put her feet up on the cushions. "Now what were you saying about a foot rub?"

****

James

Yvette was asleep within minutes of putting her feet in his lap while he pressed his thumbs into her arches.

He kept rubbing, wanting her to stay relaxed—and asleep—so he could stare at her beautiful face for as long as he wanted in the light of day.

She was as beautiful as the first day he'd met her.

He remembered that hot July day when she'd walked into Steven's house on the Cape behind Hope, her light brown hair piled in a messy bun on top of her head.

He'd been enamored from the get-go and was glued to her side the rest of the weekend. By the time he reluctantly dropped her off at the airport less than a week later, he was more certain than ever that his original instinct of her being his future wife was spot-on.

Then he flew to San Diego at the end of July to surprise her for the weekend, only to be surprised himself when her boyfriend answered the door.

A *surprise* was an understatement. He'd felt like he'd had his guts kicked in.

Doesn't matter, she's having my baby. Not his.

And it wasn't like he'd come home and joined a monastery. Quite the opposite. His brother, Zach, had been more than happy to set him up with women who worked at the strip clubs Zach liked to frequent. And James had been willing to be comforted by them. So while he'd never technically paid for sex, there was definitely a transactional element. They weren't going out with him for his personality, nor was he taking them out for theirs. It was more what they could do for each other.

For the women, it meant expensive gifts and invitations to trendy restaurants or hard to get seats to galas and balls. For him, he had a hot woman on his arm who was usually a decent lay. And there was zero chance of getting his heart broken again.

If Hope showed up and saw him with his date of the week, knowing she'd report back to Yvette, it was even better and had almost been worth the daggers she'd shoot him.

Almost.

But now... *Fuck.*

There was a lot he regretted. The way he'd handled everything from when he'd knocked on Yvette's door in San Diego to the present.

Still, there was one thing he didn't regret—that little baby in her belly.

The slate grey cat that had been in Yvette's lap last night—the same one she'd been holding before she fainted yesterday—jumped up on the back of the couch and stared at him, tail twitching as if inspecting whether the man was good enough to be rubbing his human's feet.

The cat seemed friendly enough. James guessed he'd probably have to be if he was going to have the run of the inn and interact with guests.

James scratched behind the feline's ears, letting the kitty press into James's hand before reaching for the tag on his collar.

"Jalisco, huh?"

He was surprised when Yvette murmured with her eyes still closed, "I brought him back with me from Mexico. Puerto Vallarta is in the state of Jalisco."

He was familiar with Jalisco, that's where tequila came from.

"He loves you."

James wondered if his cats, Tom and Jerry, would get along with Jalisco. Jerry probably would, he was social and outgoing. Tom, on the other hand, took a while to warm up when presented with something—or someone—new.

Although James remembered he'd taken to Yvette immediately the one and only time she'd come over. The night before she went back to San Diego.

She opened her eyes and smiled at the kitty standing guard over her on the back of the couch. "He better. He's the reason I got fired from the Puerto Vallarta property and sent back to San Diego."

"You were fired?" And here he'd thought she'd moved because she was pregnant.

"From the property, yes. Not the company. I think they were worried about a social media nightmare, so they sent me back to my old job in San Diego. They let me keep the raise they'd given me, but it was really a demotion, and I knew the chance of ever getting my own hotel again, outside of San Diego and direct corporate oversight, was nil. Then I found out I was pregnant and didn't care."

"Why would it have been a social media nightmare?"

"Because I evicted a guest when I saw him kick Jalisco. Turned out, the man was a friend of the president of Marrion International."

What a fucker. If he'd seen him do that, James would have drop-kicked the asshole before she'd even had a chance to evict him.

As if he knew she was talking about him, Jalisco gingerly walked his front paws down the back couch cushion, then dropped on her belly so she could pet him easier.

"I could see how that had the potential to get ugly. People would definitely be on your side."

"Fortunately, I knew that. So, I made sure the president himself wrote me a glowing recommendation when I left. Not that I ever plan on needing it, but you never know." She rubbed her belly affectionately. "Life has a way of surprising you."

He slowly dragged his gaze from her belly to her face before replying, "It certainly does. Sometimes in the best of ways."

****

Yvette

She quickly moved her feet from his lap and curled them under her at the opposite end of the couch.

He could save his charm for someone who was buying it—and that wasn't her. She'd learned her lesson.

"Look, I know we're having a baby together..." Yvette ran her finger through the fringe ends on the blanket, not looking at him. "But we need to set some rules."

She finally glanced up and found him with his brows knitted together. "Rules? Like what?"

Like no more looking at me like you're in love with me, for starters. Of course, she didn't say that.

"I don't know. Maybe *rules* was the wrong word. More like, expectations."

He nodded but didn't say anything as he waited for her to continue.

Suddenly, her mind was blank, and she couldn't think of anything to say—*damn pregnancy brain.*

"What are your expectations, Yvette?" he prompted.

"I'm not sure, to be honest. I guess, I expect that we'll get along for the sake of our child. Be civil, work out a schedule, and that will be the extent of our contact with each other."

"No. I don't think that's going to work."

She pulled her head back with a frown. "What won't work? Being civil? Having a schedule?"

"It just seems silly that you think our contact will be limited to handing our daughter back and forth to each other. Are you really going to want to give up holidays with her because it's technically my turn? Who will miss out the first time she goes to see Santa? Which one of us will take her to school on her first day? What happens if she plays sports? We're going to sit at opposite ends of the bleachers?"

She hadn't thought that far. Hell, she'd planned on doing this parenting thing alone until yesterday.

"No," he continued with a shake of his head. "I think we need to be together as much as possible so she feels like she has a strong family unit."

"What are you suggesting? You bring your girlfriends along, and I bring my husband, and we're all just one happy family?"

Yvette noticed his jaw clench.

"Are you engaged?"

"What? No, of course not. But I'm not going to be single forever, and you obviously aren't single now, so..."

"You're single?"

"Um, the men aren't exactly lining up to take out a woman in my condition."

Thanks for that, jackass.

"What about your boyfriend? Did you guys break up because of the baby?"

While they hadn't technically defined their relationship, at one point, she'd started thinking of James as her boyfriend.

Until the rug was yanked out from under her when Hope saw him at an awards ceremony with a beautiful blonde after he'd ghosted her.

Yvette now wondered if it was the same woman he'd brought with him to the inn yesterday. She'd be damned if she was going to ask him, though.

She didn't have a lot right now, but she at least still had her pride, and James Rudolf wasn't taking that from her.

"I haven't had a boyfriend since I graduated college. Just a few meaningless flings here and there. And then..." She paused. She'd almost slipped and said, and *then I met you.*

He raised his eyebrows with a tentative smile; his expression almost... hopeful?

"And then...?"

She huffed out a humorless laugh. "And then my last fling got me pregnant and blocked me before I could tell him."

The smile fell from his face.

"So, you didn't have a boyfriend?"

"When?"

"This summer. Back in California."

"Of course not. I would never have hooked up with you if I had." The idea was insulting. "I'm not a cheater."

The color drained from his face. "You didn't have a boyfriend?"

"Why do you keep asking me that?" Did he think he wasn't the father? "No, I didn't have a boyfriend. What kind of girl do you think I am? I hadn't even been on a date this year, until I met you."

He scrubbed a hand over his chin. "Then who was the guy that answered the door at your apartment? He said he was your boyfriend."

She was so confused.

"What are you talking about? A man answered my door and he said he was my boyfriend? When were you at my apartment?"

He leaned forward and put his hands on his knees. "The last weekend in July. I told you I was working, but I was really on a plane to California to surprise you."

Yvette started doing mental gymnastics. The last weekend in July... had she had any maintenance workers in her apartment? That was the only explanation she could think of as to why a man would have answered her door.

"Are you sure you had the right apartment?"

"Positive. He opened the door and before I could even ask for you, he told me you two were back together and to leave you alone."

Was she in the Twilight Zone? Who could have possibly done that?

"What exactly did he say?"

"He said, 'Eve and I have worked it out. You need to leave her alone.' Guess I understand why you didn't want me calling you Eve."

The realization hit her like a ton of bricks. Where she was the last weekend in July, who the man was.

"It's because my assistant is Eve and that's who the man was talking about. I let her stay at my apartment while I went to Puerto Vallarta to tour the property. Her boyfriend had kicked her out of their place. Her previous ex was staying with her because the ex who'd thrown her out was having a change of heart."

His eyes got wide. "So, that wasn't your boyfriend who answered the door?"

"No. It was *Eve's*. I was in Mexico."

James closed his eyes. "I'm such a fucking idiot."

She swallowed hard before asking, "Why?" Even though she suspected she already knew the answer.

James

It all made perfect sense now. Yvette hadn't lied to him. She didn't have a boyfriend.

Of course, she didn't.

When the man at her door had all but threatened his life if James didn't leave, it'd felt like he'd been hit with a sack of bricks. At the time, all he could think was, *how could I have been such a fool?* She'd really duped him. And he'd flown all the fucking way to California to find out what a sucker he was.

After those magical few days they'd spent together, and all those nights on the phone, he'd thought he knew her. That what they had was special.

Turns out... it was.

And he'd fucking blown it.

He felt like he wanted to puke. How could he even begin to explain what he'd done? How he'd ended their relationship *by mistake?* Who the fuck does that?

"I-I think I made a huge mistake."

Yvette gave him a tired smile. "Ya think?"

He moved from his seat on the couch to kneel on the floor in front of where she was seated. James took her hands, and she slipped her feet from under her legs to sit up straighter.

With her soft fingers in his palms, he looked into her brown eyes. "I'm so sorry. I thought you had played me. I should have known you'd never do something like that."

"Yeah." She gave a mirthless laugh. "You should have. I can't believe that's why you ghosted me. You never even gave me a chance to defend myself."

"I thought—"

She pulled her hands away and tucked them between her thighs. "You *thought* I was a liar. And I meant so little to you that you couldn't even be bothered to find out the truth. You just went home and moved on."

"I never moved on."

She raised her eyebrows. "Could have fooled me. It sure looked like that way yesterday."

"She's not—"

Yvette cut him off again. "Is she the same woman you took to the dog rescue fundraiser?"

James swallowed hard as he tried to figure out how to answer that without damning himself.

He must have taken too long to think of something because before he could even utter a word, she shook her head with pursed lips and glared at him. "Yeah, that's what I thought."

"It's not like I'm dating her exclusively. She fulfilled a need. There's plenty of women I've been—" He shut his mouth when he realized admitting he'd been seeing a stable of women wasn't helping his cause.

"How nice for you," she said with a sarcastic smile.

Fuck! Idiot! He was making things worse.

"I don't want anyone but you and our baby," he confessed quietly.

"I think we missed our chance. We just need to concentrate on co-parenting this little girl of ours."

Oh, he was going to co-parent with her, all right. Right after he wifed the hell out of her.

But James knew this was a marathon, not a sprint. He was going to have to earn her trust back before they became a happy family, and that was going to take time.

And he had nothing but time.

CHAPTER TWENTY-FIVE

Yvette

Finally, she had her answer about why he'd cut her out of his life.

It was all a misunderstanding.

And yet, that didn't make her feel any better.

He hadn't cared enough about her to talk to her before writing her off, but suddenly, now he cared? Because she's having his baby, he wanted to be with her?

Not. Happening.

Yvette grew up torn between two people who should have never gotten married but did so because of a baby. As she'd grown older, she suspected her mother may have cared more for her dad than he had for her. It had caused Nora to spend years in bitterness and misery until she finally met Jerry—Yvette's stepfather. Yvette wasn't going to allow that to happen to her. It was why she'd been so careful with birth control. Little did she know that the flax seeds she'd been adding to her morning smoothies had other ideas.

She and James could raise their daughter together in separate households, with separate spouses.

What he'd said about being a united front made sense, and maybe the couples would all get along well enough to be able to spend the holidays together and sit together at sporting events for the sake of their child. But Yvette and James were not going to be a couple.

No way would she risk becoming bitter like her mother had been. Talk about wasted years.

"I need to get some work done," she said as she gripped the arm of the couch and hoisted herself to a standing position. "Since we had a late breakfast, are you okay with having a late lunch, too?"

He nodded his head, not commenting on her dismissal of the matter as he watched her walk out of the room.

Yvette turned back with her hand on the door casing. "There are snacks in the refrigerator that Alice made before she left last night, and of course, help yourself to anything in the pantry. I don't know how much information Taylor gave you when you checked in yesterday, but the Wi-Fi password is StarsHollow—capital *S*, capital *H*—0619."

James cocked his head. "I understand the 0619, that's your birthday, but what is Stars Hollow?"

He remembered when her birthday was. That shouldn't have meant anything, but in her heightened hormonal state, every little thing meant something. She needed to get to her office before she started crying.

With a shrug of her shoulders, she quipped, "Either you get it, or you don't. I guess you don't." Then she escaped from view before the first tear began to fall.

*

She was in her office, playing with colors on their ad for a New England travel magazine, when James appeared in her doorway holding one of the trays guests used to take food to their rooms.

"Knock, knock," he said with a sheepish grin, his dimples on full display. "I brought you some lunch."

Yvette couldn't help but smile at the handsome man. God, she hoped their daughter looked like him.

She stood and walked around her desk. "I'm supposed to be making you lunch, not the other way around."

"Well, you were busy, and I'm not. And I knew you needed to eat soon."

Goddammit. There he went being thoughtful again.

Her stomach growled at the same time she glanced at the croissant-style sandwich, chips, and pickle on the plate he'd brought.

Part of her wanted to thank him, take the tray, and close the door to eat at her desk away from him. But she hated eating at her desk. It reminded her too much of her old job. She gave up that lifestyle when she moved to Massachusetts.

Besides, she didn't want to be rude—after all, he went to the trouble to make lunch for her. That was the *only* reason she said, "That looks delicious. Did you already eat?"

The *only* reason. His smiling ocean-blue eyes had nothing to do with it.

"No. I was hoping to convince you to join me in the breakfast nook. The snow is falling again, so it's really beautiful outside."

"I haven't decided yet if I'm a fan of the snow or not."

He grinned. "Like I said, you can take the girl out of California..."

"It's going to take some getting used to."

They walked toward the kitchen without verbally committing to having lunch together. If she didn't say it out loud, she didn't have to cop to it.

"Next year, I'll take you skiing and sledding and ice skating. You'll see there are a lot of fun things to do in the winter."

She glanced down at her protruding belly. "Yeah, the most I can do this year is build a snowman, or maybe have a snowball fight. I think if I tried to make a snow angel, I wouldn't be able to get back up."

He set the tray on the counter and pulled out a chair for her at the table. The falling snow outside caught her attention.

"It's coming down pretty hard."

"The news says we're supposed to get two feet over the next few days."

"Shouldn't you get back to Boston then? You're going to get stuck here!"

He grinned as he sat down in the chair next to her. "That's the idea."

****

James

He decided it was fate when he heard they were in for a blizzard. Mother Nature wanted them together as much as he did, and she'd given him a gift in order to be alone with her and win her back without any outside distractions.

He wasn't going to squander it.

"It looks like good packing snow. We could build a snowman after lunch, and you can even try making a snow angel. I'll be there to help you up."

Her eyes lit up. "You know, I've never made one before."

"Which a snowman or snow angel?"

"Well... both."

"What? Oh, we are rectifying that this afternoon! You're a New Englander now. It's part of the initiation."

She bit her bottom lip as if trying to disguise her excitement. "Okay. But only if we have hot cocoa afterward."

"There are even plenty of marshmallows. I saw them in the pantry."

"Then it's a date." Her eyes grew wide as the words came out of her mouth. "I mean, not a date-date, obviously."

"Of course."

Oh, it was a date-date.

CHAPTER TWENTY-SIX

James

She was adorable in her grey faux fur-lined boots, purple striped matching hat, scarf, and mittens. The purple bubble coat she had on was two sizes too big for her tiny frame. It consumed her.

"I'm guessing you bought your coat online," he mused with a smirk.

"Actually, I got it at Goodwill. Hope and I were there looking at furniture for the inn, and I saw this and thought it'd be perfect. I'm not sure how big I'm going to get, and this will accommodate whatever size I become. At least I hope I don't get so big that this won't work. I'll buy a better-fitting one next season."

He carefully tucked her scarf into her coat and zipped it all the way up, resisting the urge to kiss her when she looked up at him.

James didn't let go of her jacket, maintaining their proximity. "There," he said softly. "Now you won't get any snow down your front."

She stared at him for a beat with a tender look, like she had the first weekend they'd met, and he *almost* leaned down to touch his lips against hers. He knew the moment the spell was broken because she looked down and took a step back.

"Let's go build my first snowman!" she said cheerfully—*too* cheerfully.

They'd barely stepped off the porch steps when he realized this was a bad idea. The snow was falling harder than it had been when they ate lunch. It was hard to keep his eyes open against all the snowflakes coming down.

He reached for her hand and pulled her back on the covered porch.

"Why don't we do this when the snow has stopped? It isn't going to be very fun in these conditions."

She let out a deep sigh. "Oh, thank God. I thought people actually did stuff in this."

"No. Not like this. Although, I am going to bring in some more wood from the woodpile I saw around back. I want to make sure you're nice and cozy."

"I'm still in my pajamas. I think I got that part covered."

"Put on warm socks, make some hot chocolate, and go sit by the fire. I'll be in in a minute to join you. We'll play some cards or watch a movie."

Yvette looked like she wanted to argue but then decided against it. With a single nod, she said, "Okay, yeah. Cards sounds fun." Then she went inside.

They'd played a lot of games over the Fourth once the sun went down on the Cape. The night they'd met, they'd stayed up late playing cards, laughing, and getting to know each other. He kissed her for the first time after she beat him in a hand of blackjack.

That kiss quickly became heated, and before he knew it, they were getting naked in his guest room.

Is that the night our daughter was conceived? he wondered with a smile as he stacked logs in a wheelbarrow.

They'd decided to go without a condom, which was convenient since neither of them had one. She said she was on birth control, and he'd watched her pop a pill the next morning at breakfast, so he didn't think that was a lie. They were just the one percent where contraception failed.

And James was perfectly okay with that.

Of course, their chances were probably improved astronomically by the number of times they'd had sex that weekend and again when she stayed at his house the night before she went back to San Diego.

He'd loved how comfortable he felt with her in his space. Like she belonged there. He'd almost dropped to his knee and proposed right then, but the logical part of him told him it was just because he didn't want her to go back to San Diego.

The first day she left, he found himself calling her the second he stepped out of the hospital doors, and they talked into the middle of the night. They repeated that every night for weeks until he knew he couldn't wait for her trip to Boston at the end of September to see her again.

The purpose of his trip to San Diego had been to ask her to move in with him. He hadn't cared if she worked, went back to school, or watched TV all day, he'd just needed her with him.

Now, he needed her and their daughter with him. Maybe he could convince her to live in Boston with him most of the week, and then they could come to the inn on his days off.

You're getting ahead of yourself there, buddy.

James didn't care. He was going to make it happen. There wasn't another option.

CHAPTER TWENTY-SEVEN

Yvette

She found herself humming "Frosty the Snowman" as she took mugs from the cupboard while waiting for the tea kettle to boil.

Humming. Christmas carols.

Who *was* she? Yvette didn't hum, and certainly not Christmas songs.

Her phone dinged with a text.

Hope: Everything going okay?

No way would she tell her friend what she'd just been doing.

Yvette: Everything's fine. How's Olivia?

Hope: She had a little boy. We didn't make it back before she had him, but everything worked out. It was an easy delivery, I guess. Although, I'm not sure how expelling a human from your body— regardless of the method—can be considered easy. But he's healthy and beautiful.

Yvette: I'm sorry you didn't make it back in time. Did she get to the hospital okay?

That was Yvette's biggest fear being so far from Boston— not making it to the hospital and delivering in a car on the side of the road. It was part of the reason she'd decided to move back in March until the baby came.

Hope: Thank God the kid plowing her driveway was there to take her... But I feel bad for him, poor guy. He's like nineteen. He's got to be traumatized. He was really sweet and stayed with her the whole time. I don't think he's left the hospital yet. LOL

Yvette: Aw, he's an honorary uncle! But I'm glad everything turned out okay.

Hope: How's the weather there?

Yvette: It's snowing hard here. James said we might get two feet in the next day?

Hope: That's what the weatherman is saying. I wouldn't be surprised if our weekend reservations have to cancel.

Yvette: Oh no! You think it will be that bad?

Hope: That's what I hear.

Yvette sent back a worried face emoji.

Hope: All you have to do is say the word, and I'll have the kid who brought Olivia to the hospital drive his big 4-wheel drive truck with the plow on the front to the Dragonfly and bring you back to Boston.

Yvette shook her head, even though her friend couldn't see her.

Yvette: It's fine. Really. I just feel bad for James if he can't get back to the hospital.

Hope: Trust me. I have a feeling James couldn't be happier about this turn of events.

Yvette: He mentioned something like that.

The memory made her smile as the kettle whistled. She took it off the burner and put heaping spoonfuls of hot cocoa powder at the bottom of their mugs. The marshmallows were already on the counter. Alice, their chef, said the only hot cocoa is one that's made with milk and cocoa powder. Yvette begged to disagree. So, they compromised and kept supplies on hand for both.

Hope: Although thank God he'd already sent the stripper home. Could you imagine being snowed in with her there, too?

And just that like that, she didn't feel like humming anymore.

Yvette: No, I can't.

Hope: Sorry, babe. I didn't mean to bring that up. But, if it's any consolation, Evan said he only brought her to make you jealous.

Yvette: Not really a consolation. Just a reminder that he'd moved on. Oh, I found out the reason he ghosted me.

Hope: Do tell!

She gave her friend the *Reader's Digest* version of what happened.

Hope: Wow. I knew there had to be a reason. Everyone said serial dating wasn't his style.

Yvette: Not sure him thinking I had a boyfriend is a valid reason to turn into a manwhore.

Hope: I didn't say it was a good reason. It just helps explain things. And, come on. Think about it. Having lots of meaningless dates kept his heart, and probably his pride, safe.

She scowled as she read her friend's text.

Yvette: I'm not buying it.

Hope: I love you, and I'll support whatever you decide to do. All I'm saying is maybe he's not as bad as we originally thought.

Yvette: Maybe.

Hope: At least you know he'll be a good dad.

Yvette: That's true. We'll just have to establish some rules about when the baby can be introduced to people we're dating.

Hope: *If* you date other people.

Yvette: I'm guessing he's not going to become a monk just because he's having a daughter.

Hope: I didn't say anything about him not having sex... I just meant not with someone *else*. Other than you.

Yvette: I love you, even when you're delusional.

Hope: We'll see...

No, no, they wouldn't. She might have fallen for James Rudolf once, but she wasn't going to make the same mistake twice.

****

James

He stomped his boots as he walked up the porch steps with his last armful of firewood, trying to dislodge the snow in the contours of his boot tread. After stacking the logs in the little pile he'd made next to the door, he quickly brushed off the fresh snow on his coat before going inside.

James liked the idea of Yvette pregnant and in the kitchen making them cocoa while he did manual labor outside. It brought out his inner-caveman caring for his woman and child while she, in turn, took care of him.

After taking his boots off, he made his way to the kitchen and found her pouring steaming hot water into two large blue stoneware mugs.

"We should have enough firewood to last a week, should we need it," he said with a warm smile as he approached the island where she stood.

"Thank you, but why would we *need* it?"

"If we lose power. Blizzards are notorious for knocking out power for days."

Her eyes got big. "A generator is on our list of things we need, but we decided to wait until we're making a profit to buy one."

A generator was going to the top of James's list of things to buy his baby mama. If he couldn't be around to make sure she was kept warm, there was no way he was leaving her here without a backup power supply.

"We'll be okay if something happens. We have plenty of food, and I saw the cases of bottled water in the pantry. We'll just close the French doors of the living room. The low ceiling and fireplace in there should help keep the room warm."

A look of relief washed over her. Still, he couldn't help adding with a wink, "And we can always get naked under a blanket for body heat if it gets too cold."

She didn't even flinch.

"I'm sure Jalisco will keep me warm, if I need it."

He shrugged, like her shutdown of his idea to get naked didn't bother him. "I don't know... I generate a lot of heat. You might find yourself wanting in on it."

She raised her mug at him, the corner of her mouth hiking up as she walked toward the door. "Good to know I have options."

"Where are you going? I thought we were going to play cards?"

"Maybe later. I have to get some work done while I still have electricity."

Well, that backfired.

CHAPTER TWENTY-EIGHT

Yvette

In a way, it was good that Hope had reminded her about James bringing Brandi to the inn. It brought her back to reality. She'd almost got sucked into the daydream.

Almost.

It was easy to do when she was with him, especially when he tried to act like they were still a couple.

They weren't a couple anymore. Not that they ever had been. But the possibility had been there—once. But that ship sailed.

If she were being honest with herself, she was glad he discovered she was pregnant, and he wanted to be a part of their daughter's life. Hope was right, he was going to be a good dad. Involved, attentive, probably spoil their little girl rotten. Yvette had grown up without a father to take her to the father-daughter dances, come to her piano recitals, or cheer her on in seventh grade when she made a misguided attempt to play volleyball. Or any of the other things a girl needed her dad for. She was happy her daughter was going to have that. James was just going to have to keep his extracurricular activities on hold on the nights he had their child. Yvette was going to insist on that.

She wasn't a hypocrite. On the contrary, she had every intention of doing the same, not that she could even imagine dating anyone right now.

That wasn't entirely true. She could imagine having her brains fucked out; these pregnancy hormones were out of control. Too bad the man she imagined doing the deed with was the same one who'd threatened her with his naked body heat.

When he'd said it, she envisioned a days-long power outage and spending the entire time naked, wrapped up in his arms, under a blanket in front of a fire.

But that would be a bad idea. Besides, the second he saw her round, naked body, he'd probably wish Brandi was still here.

As if she'd willed it, the screen on her computer flashed before going black at the same time the small lamp on the credenza flicked off, and her office went dark, except for the waning late afternoon light coming in the window.

What was the saying? Be careful what you wish for?

James appeared within minutes.

"Do you know where you keep the candles and flashlights?"

"As a matter of fact, I do." Yvette was proud of the fact that she'd inventoried every single thing the first week she and Hope took over the inn. "They're in the supply closet behind the front desk."

He came around to where she was sitting and held out his hand. "Come on, I've already got the living room nice and toasty."

She reluctantly took his hand and let him help her out of her chair. Walking behind her with his hands on her hips, he guided her toward the door and dipped down to murmur in her ear, "There are snacks, too. I made sure to include some sweets in addition to the healthy ones."

He was speaking her love-language.

When they approached the living room, she noticed he'd already closed the French doors they usually kept open. Through the glass, she saw a roaring fire in the fireplace and a platter of food on the coffee table, complete with a stack of small plates next to it. There was even a pitcher of water and glasses.

"You thought of everything," she mused as they walked through the door. It was noticeably warmer than the drafty lobby with the fifteen-foot ceiling. "And you're right, it is nice and cozy in here."

He led her to the couch, his hands out at her sides as if he might need to catch her like she was a fragile old lady. It was sweet, in an annoying kind of way.

"I'm capable of walking, you know. Been doing it going on twenty-eight years now."

He sat down next to her with a grin. "Yeah, but you've only been doing it with my daughter in your belly for six months, and after your fainting spell the other day, I'm not risking it."

She wasn't about to tell him that *he* was the reason she fainted.

"That was because I hadn't eaten. I've learned my lesson. You see how much I've eaten today. Besides, are you going to walk me everywhere for the next four months? Maybe wrap me in bubble wrap?"

He raised his eyebrows. "Now *that* is a good idea. I need to look into that."

She couldn't help but smile. "You're impossible."

"Just want my girls safe."

Yvette played dumb. "Girls? I'm not having twins."

He gave her a pointed look. "You know perfectly well who I mean."

The idea of him taking care of her and their child and keeping them safe should not make her feel the sense of peace that it did. But she couldn't help it—it was a primal instinct to want the big strong man who knocked her up to take care of her. Still, she refused to acknowledge it. At least out loud.

"I promise I will be careful with our daughter. You have nothing to worry about."

His smile was soft when he replied, "I know. You're already a great mom."

That sounded like a line. Yvette narrowed her eyes at him. "What makes you say that?"

"Lots of things. The fact that you walked away from your career to open a bed-and-breakfast so you could slow down and have time for our daughter. How you take care of yourself: you eat right, for the most part, get plenty of rest, and Hope said you try to take a walk every day."

Yvette was embarrassed at his kind observation, so she simply asked, "Hope told you that?"

"She wanted to make sure I went with you if you wanted to go, so you didn't slip and fall."

"I'm not an invalid," she said with a scowl.

He gave her a sidearm hug. "Aw, don't be mad. We just care about you. That's not a bad thing."

Now she felt like an asshole, and tears filled her eyes. "I know. You're right. I don't mean to sound like an ungrateful jerk."

Embarrassed, she tried to discreetly brush the tears from her cheeks without him noticing.

Of course, he noticed, and immediately dropped to his knees between her legs, holding both her hands in his. "Oh, sweetheart. You don't sound like a jerk. I know it's hard for you. You're a strong, independent woman and everyone is treating you like you're made of glass. It has to be frustrating."

"But I know it's because they care."

James released one of her hands so he could run his thumb under her eye to wipe the tears. "Yeah, baby. We do."

She didn't want to include him in that equation of people who cared, but he made that harder every time they were together. The solution obviously would be to not spend time with him.

Unfortunately, Mother Nature had ideas of her own.

****

James

She looked so vulnerable, sitting on the couch with tears in her eyes. He wanted to scoop her up, hug her close to him, and protect her from everything that made her sad. Her wanting nothing to do with him was killing James.

He decided to press his luck and stroke her hair with his free hand while simultaneously caressing the webbing of her hand with his other thumb.

She didn't pull away, so he pushed further, murmuring, "*I* care about you," before he brushed his lips against across her cheek.

James half-expected her to pull away or at least stiffen at his touch. But, instead, she turned to look directly at him. There was longing in her mocha-colored eyes that seemed to mirror how he was feeling.

With only the slightest hesitation, he captured her lips with his, nipping gently at first to allow her a chance to stop things if she wanted. Instead, she wrapped her arms around his neck and sighed contently when he deepened the kiss.

Their tongues began to tangle, and she gave as good as she got, whimpering when he slanted his mouth and pressed her down on the couch.

Her taste, her smell, her noises... that's what he'd been missing these last months. What he'd desperately been trying to forget, or at the very least, drown out.

Nothing had worked: the other women, the drinking, working nonstop. She was still who he saw when he closed his eyes. Then the anger at being duped would swell in his chest and eat at him as he wondered how he could have been so stupid.

James slipped his hand under her blouse and felt the roundness of her stomach. Now he was wondering how he could have been so stupid to not believe what they had was real and to fight for her. He'd wasted four and a half months without her.

Resting his weight on his forearms so not to crush her, he pressed his hips against hers. She shifted to move his cock right where she wanted it, where it belonged, and lifted up to create even more fiction.

"My sweet California girl," he murmured against her neck. "I've fucking missed you so much."

She reached for his cock over his shorts. "Less talking."

But he *wanted* to talk. Whisper how he felt. Make promises to her about forever.

He sat up. "Baby..."

Yvette reached for the drawstring on his pajama pants, untied it, and then slid her hand inside to grasp his hard cock. Her tiny hand was soft; her grip felt like silk.

"James, don't ruin this. Just shut up and fuck me."

Ruin it? By telling her how he felt?

His throbbing cock told him to shut his damn mouth and do as she asked.

James could smell her arousal as he tugged on her flannel bottoms. She lifted her bum so he could pull them down her thighs and groaned out loud when he found her without any panties on. Her round belly with *his* baby growing inside her made his dick even harder.

He wasted no time pulling her lips apart to peer at her glistening, pink center. "There's my pretty pussy," he growled before darting his tongue along her folds. "Fuuuuck, you taste good."

Yvette bucked her hips against his mouth when he circled her clit with his tongue. He felt her hands in his hair as she moaned loudly. He slipped one finger inside, then a second.

"Goddamn, baby. You're so tight."

She was as responsive as she had been when they were together in July. She'd confessed one night on the phone that no one had ever touched her like he had.

"I thought multiple orgasms were a myth before I met you."

Even though she had been three thousand miles away, his cock had stirred as if it was displaying like a peacock.

"Not a myth, baby."

"No," she'd whispered. "Not a myth."

He'd wanted to beat his chest like a caveman that night. Kind of like he wanted to right then as she pulled his hair, holding his mouth tight against her pussy while her legs quivered.

"Oh my god, James. Yes! Yes! Yes!"

She arched her back, her mouth slack in a silent *O* as she came apart around him. His ego made him keep going, wanting to make her come again.

Instead, she squeezed her thighs around his head, causing him to cease his efforts.

He looked up at her with raised eyebrows.

"Condom?" she replied to his unspoken question.

Fortunately, he'd brought his suitcase into the living room and retrieved one in a flash.

She didn't take her eyes off his cock as he walked back to where she was still sprawled on the couch.

"See something you like?" he asked with a smirk.

"God yes. You have a beautiful cock."

"I think you mentioned that once before. The first time you saw it, although I still don't understand how a cock can be beautiful."

She sat up and stroked his dick while she continued to examine it. "Yours is. It's perfectly straight with just the right amount of veins, and the length and girth are ideal. Big and thick, but not too big or thick."

"Good to know." He was still smirking as he knelt between her legs, but he secretly loved her observations of his dick.

Yvette snatched the square package that he'd just ripped open and pulled out the condom. "I also recall you know exactly how to use your beautiful cock." Her voice was husky as she rolled the latex down his shaft.

This was a new side to his California girl. He liked her aggressiveness almost as much as he'd liked her sweet submission back in July. Hell, he just wanted her naked. He didn't care how: forceful or timid, sweet or spicy; he'd take her however he could get her.

Guiding his cock to her opening, she pushed the tip inside as she leaned back on the couch with her legs wide.

James wrapped his arms around her thighs and pulled her body closer. "Is this okay for the baby?"

"It's fine."

He didn't thrust any deeper. "Are you sure?"

It was her turn to smirk. "I thought you said you went to medical school?"

"I—"

She cut him off. "I use a vibrator regularly and haven't had any problems."

His left eyebrow went up. "Regularly, huh?"

Yvette looked him dead in the eye. "Regularly. My hormones are off the rails lately."

"You won't be needing a dildo anymore, baby. I'll take care of all your needs."

"For the next few days," she amended his statement.

"For always."

She shook her head and impaled herself with his cock.

"Shut up and fuck me."

He was nothing if not obliging.

CHAPTER TWENTY-NINE

Yvette

After he'd wrung the fourth orgasm from her body, she collapsed on the couch feeling like her limbs were made of Jell-O. She heard the French doors open, and a blast of cold air hit her naked body, but she didn't have the energy to even open her eyes to see where he was going.

She woke up and found a mattress on the floor in front of the fireplace, complete with sheets, pillows, and blankets.

Rubbing her eyes as she sat up, wrapping the blanket around her, she asked, "What's this?"

"There's not enough room on the couch for the two of us," he said as he sat down on the couch next to her, wearing only his pajama pants. "And I'm holding you in my arms tonight."

They were nice arms, she'd give him that.

James gestured to the snacks on the coffee table in front of them. "You need to eat something."

Yvette reached for a carrot stick. "Jeez, it's like having Hope here."

"Considering how much I know she cares about you, I'm taking that as a compliment."

Her phone dinged with a text message. "Speak of the devil..." Hope had sent her a picture of Olivia's new baby.

"Aw, he's beautiful," Yvette said and handed her phone to James.

He stared at the picture a long time before looking up at her. He whispered in awe, "He's so little."

"Thank goodness they don't come out any bigger. I'm already scared for my poor vagina."

He leaned over and kissed the blanket covering her belly, then spoke directly to their baby. "Take it easy on your mommy's vagina. Your daddy and future siblings thank you in advance."

She quirked a brow. "Future siblings?"

He grinned as he sat up straight but kept a hand on her stomach. "At least one more, but I wouldn't hate it if we have four."

Yvette turned her body, so his hand fell away, and she was facing him head-on. "Hold on. *We*—as in you and me?"

He cocked his head with a confused expression. "Who else would *we* mean?"

"That would imply we are going to be together in the future. We already agreed we aren't doing that."

"I never agreed to that."

Her traitorous heart skipped a beat. Thankfully, neither her heart nor her hormones were in charge right now.

She gripped the blanket at her chest to ensure she was covered. "Okay, *I* already told you, *I'm* not doing that with you. We'll co-parent our daughter, but we're not going to do it as a couple."

"Then what just happened between us?"

Borrowing something he'd said earlier about Brandi, she said, "Fulfilling a need."

He pulled back like she'd slapped him and stared at her for a few beats before shaking his head.

"Bullshit. We have something special, California girl. You can deny it all you want, but you feel it, too."

His words were the balm her heart needed after all these months of feeling rejected. *My heart's not in charge anymore*, she reminded herself. *I have a little girl to protect now.*

She shook her head, but he was undeterred. "It's okay. I know I need to prove myself again. Fortunately, I'm not going anywhere."

"Mmm, but you are. Once we dig out of this blizzard."

"Going to work doesn't count, Yvette." He winked at her. "I've got to be able to support my family."

Her pride made her say it before her brain had the chance to tell her it was a bitchy thing to say, even if he deserved it. "You don't have to. We don't need your money. I planned on doing this without a dime from you."

He frowned. "Too bad. Plans change."

"Don't I know it," she muttered.

He stood up and started toward the door.

She hadn't been trying to chase him off, but she didn't blame him for bailing. She was being awfully snotty for someone who'd spent her afternoon having orgasms and a nap. Although she was surprised that's all it took to get him to leave.

He paused at the door. "What do you want on your sandwich? You need some real food—you're hangry. To quote the candy commercial, 'you're not you when you're hungry.'"

Yvette blinked rapidly at him. "You're going to make food?"

He wasn't bailing, he was making her food. Dammit, he needed to stop being nice.

"Yeah, where did you think I was going? Unfortunately, our choices are limited without a power supply—although we can always heat soup or cook something in the fireplace if we need to."

Yvette pictured her camping trip with the Girl Scouts when she was a kid. Her one and only camping trip. It had been a disaster. Her troop leader was as ill-equipped to handle the wilderness as the rest of the city girls.

"Let's hold off and see how long the power stays out before getting crazy. How long do you think the food in the refrigerator and freezer will be okay before I should move it outside?"

"We've still got a while."

"Okay." She reached for her pajamas and tried to get dressed under the blanket covering her.

He watched from inside the doorway with the corner of his mouth turned up. "What are you doing?"

"Getting dressed."

"Why?"

"I should be the one making you something to eat, not the other way around."

He stalked over, snatched the flannel from her hands, and situated the blanket around her naked body. "You'll do no such thing. Now, lie back down and rest. I'll wake you up when I come back with your sandwich."

"Stop trying to be likeable," she grumbled.

"Is it working?"

Yes.

"No!"

"I've got nothing but time," he said with a grin, then slipped through the French doors.

Yvette flopped back on the couch with a sigh. She hated to admit it, but she was glad he was here. Being stuck in a blizzard alone would have been miserable.

****

James

She never did tell him what she wanted on her sandwich. But he remembered during the summer, she ate peanut butter and strawberry jelly. He remembered her making him one too, and when he took a bite, he was transported back to being a kid, probably the last time he'd had a PB & J. He voiced the sentiment out loud, and she quipped, "You're never too old for a classic."

"A true classic would be grape jelly," he pointed out.

"Pfft, says you."

He wondered if peanut butter or jelly was on the list of foods that now made her sick. Hope had given him a crash course last night, but he didn't remember either being mentioned.

When he opened the refrigerator and saw a bottle of strawberry jelly on a door shelf, he decided it was safe. The peanut butter would be good for protein, and the jelly would satisfy her sweet tooth. He grabbed the milk carton—she needed calcium, too.

The tray carrying sandwiches, milk, and potato chips was a far cry from what he'd like to prepare for her, but he decided he'd take PB & Js and being snowed in with her than the best steak dinner and sharing her with other people any day.

She clapped like a little kid when he put the tray down on the floor in front of her. The coffee table still had the snacks he'd made earlier.

"You made my favorite!"

"I remembered. They're not on the off-limits list, are they?"

She grabbed one of the sandwich halves and took a bite, smiling as she chewed. "Nope. Not yet, anyway. Although my doctor seems to think my morning sickness has subsided. I still won't risk eating cheeseburgers or burritos right now, though. That was terrible."

A pang of regret hit him in the solar plexus. Not for the first time since he'd arrived at the Dragonfly. "I wish I would have been there to help you through that."

"Well, you would have to have been taking my calls, so..."

"I'm so sorry, Yvette. I'd give anything to be able to go back in time and fix it, but unless you have a time machine in the barn, I can't. All I can do is acknowledge how badly I fucked up and beg for forgiveness. I want to be with you and raise our daughter together."

He cut her off when she opened her mouth, suspecting he knew what she was going to say. "In the same house."

She pressed her lips together, and they sat in silence while she took a bite from the other half of her sandwich.

"Do you want some milk?" he asked as he lifted a glass.

Swallowing hard, she reached for it then took a big drink before handing it back to him. "Thank you."

"My pleasure." That wasn't a lie. He liked taking care of her.

"I appreciate what you're trying to do, but you don't have to wait on me."

"What am I trying to do?"

She shrugged before taking another bite. "Serve your penance. But honestly, it's not necessary."

"Oh, it's very necessary. Even if I wasn't 'serving my penance.' He put air quotes around the words. "You're carrying my child, of course, I'm going to take care of you."

She gave him a weak smile. "You're going to be a great dad."

And husband.

He left it unspoken, for now. It, by no means, meant he'd given up. On the contrary, she was naked under that blanket; James was just getting started.

CHAPTER THIRTY

Yvette

He took the tray of empty dishes back to the kitchen but left the uneaten chips at her suggestion. When he returned, he carried an armful of logs that he deposited in the metal rack on the hearth next to the fireplace.

"There, now we should have enough to keep the fire going until morning."

"I don't know what I would have done if you weren't here."

"I'm sure Isaac would have come back to help; or Hope would have hired a snowplow driver to come get you."

He wasn't exactly wrong. She had offered to send someone with a plow. And Isaac did have a snowmobile that he already said he would use to come back anytime they needed him.

"Speaking of our staff... I should text Taylor and make sure she's okay."

She looked around the room for her phone. Before she could move from the couch, James was reaching for it, then handed it to her.

"Thanks."

She wasn't used to having her every whim met.

Yvette: Hi! I'm just checking on you. We lost power, but we're managing to stay warm in the living

room with the fireplace. How about you? Are you okay?

There wasn't a reply until an hour later.

Taylor: I lost power, too. But I'm okay. Isaac has a generator at his place. He came on his snowmobile to get me.

"Everything okay?"

"Yeah. Isaac has a generator so he went and checked on her and took her back to his place."

James gave a lecherous grin. "I'll bet that was just awful for him."

She laughed. "Isaac's a good guy."

"I'm not saying he's not. It was very chivalrous of him to check on Taylor. She's a single girl alone in the country without power. Of course, he didn't check on you..."

"Because he thought Hope and Evan were still here."

"And me. I'm here with you, too. But probably more importantly, he's not in love with you."

As much as she wanted to, if for no other reason than to be disagreeable, she couldn't argue. Everyone knew how he felt about Taylor, except maybe Taylor.

"Maybe he'll finally pull the trigger and do something about it. Although maybe he won't. That would be really awkward to be snowed in with her if she didn't feel the same way."

He gave her a pointed look. "Tell me about it."

"Oh, please. This is hardly the same thing and you know it."

"Mmm, it's kind of the same thing."

"Well, if it is, it's your doing. I was trying to find a way to get transferred to Boston when you pulled your disappearing act."

He cocked his head, his expression somber. "You were?"

She shrugged, embarrassed at having revealed that. "It doesn't matter anymore."

"Yes, it does."

"Why?"

"It means we were on the same page. I had come to San Diego to ask you to move in with me."

His revelation made her heart beat faster.

"That was the past, James."

"It can be our future, too. We can get there again." He put his hand firmly on her stomach. "We have the best reason to try."

She shook her head. "No. This baby is the best reason *not* to try."

****

James

Was that pregnancy hormones talking? Because she wasn't making any sense.

Of course, he was smart enough not to ask her such a question.

"I don't understand."

She sighed. "James, my parents got married because my mom was pregnant with me. They should have never gotten married, but they did. And they let me have a mom and a dad under the same roof for six years of my life. Then they got divorced, and I was devastated. My dad moved back to France, so I hardly ever got to see him. He and my mom bickered whenever they talked and did everything in their power to make the other one miserable. My mother became bitter and resentful. I don't want to end up like her."

"I'm sorry that happened to you. But one, I'm not moving anywhere—certainly not out of the country, so I'm always going to be here for our daughter. And two, if I'm ever lucky enough to be living under the same roof as you and our children, I'll do everything in my power to make you want to stay." He reached for her hand. "We're not your parents, Yvette, and no matter what, you'll never do this alone."

She squeezed his hand and gave him a weak smile. "I'm glad you're going to be in her life. A girl needs her daddy."

"What about her mommy? Don't you need a partner in your life?"

"Maybe someday I'll find someone."

She might as well have slapped him. He did his best to school his expression.

You're playing the long game, he reminded himself.

"I'm not going anywhere, baby. And I've got nothing but time to prove that to you."

"Good to know," she said dismissively. "We can keep having meaningless sex though, right?"

Gee, twist his arm. It was, however, anything but meaningless.

Chapter Thirty-One

Yvette

The power stayed off the rest of the night, and they ate dinner by candlelight. James must have been a Boy Scout because he made them what he called tinfoil dinners: meat, potatoes, and vegetables wrapped in tinfoil and put in the fire to cook.

"This is the best thing I've ever eaten!" she crooned as she dug in.

He smiled while he unwrapped his meal and put it on a plate.

"I'm glad you like it. We might be having a few of these if the power doesn't come back tomorrow."

"I should move the stuff from the refrigerator and freezer outside..."

"Already took care of it," he said before taking a bite.

"You did?" She felt the tears forming in her eyes—again.

He reached across and grabbed her hand with a sympathetic smile. "Aw, baby. Don't cry."

She sniffled. "It's the hormones. I'm not used to people taking care of me."

He gave her a wink. "I got you, Mama."

So he was proving. And it scared the shit out of her.

****

James

After dinner, James propped his back against the throw pillows they'd piled on the mattress while Yvette laid her head in his lap as he read from her favorite romance novel by the light of the fire. She'd put on an oversized T-shirt and a pair of panties before dinner, he'd get a semi every time she flashed the pink satin, or her nipples got stiff under the white cotton.

"You have a really sexy voice," she murmured sleepily when he came to the end of a chapter.

He ran his fingers through her hair. "I'm glad you like it."

"I do. I remember when we used to talk on the phone for hours. I just loved listening to you."

"I loved listening to your voice, too."

He paused before starting the story again. It felt like she had more to say. Finally, she whispered, "You really crushed my heart, you know."

"I know, baby. I'm so sorry."

"How could you just forget about me like that?"

"I never once forgot about you. Not ever. I hated that you were all I could think about. I couldn't get you out of my head."

"I don't know if I believe you. You didn't waste any time finding women to sleep with."

He closed his eyes; her words were like an icepick to his chest. He knew any excuse he offered would be lame, but he owed her some sort of explanation, so he went with the truth.

"I was hurt. I thought you'd played me. I'd been head over heels in love with you, and it felt like someone had come along and cut me off at the knees. I didn't want to risk getting serious with anyone again. I didn't trust my judgment, so I decided to only date women who I knew for sure weren't relationship material. My brother was more than happy to help me out in that department."

"I can't decide whether to hug him or punch him in the face next time I see him."

"Oh, go for punch him in the face. Definitely."

That made her laugh.

"I think we should establish some rules about when we let our daughter meet the people we're dating."

"It's not going to be an issue for me, since I'm only dating her mother."

"You say that now..."

"I'll say it next week, next month, next year, next decade. You're it for me. I want to have a family with you. I'm not just saying this because you're pregnant. I came to San Diego to ask you to move in with me before I knew you were pregnant."

"And then you just gave up on me. On us."

She'd taken the icepick out of his heart and jabbed it into his stomach.

"I didn't know. I thought..."

She interrupted him with a sigh. "I know. You thought I had a boyfriend and had lied to you."

James played with her hair absent-mindedly, unsure what else he could say.

Finally, she sat up straight to look at him.

"How about this? We leave the past in the past. I know you're sorry, and I accept your apology. We start fresh, starting now. No obligations or expectations of each other, just a friendship with benefits."

"I like the idea of you forgiving me for screwing up, and the two of us starting with a clean slate. I really like the idea of still being able to pleasure you sexually on a regular basis. And while I'm not really a fan of the friends with benefits part, I'll take it—for now. But you need to know, my intention is to be with you. Permanently."

He was marrying her by Valentine's Day. They were moving in the right direction; he just needed to prove to her that he wasn't going anywhere, and he didn't just want to be with her because they had a daughter on the way.

He'd tear down the walls she'd erected around her heart. Brick by brick if he had to. But hopefully, they'd all come crashing down before he even left here.

Hey, a guy could dream.

CHAPTER THIRTY-TWO

James

He woke up in the middle of the night with her snuggled against him. He loved feeling her soft skin against his and her familiar scent filling his senses. He felt content.

James realized what had woken him up. The fire had begun to die, and the room was getting cold. Part of him didn't care because he knew that was why she'd snuggled against him—for his body heat, but the protective part of him didn't want the room to get too cold, and it certainly would if he let the fire die out completely.

Slipping out from under her arm, he placed another log on the fire, then settled back in beside her.

"Thank you," she murmured as she turned over and wiggled her ass as close to his groin as she could.

If she was trying to get him hard, she succeeded. However, her soft snoring told him that probably wasn't her intention.

There's always tomorrow he consoled his cock before he fell back asleep next to her.

****

Yvette

The truce between them was nice. Letting go of her hurt and anger made her feel a hundred times lighter and allowed her to accept and appreciate the way he was doting on her without having to overanalyze it.

His phone beeped, and he glanced at it and made a face.

"Good thing you had those power packs in your car so we could charge our phones," she said with a laugh.

"Yeah, good thing," he grumbled as he tapped out a message.

"Everything okay?"

"The hospital is slammed and short-staffed. Parker just sent out a mass plea to everyone on the payroll to do what they can to make it in."

"I'm sorry. It's probably hard for you to be stuck here when you're needed there."

He pocketed his phone with a smile. "I'm needed here more."

"Well, if it means anything, I'm really glad you are here."

Leaning down to kiss her lips, he murmured, "That means everything."

Goddammit, her toes should not be curling over that.

His phone dinged again. This time he burst out laughing when he read the message.

"Hope has threatened me with bodily harm if I even *think* about leaving you alone to try and get back to the hospital."

He typed out a response, then looked up at her with a smirk when he was done.

"What did you say?"

"I told her not a chance."

Just then, Yvette's phone dinged.

"Gee, I wonder who that could be," she laughed.

Hope: What is going on there? Is everything okay? Do I need to call Isaac to come and check on you? Maybe have Olivia's snowplow guy come and get you after all?

Yvette: Everything is fine. We called a truce.

Hope: Truces are good, right?

She looked over at the gorgeous man with his hair still messy from sleep, smiling softly at her.

Yvette: Truces are great.

Hope: Squeal! When can we start planning your wedding?

Yvette: Slow down there, turbo. There's a big difference between getting along for the sake of our daughter and getting back together.

Hope: Have you had sex??

Yvette: Worry about yourself.

Hope: Double squeal!! That's a yes!!!

Yvette: It's just pregnancy hormones.

Hope: Keep telling yourself that, my little smitten kitten friend.

Yvette sent her a GIF of a roaring tiger with the caption, **Kitten my ass.**

Hope: You go, mama tigress! Get ya some!

Yvette: I have to go. She included an eye roll emoji.

Hope: Yeah, you do. She sent back a winking emoji.

Yvette: Love you.

Hope: Love you, too. I'll get there as soon as the roads are clear. BTW—I know you don't have internet, so I checked. The weekend reservations canceled.

Yvette sighed. While she was relieved because they were in no position to take guests and probably would have had to cancel with them if they hadn't first, it worried her to lose the revenue.

As if her BFF read her mind, she sent another text.

Hope: We planned on taking a loss until summer. This was in the business plan. Don't sweat it.

Yvette: You're right. Thanks for the reminder. See you soon.

****

James

The power stayed off until the early morning on Friday. When they woke to the lights on and the sound of the furnace running, he couldn't help but feel a pang of disappointment. He'd had such a great time having all her unoccupied attention.

They'd played games, read books, talked about everything and nothing, and had even gone outside Thursday afternoon when the sun was shining to build a snowman and make snow angels.

She'd looked like an angel herself with her smiling eyes and rosy cheeks.

They'd also had a lot of naked time. If she hadn't already been pregnant, she damn well would have been before he left to go back to Boston.

Friday morning, as she sat at the kitchen island while he made breakfast, she asked, "Are you leaving today?"

He nodded slowly. "The roads should be clear. I'm scheduled at the hospital tonight, but I don't have to go. I don't want to leave you alone."

"Isaac and Taylor should be here soon. I won't be alone."

But would they stay with her if she lost power?

"Since you don't have any guests this weekend, why don't you and Jalisco come stay with me in Boston?"

Jalisco was fiercely independent and hadn't liked being cooped up in the living room with them, so he'd sneak out to roam the inn whenever one of them went out the French door, then meow loudly when he wanted to come in and warm up. Or eat. Yvette had said to leave his litter box where it was, and James didn't argue with her.

He was curious to see how the three cats would get along.

Tom and Jerry were pampered babies he'd had them since they were kittens, whereas Jalisco had some street smarts. Maybe the former tomcat could teach his felines a thing or two.

"Oh my God!" she gasped. "I forgot about Tom and Jerry! Who is taking care of them?"

"The neighbor girl."

"Isn't she in college?"

"The little sister. She helps me out when Tracey's at school."

"Oh, that's nice."

He put her omelet and pancakes in front of her, then cracked eggs to make his own. "You didn't answer my question."

Yvette spent a long time buttering her pancakes, not looking at him. He somehow felt like their future was riding on her answer. If it was a yes, he was ordering wedding invitations for their Valentine's Day nuptials. If she said no, well... he wasn't ready to admit defeat, so he'd just keep trying.

He set his plate down and took the seat next to her, still waiting for her reply. Finally, she murmured, "I don't think that's a good idea."

He swallowed hard but tried to keep his face neutral.

"I have a lot of work to do, especially since I haven't done anything these last few days."

"Can't you do it from my place?"

"No."

He could tell by the look on her face that she was lying, but he let it go.

"Okay. Well, I'll be back in four days. And we can text a lot in between."

****

Yvette

"You're coming back?" she squeaked.

"Yvette, I'm going to prove that you can count on me. I'm going to be there for you and the baby."

She wasn't convinced, but there was a part of her that wanted to hope.

"Then I'll see you in four days. Do you have to leave soon?" *Do we have time for one more round of sex?*

He gave her a crooked smile as if he read her mind. "I've got a little time."

"I need to shower."

"Want some company?"

She did, but she also had two days of armpit and leg hair growth.

"Maybe next time."

****

James

By the time she reappeared after her shower, he'd already put the mattress back on the bed he'd pulled it from, straightened the living room, and was loading the dishwasher with the stack of dishes that had piled up when they didn't have electricity when she appeared in the kitchen. Her hair was styled, and she'd taken the time to put makeup on. She looked adorable in her black leggings with knee-high boots, baggy sky-blue angora sweater, and tweed scarf.

"You look beautiful."

She glanced down at her ensemble. "Thanks." She looked around at the kitchen. "Wow, you work fast."

"I do." He walked her to a chair and helped her sit down. "There's nothing left for you to do. Hope asked the staff to come back, and they're going to deep clean, so you don't have to lift a finger."

That elicited a grin from her. "I think you're worse than Hope. I'm not going to break, you know."

He leaned down and kissed her forehead. "I'm not taking any chances. Now, let me hop in the shower so I can fuck you before I leave."

****

Yvette

Isaac and Taylor showed up together on Isaac's snowmobile while James was still in the shower, leaving her disappointed she wouldn't get one last orgasm before he left.

"I thought the roads were plowed?" Yvette asked when they came through the door all smiles with red cheeks.

"They are." He gestured to where Taylor was taking off her coat and hat. "She just wanted to go for another ride on my sled."

"It looks fun."

"I'm happy to take you."

She sighed wistfully. "Maybe next year. Hope and James would have a heart attack if they saw me even looking at a snowmobile right now."

James walked into the lobby in a faded pair of jeans, Northwestern sweatshirt, and the boots he'd worn the first day he showed up there. His hair was still wet, and he smelled clean and woodsy. "Yep, I would." He dropped his duffel bag at his feet, slipped an arm around her waist, and then kissed her cheek. "But you're a grown woman. If you think it's a good idea..."

"Of course not."

He winked and squeezed her hip. "Good."

"Are you leaving?"

"I should get back to Boston so I can get a nap before work." He looked at Taylor. "I just need to settle my bill."

Yvette rolled her eyes. "I think it's safe to assume the lack of water and electricity during your stay, *Mr. Randolph*, means management will comp your visit."

"I insist. I was still a guest."

She knew it was charity, and she wasn't about to take it.

"No, *I* insist. There's no way I'd take your money. Especially after all that you did for me."

Thankfully, he didn't argue. "Talk about great customer service. You can bet I'll be back. In four days, to be exact, and next time, I'm paying." He leaned next to her ear. "Even though I'll be sleeping in the owner's suite, with the owner."

Her toes curled. She found herself wishing she would have agreed to having him join her in the shower after all.

"Tell your friends, too," Taylor chimed in.

He picked up his bag and winked at Yvette. "Oh, most definitely."

CHAPTER THIRTY-THREE

Yvette

James called her Saturday morning when he got off work before going to bed. And when he woke up before he went to work.

He did that every day he was gone. On Tuesday afternoon, a white Chevy suburban pulled into the Dragonfly's parking lot, and James got out of the driver's door. He saw her watching through the picture window and raised his hand to wave before getting his bag out of the back seat.

"Did you rent that just to drive here?" she asked when he came through the door.

"No, I bought it. It's four-wheel drive, so I can get here easier. Plus, I figured we'll need something bigger that can hold car seats."

She didn't miss seats—plural—but she ignored it.

"You traded in your Porsche for a Suburban?"

"Of course not. We'll still want to take the Porsche on dates."

She smiled as she shook her head. He made it hard not to like him.

"Come on, I'll show you to your room."

"Don't I need to check-in first?"

"We have your information on file. You're all set."

As they walked out of the lobby, he growled behind her. "You better be taking me to your apartment, California girl. We have some unfinished business."

"We do?" she teased. "Like what?"

His hand settled on her hip, and she stopped as he closed the distance between them. She could feel his hard cock against her ass. His hand moved from her hip to her chest, where he squeezed lightly as he nipped below her ear. "I think you know, baby."

****

James

They spent more time in bed than out that weekend. She wasn't joking—her hormones were off-the-charts horny, not that he was complaining.

If her staff noticed that they didn't come out of her apartment much, they didn't say anything.

Yvette had told him that Taylor and Isaac had been more than curious about him, so she ended up confiding that he was her baby daddy. That must have been why when he did appear in the kitchen for food, everyone seemed to bend over backward to help him.

As they ate at the kitchenette table in her apartment, he asked, "Christmas is next week. Are you coming to Boston, or am I coming here?"

She stared at him for a long time. "You want to have Christmas together?"

He furrowed his brows. "Of course. Who else would I want to have it with?"

"I don't know... your family?"

"You and that baby are my family."

She looked at her plate and quickly took a bite of food, but he could tell she was smiling.

The long game.

"So? Here or my place?"

"Here, I guess. Hope and Evan, and Steven and Whitney are arriving on Christmas Eve, then the day after Christmas, we were going to start preparing for their wedding. I think even Zach is planning on coming a few days before New Year's Eve."

James had been, too. Before he knew Yvette was the co-owner of the bed-and-breakfast and that she was pregnant with his daughter.

"When were you planning on leaving?"

She gave him a quizzical look.

"Evan... he had said you weren't going to be at the wedding. I'm assuming because you didn't want to run into me?"

"Yeah." She took a bite and proceeded to chew slowly as if buying time to think. She swallowed, then said, "I was going back to Boston on the twenty-seventh."

"But you're not now."

She smiled. "Well, thanks to Evan, I don't need to hide from you anymore."

"That's a good thing, though. You're not mad that he told me, are you?"

"No. I'm glad you know and are going to be in her life."

"Both your lives," he corrected.

CHAPTER THIRTY-FOUR

Yvette

James showed up the evening of December twenty-fourth with his normal duffel in one hand and the other clutching a multitude of different colored shopping bags.

"I told you, we aren't doing presents," she scolded when he walked through the door, still wearing dress slacks and a shirt and tie. He'd obviously come directly from the hospital and looked tired but still managed to pull off looking sexy as fuck.

He dropped his duffel, handed her the bags with the different store names on the sides, and took off his coat to hang on the hooks by the door. Then he slipped off his shoes.

"These are for the baby."

"Oh," she said with a smile.

"And maybe there are one or two things for you, too."

"James! We agreed... no gifts!"

He tapped her nose. "Relax, it's nothing big. You're not charging me to stay here, even though I can afford it and you should. Think of it as a hostess present."

"I've told you, I don't want your charity."

"It's not charity, it's helping my..." He paused before continuing, "future wife's business."

She raised her eyebrows. "Future wife?"

He walked past her with a smirk. "I said what I said." And then he continued walking into the living room where everyone was.

Yvette heard a chorus of "James!" and smiled. It made her feel good that everyone liked him.

She set the shopping bags on a chair in the lobby and followed him into the living room. Hope handed him a glass of sparkling cider. They'd all agreed earlier to no alcohol over the next few days, in solidarity with her, even though she said she didn't mind. But everyone had insisted, which, of course, made her bawl like a baby.

"Don't get too sentimental, we're still having booze at the wedding," Hope said as she handed her a tissue.

"I would hope so." Yvette dabbed her eyes then looked at the future bride and groom. "I'd feel awful if you felt like you couldn't drink at your reception because of me."

James didn't even comment on the drink Hope had handed him and instead raised his glass in a toast. He waited for everyone to pick up their glasses before proclaiming, "To new beginnings."

Everyone repeated, "To new beginnings," and clinked glasses. James wrapped his arm around her waist when he tapped his glass against hers.

He dipped his mouth to her ear. "You look beautiful, by the way."

Even though she didn't feel it—her ankles were starting to swell, and she'd had trouble getting up from a chair earlier, she said, "Thank you. So do you. Although I can tell you're tired. Are you hungry? There's a whole table full of food in the dining room."

"I'll grab a quick bite."

Yvette walked with him to the dining room and talked to him while he picked up a green paper plate with a big picture of Santa on it and a red napkin before walking around the table to look at the food selection. Alice had outdone herself, as usual.

He asked how she was feeling—like he always did.

"She's been really active today," she said while rubbing circles on her belly.

That elicited a smile from him as he picked up a sandwich roll with deli meats inside.

"No morning sickness? Lightheadedness?"

"No and no. And before you ask, I haven't overdone it. Thanks to you and Hope no one will let me do anything around here."

He shrugged. "Sorry, not sorry."

She stifled a yawn. "I didn't expect you would be."

With a full plate, he motioned to the door. "You must be tired, too. Maybe we can turn in soon?"

That sounded perfect.

****

James

They sat in the living room while he ate, both of them participating in conversations where it was expected of them, but he couldn't wait to put her to bed. Not to fuck her, although he suspected she would have other ideas, but to make sure she was getting enough rest.

He believed her that the staff wasn't letting her overdo it, but James still suspected she was pushing herself too hard preparing for Steve and Whitney's wedding. She saw it as the Dragonfly's debut for her and Hope's friends and family since so many would be in attendance and seeing the inn for the first time, and she'd been stressing about making it look perfect.

Every time he came to the inn, there were more decorations and added Christmas trees. She'd gotten this crazy idea that in addition to each communal room, each guest room needed a tree.

Now there was a Christmas tree in the cozy living room where they'd spent their time snowed in, the "salon"—a large formal living area—the dining room, each guestroom, and two twelve foot ones in the lobby. There were even miniature trees in the half bath on the main floor and at the front desk. Plus, one in her apartment.

He'd sought Hope out at the hospital earlier that week to express his concern that Yvette was working too much and to ask her opinion about something.

"I know, I know," Hope said when he stated he thought she was overdoing it. "Taylor has assured me that she, Isaac, and the rest of the staff are the ones doing the actual labor. She's just giving instructions."

That had made him feel better, although seeing her now with dark circles under her eyes, he had his doubts.

The other thing he'd wanted to talk to Hope about was what kind of engagement ring he should get his baby mama.

Hope narrowed her eyes at him. "When were you planning on doing this?"

"I don't know. I just want to have it when the time's right."

Hope pursed her lips like she was suspicious. "She's not ready. But if you must know, she's always been partial to round cut solitaires—big, but not gawdy, and I would go with simple pave diamonds on the band with a matching one for her wedding band."

He was astonished at the detail she'd just given him. "How do you know this?"

"We've been best friends since middle school. You think we haven't looked at engagement rings together?"

"Does she know what you want, too?"

"She does, Evan does... hell, even my mother does. I'm not leaving that to chance." She looked at him for a beat, then said, "Just make her happy. You do that, and I'll call a truce with you, too."

He grinned. "She told you."

"We're worse than an old married couple, there are no secrets between us."

He believed that. He'd taken advantage of it when he was bringing strippers to dinners and galas, knowing Hope would tell Yvette.

"Does Evan know you two have no secrets?"

"Of course."

"Have you forgiven him for telling me? You should. I needed to know."

"We'll see how things between you and Yvette go before I decide if he's forgiven."

"You know, *you* should have told me—months ago."

She snorted. "My loyalty is, and always will be, to Yvette. It wasn't my place to tell you. And you probably should drop it before I get pissed at Evan all over again. He just got out of the doghouse."

"Okay, okay. See you Christmas Eve."

Now sitting in the inn's living room the night before Christmas, Yvette disappeared, he assumed to use the bathroom, and Hope plunked down in her empty seat.

"So? What's in the bags?"

He laughed. "Some baby clothes, a few maternity outfits, and the next book in the series she's reading."

She raised her eyebrows and cocked her head. "That's it?"

"In the bags, yes."

A smile of recognition crossed her lips. "Tread lightly. You're making a lot of progress, don't blow it by jumping the gun."

She got up and went back to her seat before Yvette returned.

James knew Hope was right, and he had no plans of asking Yvette over the holidays while things were frantic for her.

Valentine's Day, however... that was his goal of when he wanted to ask her. He wanted to be married before their daughter arrived. If he asked her on February fourteenth, that gave them time to still have a small, intimate ceremony before her due date.

They just needed to get through the rest of the holidays and this wedding.

She appeared at the threshold of the living room, and James hopped from his seat to meet her before she came back in and sat down.

"Good night, everyone. I need to get this pregnant woman in bed."

He realized how that probably sounded, and if his brother had been there, he would have picked it up and ran with it. Fortunately, everyone in attendance was scared of Hope and kept it clean.

Yvette offered a small wave as she said good night.

"Good night!"

"See you in the morning!"

"Sleep well!"

"Love you!"

That last comment was from Hope, of course.

"Love you, too!" Yvette replied.

James knew he and Yvette hadn't said it to each other, but in his heart, he knew she loved him as much as he did her.

Now to figure out the right time to tell her. When she'd be willing to admit it and say it back.

CHAPTER THIRTY-FIVE

Yvette

James went to Boston the morning after Christmas to work four shifts, then returned after his last one on December twenty-ninth. She knew he was running himself ragged, going back and forth, but she also suspected he wouldn't stop, even if she told him to.

Zach showed up just after James on the twenty-ninth, looking tanned and rested. Although there was no doubt the two were brothers, there were definite differences. Aside from Zach being gregarious to James's quiet stoicism, James was a little taller, while Zach had a wider chest and shoulders. Even though James had the sexy silver fox look going, and Zach's hair was darker without any grey, you could still tell by the crinkles around his eyes that Zach was older.

"How was Jamaica?" Whitney asked after Zach had pulled her in for a long hug.

"Perfect. I still say you guys should do your honeymoon there."

"Who'd you go with?" Steven asked with a smirk, drawing his future bride from Zach and into his embrace. He kept his arms firmly around her.

"Bambi."

Yvette spit her drink out, and Hope asked incredulously, "Like the deer?"

Zach grinned shamelessly. "Yeah."

"Wasn't the last one Barbie?" Yvette asked.

"Barbie's still on the roster."

"Bambi. Barbie. How do you keep track?" Hope asked.

"Easy. Barbie has implants. Bambi's tits are real."

"So much for substance," James muttered.

"Hey, until I find my own Whitney," he winked at the bride-to-be, "I see no harm in playing the field."

"Maybe you should widen your field," Steven observed. "I didn't find Whitney in a strip club... just sayin'."

"There are a lot of single lawyers out there, Zach," Whitney added.

"Eh, maybe someday. Since all my wingmen are getting domesticated, I'm sure it's only a matter of time."

"Definitely a punch in the face," James grumbled, reminding Yvette of when she'd once said she didn't know whether to hug his brother or punch him in the face for setting him up with meaningless flings.

Zach turned his attention to James and Yvette. She was expecting some sort of sarcastic remark about how round she was, but Zach gave a sincere smile then pulled James in for a hug.

"Congratulations, man. I'm so excited to be an uncle."

He didn't hug Yvette, just held her hand between both of his and didn't let go. "Yvette, you're the most beautiful pregnant woman I've ever seen. You're glowing, sweetheart."

She felt a blush creep up her chest. "Thank you."

He released her hand and kissed her cheek with a soft smile. Yvette caught a glimpse of what he was like under all his bravado and felt a soft spot grow in her heart for the man who was going to be her daughter's uncle.

Zach made his way to Evan and Hope, and James said with a soft sigh, "I wish he would settle down. I think he'd be so much happier."

"He just needs to find the right woman. I thought he was going to ask Zoe out last summer? It seemed like they were perfect for each other."

"I thought so, too, but he never did."

"Well, she's set to arrive tomorrow. Who knows what will happen?"

****

James

He made sure that Yvette didn't overdo it the next day and slipped Taylor and Isaac each an extra five hundred dollars to thank them for making sure she was taking it easy when he wasn't around.

"You don't have to do this," they'd both protested. "We love Yvette. Of course, we're going to take care of her."

He shrugged. "Consider it a Christmas bonus, then."

James gave the rest of the staff money, too, with the same speech. It was a thank you gift for watching out for

Yvette, and when they'd protest it wasn't necessary, it became a Christmas bonus.

Hope came up to him during the rehearsal dinner's cocktail hour and bumped his shoulder with hers. "I hear you're bribing my staff."

"Just thanking them."

"Steven is paying them really well for their time this week, in addition to their salary. And even though we gave them a holiday bonus, I had still wished we could have done more, so, thank you."

"I'm no business owner, but maybe you should start charging people when they stay here... I know damn well you practically gave the rooms away for the wedding."

"It didn't feel right... they're my brother's guests."

"They would have paid for a hotel if he'd gotten married anywhere else. You're entitled to make a profit."

"I know. Yvette says it's harder being the owner. Before, she could chalk up not comping rooms to friends and family as 'company policy.' Then make them feel like they were getting a steal by giving them a twenty percent discount off the rack rate. When in reality, they probably could have gotten as good a deal on a travel website. Now, she feels bad for charging them anything."

"Taylor needs to handle all the bookings. Or you need to hire someone else. That way you're not the ones saying no."

"That's a great idea. I'll talk to Yvette about it. Speaking of..." Hope looked around the room. "Where is she?"

"I convinced her to take a nap and get ready during cocktail hour, since she's not imbibing anyway."

"And she agreed?"

James grinned. "I have my ways of convincing her."

Hope stuck her fingers in her ears. "La la la... I can't hear you!" She pulled them out and said, "I have to go find my mother. I have a feeling she's in the kitchen trying to 'help' Alice with the menu. Talk to you later."

James couldn't help but smile when he thought about how he'd convinced Yvette to take a nap. Licking her pussy until her little body quivered in orgasm and she passed out seemed to do the trick. It was one he enjoyed employing frequently. His baby mama was well-rested when he was around.

He noticed Zach hadn't left Zoe's side since she checked in. Good for his brother. James would love to see something happen between them. They seemed good for each other.

Yvette appeared in a long-sleeved dark red velvet maternity dress with a matching sash and rhinestone clasp that sat right above her bump. It fell just below her knees, and thankfully, she was wearing flats instead of heels. Her brown hair was in an updo with little ringlets framing her face. Her makeup had been carefully applied, with her lips matching the wine color of her dress. She was fucking stunning.

James heard Zach's voice at the same time he felt his brother's hand clasp his shoulder. "Close your mouth, you'll catch flies."

James hadn't realized it, but his mouth *was* hanging open. He quickly closed it, embarrassed at being caught so starstruck.

"She's beautiful," Zach observed. "God, I hope your kid looks like her."

"Me, too."

"Are you going to make an honest woman out of her?"

"That's the plan."

Zach gestured toward Yvette with his drink. "Does *she* know about this plan?"

"Not yet."

"I'm rooting for you, brother. Go, charm the pants off her." Then he chuckled. "Oh wait, that's what got you into this situation."

"Fuck off," James said, not waiting for a reply before heading toward her.

****

Yvette

James approached her looking sexy as sin in a dark grey suit and red tie. It was like he'd matched his tie to go with her dress, which was impossible since she hadn't told him what she was wearing.

He handed her a champagne flute filled with sparkling cider and clinked his matching glass against hers.

"You look stunning. I feel like the luckiest guy in the room to be your date."

"I never agreed to be your date," she teased.

"Too bad. I can still taste your pussy on my lips, that makes you mine."

Yvette had to admit, she enjoyed getting a growly rise out of him. It turned her on when he got all possessive alpha male with her.

"Come on." She reached for his hand. "I want to introduce you to Hope's mom and dad."

"Oh, I already know them."

"You do?"

"Of course. Zach was Steve's roommate in college, remember? I've known them since I was in high school, when I helped Zach move into his dorm his freshman year. Frannie and Robert were there helping Steven."

"Wow, small world."

Frannie said the same thing when the two went over to say hello.

There was no doubt Hope got her spitfire personality from her mom. Francine Ericson was just much more refined about hers. Yvette guessed she probably had to be, being married to a federal judge.

She grabbed Yvette and pulled her in for a long hug. "I have missed you, so much. It's weird not seeing you and Hope every weekend for Sunday dinner. But I'm glad you two are together again."

The elder Ericson woman turned her attention to James and hugged him. "And James, look at you, a handsome doctor. You two are going to make great parents."

"Thank you, ma'am."

Frannie laughed. "My dear boy, I've known you since you were a gangly teenager. You should know better than to call me ma'am."

He laughed. "Yes, of course, Frannie. I'm sorry about that."

Her face got serious. "So. You must also know I love Yvette like a daughter, and I can tell you make her happy."

Yvette loved that Fran could tell she was happy.

Then the woman continued, "Which means I'm a little disappointed that I haven't received my wedding invitation yet."

"I'm sorry?" James asked at the same time Yvette said, "What do you mean? Of course, you got one, you're the mother of the groom."

"Not to *this* wedding. To *yours*. When are you getting married?"

Yvette braced herself when she replied softly, "We're not."

Francine's eyebrows went up, and she shot her gaze at James. He quickly said, "What she means is, we're not *sure*. We haven't set a date."

Mrs. Ericson's eyes softened, but there was still a look of censure in them. Not in a judgmental way—that wasn't

Frannie's style. It felt more like she wanted what was best for her honorary granddaughter. To her, that meant James and Yvette should be married.

"Well, I hope I'm invited when you do set a date."

"Of course," they both said at the same time.

"If you'll excuse us," James said. "I think we need to find our seats. It's almost time for dinner, and I need to get Yvette off her feet."

Frannie patted his cheek. "Good man. Keep taking care of our girl."

"I will."

They found their seats, and Yvette let out a deep breath. "Wow, I'm sorry about that. She's always been protective of me."

James smiled. "That makes me like her even more now."

CHAPTER THIRTY-SIX

James

The wedding was held in the inn's salon, and it was perfect. Simple. Elegant. A true reflection of the bride and groom. And the way they stared and smiled at each other like lovestruck fools the whole day, it couldn't have been more obvious how much they adored each other.

If anyone deserved happiness, it was those two. They'd gone through hell to get their happy ending.

James noticed Zach was also grinning from ear to ear, before and during the ceremony. His brother wasn't exactly subtle about who was making him smile when he'd look out into the audience, and his focus would land on Zoe. The gorgeous woman was far more discreet and just turned the corner of her mouth up in return.

She was so different from the women Zach had dated since breaking up with Bridget. They'd fawn all over him, display their sexual prowess, feed his ego, and in return, he bought them expensive things and took them on exotic trips.

But James knew they weren't feeding his brother's soul. And he wanted that for Zach. James understood better than anyone why Zach was with women he had no future with. What he didn't understand was why.

James just wanted his brother to find happiness like he had. He watched Zach grin broadly again at Zoe. Maybe he was on his way.

Zach was a big boy, he'd figure it out, or he wouldn't.

The needle moved toward *he wouldn't* when Barbie, his Fourth of July date, showed up at the reception.

****

Yvette

She noticed James's face fall in the middle of dinner and immediately looked where he was staring.

A gorgeous young blonde who looked an awful like Barbie, the woman he brought to Steven's beach house over the Fourth of July, was standing next to Zach with her hand on her hip, shaking her finger at him.

Zach stood and discreetly ushered her out of the room while Zoe, who was sitting next to Zach, maintained her regal composure like nothing had happened.

Frannie would be so proud.

Zach didn't return for a while, and when he did, he was no longer all smiles, like he had been most of the day. The body language between Zach and Zoe changed considerably, too. It was apparent something had happened.

The rest of the reception went off without a hitch. Alice, with the help of the temporary staff, rocked the food the entire weekend, and dinner was no exception. Even Francine had been impressed.

They'd transformed the lobby into a dance floor, and the DJ had people dancing all night, then helped everyone noisily usher in the new year.

Steven and Whitney were beaming, and they kept thanking her and Hope for such a great wedding.

"I couldn't have wished for a more perfect day," Whitney gushed after hugging them for probably the fiftieth time that day.

That made all their hard work worth it.

It was funny, when the brides in Puerto Vallarta had hugged her and thanked her for making their special day perfect, Yvette had fought to smile and be gracious, let alone share in the couple's happiness.

Today, she felt nothing but joy.

She glanced at the dashing silver fox in the tux and knew he was the reason.

CHAPTER THIRTY-SEVEN

James

The bridal party and the rest of the guests who stayed at the inn last night all had a late breakfast together on New Year's Day. James sighed when he noticed Zach and Barbie at one table while Zoe sat making conversation with guests at another.

He was sure he'd find out what was going on soon enough. He and Zach usually met at least once a week for lunch or dinner, with an occasional happy hour with Steve and Evan.

After breakfast, Yvette walked him back to her apartment so he could get ready to return to Boston.

She sat on the bed and watched him fold his clothes. "What time do you have to leave?"

She sounded sad—that shouldn't make him happy, but it did.

"I need to head out by noon, so I have time for a nap before work."

She looked at him wistfully. "I had a lot of fun with you this weekend."

James stopped what he was doing and kneeled in front of her, grabbing her hand. "Me, too. Why don't you and Jalisco come to Boston with me for a few days."

He knew it was a longshot, but he had to ask. He thought he'd imagined it when she replied softly, "Okay. But I need to be back here by Thursday morning."

He had no idea if he was scheduled at the hospital on Thursday, but he didn't care, he'd make it happen.

He kissed her hand and said, "That's great!" Then he took great pains to slowly stand instead of doing a happy dance like he wanted to. "Do you need any help packing?"

"No, it won't take me long. I should try and help clean up as much as I can before we go. Not to mention, I need to find Jalisco."

"I saw him under the kitchen table earlier." There wasn't a chance in hell he was letting her do any cleaning. "By the way, you're not the one changing Jalisco's litter box, are you?"

"No, Hope was adamant that be one of the maid's jobs."

He needed to give Hope some serious props. She was a great friend to his baby mama.

"Go take a shower, I'll go see what needs to be done."

"Okay," she replied with that sweet but sexy smile that he loved so much. The one that made her face—and his heart—light up.

He suddenly had an image of a little girl with the same smile. He had a feeling both women were going to have him wrapped around their little fingers. And that made him happier than he could have ever imagined.

He ran into Hope the second he stepped out in the hall.

She was thrilled when James told her he was taking Yvette with him to Boston and scoffed when he told her Yvette was worried about helping clean up.

"We've got it all under control," Hope assured him. "Just get here out of here before the next storm blows through."

"I haven't checked the news, are we expecting another one?"

"Yes, tomorrow night. But do *not* tell Yvette until you're in Boston, otherwise she might decide not to go. Maybe she'll get snowed in there until she has the baby."

"You don't want her to stay here?"

"Hell, no. I would much rather she be in the city in her condition. But if staying at the inn is what will keep her nearby instead of in San Diego, then I'm not going to say anything."

"So, if I could talk her into staying with me...?"

"That would go a long way toward getting you off my shit list."

"I thought I already was?"

"Eh, the jury's still out."

He couldn't help but smile at her response, then asked, "What about the Dragonfly?"

"We have phenomenal staff. They are more than capable of handling the day-to-day things."

"I'll see what I can do."

"Just get her there."

"That's the plan. But you realize I'm scheduled at the hospital tonight."

"Then she and I will have a sleepover—at your house."

"You're leaving today, too?"

"Yes, my parents are getting on a plane this afternoon and Evan has to work tonight, so a sleepover at your place works out perfect. You've got a hot tub, right?"

"I do. But Yvette shouldn't sit in it for more than ten minutes. Promise me."

"Of course. Do you have good snacks?"

"Shit. No. I don't really have anything. I get takeout and I eat out a lot."

She sighed and looked at him like he was a helpless toddler instead of a fucking medical doctor with multiple degrees.

"I'll take care of it. I know what she likes. What's the nearest grocery store to your house that delivers?"

He blinked at her. "Grocery stores deliver?"

She rolled her eyes. "Oh my God. Never mind. I'll figure it out."

"Thanks, I owe you one."

"Pfft, one?"

"Fine. Put it on my tab."

"You say that like you don't think I'll collect."

"Oh, I have no doubt. But remember, I have a cousin, and I'm going to be her baby's godfather. I probably should return the favor."

Hope audibly gasped. "You wouldn't dare."

No, he probably wouldn't, but he wasn't going to let her know that. Although, he was going to have to figure out how to smooth things over with his cousin. Maybe they could have two godmothers. He was sure if he made a big enough donation to the church, he could make that happen.

"I'm just saying... that's gotta be worth something."

"Send me a picture of the front and back of your credit card so I can order your groceries," she grumbled. "I'm not paying for them."

He laughed. In some ways, Hope and Yvette were so much alike it was scary. That's exactly how his California girl would've reacted if she didn't have a good comeback.

He pulled out his wallet and snapped a picture, then another. "Sent. Oh, hey, will you see if they can include a litter box? We're bringing Jalisco and I don't want to bring..."

"Say no more. I will take care of that, *too*."

"I appreciate it."

"You say that now, wait till you see your grocery bill."

James chuckled at her empty threat. "I will happily pay any amount of money necessary to keep my baby and my future wife happy and fed."

"Whoa! *Future wife?* Did you ask her?"

"No. But it's just a matter of time. I'll wait for the right one."

"Good for you, Dr. Rudolf."

That wasn't at all how he was expecting her to reply.

"You think so?"

"Well, a few weeks ago, I would have said 'over my dead body,' but I *kind of* understand why you were such an asshole. Kind of. But I swear to God, I will personally castrate you if you pull something like that again. But as long as you take care of Yvette and *my* goddaughter like I think you will, then I'm rooting for you."

He hugged her. "Thanks, Hope. That means a lot."

She hugged him back, then pushed him away.

"I gotta go order groceries."

"See you later."

He walked back into the apartment feeling like he'd cleared one more hurdle toward getting Yvette to marry him before the baby came.

She walked out of the bathroom, naked, and jumped when she saw him.

"I thought you were gone."

James took her in, from head to toe. Her beautiful face, free of makeup. The perfect swell of her heavy breasts, the wonder of her round belly carrying his little girl, her flared hips, her toned arms and legs, and that gorgeous pussy.

"No," he said huskily as he slowly walked to where she stood in front of her closet. He ran the tip of his finger under her breasts. "I'm right here."

She traced the outline of his hard cock over his jeans. "Yes, you are."

He dipped his head and sucked her hard nipple in his mouth, drawing a soft moan from her while her fingers wove through his hair.

James swirled his tongue around the tip then switched to her other boob at the same time he reached between her legs.

"I love that you're already wet for me."

"I love that you're already hard for me."

Touché.

He slid his finger down her slit, then back up and circled her clit. She let out a whimper and pressed against his hand.

"Do you want me to fuck you before we go, baby?"

"Yes," she moaned.

"Get on the bed."

She scrambled to do as he instructed, and he pulled his shirt off then his jeans before climbing on the bed and crawling between her spread legs.

Thank God he'd gotten tested the day he got back after the snowstorm. He loved there was nothing between them when he pushed his cock inside her waiting cunt.

Her fingernails dug into his back as she raised off the bed.

James sat up on his knees and moved in and out of her with a steady rhythm while his fingers played with her clit.

"Oh yes," she moaned and hooked her feet behind the middle of his back at the same time she cupped her breasts in her hands.

He had to close his eyes. The sight of her, wanton and touching herself was going to make him come before he was ready. He needed her to come first.

"Such a pretty pussy," he growled. "Whose pussy is this?"

"Yours!"

"Whose baby is in your belly?"

"Yours," she moaned. Her mouth was slack.

He increased the tempo of his cock and his fingers on her clit. "Whose cock is fucking you?"

He felt her pussy tighten around his dick. "Oh my god, James, yours!"

"Say my name when you come all over my cock," he commanded.

He thrust in and out. "That's it, take it. Take my cock in your pussy."

She clenched around his dick and let out a long moan.

Before she started to spasm, he snarled, "Say my name!"

"James, oh my god, James! Yes! Oh god, yes!"

Her body convulsed, and he held her hips to fuck her hard and fast, thrusting in deep when he spurted ropes of cum.

Yvette cried out, "Oh my god!" as her body quaked again.

"Did you just come again?" He grinned as he dropped his weight on his forearms on either side of her and tried to catch his breath.

"Holy shit!" was her only reply. Her pussy was still milking his dick, and she repeated, "Holy shit!"

He wanted to buff his nails against his chest. *Fuck yeah. There's more where that came from, baby.*

She brought him back to earth. "We need to finish getting ready."

Oh yeah. They had to get out of bed.

It was okay, though; he was taking her home to his.

****

Yvette

James steered her toward their coats, hanging on hooks next to the front door.

"I'll be over tonight," Hope assured her. "We'll binge on Netflix."

She hugged Hope's dad, then her mom. Frannie whispered in her ear, "I'll look for my invitation." Then she pulled away with a wink.

James slung the strap of her laptop case over his shoulder, picked up his duffel bag in one hand, gripped the handle of her roller in the other, and walked toward the door. "Ready?"

She hesitated. She felt guilty leaving everyone to clean up without her. "If you need anything, I'll be available on my cell."

Isaac stood next to Taylor. "We've got it under control. Mary Sue will be in tomorrow after everyone leaves to deep clean. We'll have this place spic and span in no time."

"You guys are great. Thank you."

"Yes, thank you," James said, guiding her by her elbow out the door with one hand after having moved both their bags into the other.

She gasped. "We almost forgot Jalisco!"

"He can stay here," Taylor said. "We're happy to take care of him."

"Are you sure?"

James interjected. "I think we should bring him with us. I want to introduce him to my cats."

"Do you think that's a good idea, doing it on their turf? Shouldn't we have them meet somewhere neutral the first time?"

"Like where?"

Yvette wrinkled her nose. "Good question."

"They'll be fine. If worse comes to worst, we'll lock Tom and Jerry in the basement. You get Jalisco, I'll put the bags in the car."

Five minutes later, with an annoyed Mexican alley cat in his carrier, they were in his car heading toward the city.

"I haven't been to Boston for anything other than doctor visits since I moved here."

"We'll go out to dinner one or two nights if you're up to it. Maybe see a show and do some shopping?"

"That sounds fun. It'll be nice being able to go out and not worry that I'm going to run into you."

He glanced at her, then back at the road. "You worried about that?"

"Of course. My doctor's office is near the hospital. I thought it'd be just my luck. Hope would always want to grab lunch at the corner café near the hospital, but I'd insist we go somewhere else."

"So, Hope went to your visits with you?"

"Yeah."

"I want to go with you to everything from now on. Doctor's appointments, ultrasounds... hell, I want to be there even if you're just going to pee in a cup."

That made her laugh, but his words were like a warm hug. She could get used to this protective side of him.

"Okay."

"Okay?" He looked back and forth between her and the road, as if he didn't believe she would acquiesce so easily.

"Yes."

He grinned when he looked straight ahead. "That's two okays in one day."

Yvette closed her eyes with a smile while leaning her head against the headrest. "You're a dork."

"Yeah, but you're having my baby, so I'm not sure what that says about you."

She didn't bother opening her eyes when she quipped. "I'm a dork, too. Our kid is doomed."

His warm hand came around hers, and he squeezed. "Our kids are going to be the luckiest kids on the planet."

There he went with kids—plural—again. As she drifted off to sleep, she realized she didn't mind the idea.

CHAPTER THIRTY-EIGHT

Yvette

James crawled into bed with her the next morning at seven a.m. Hope had stayed in one of the guest rooms downstairs.

She rolled to burrow into his chest. "Are you just getting home?"

"Yeah."

She did the calculation from when he'd left yesterday. "Wow. Fourteen hours is a long shift. Is that normal?"

"Honestly, it depends. There are surgeries that are scheduled to be that long but those are rare. We had a lot of emergency surgeries last night. Couple that with being short-staffed, it's going to make for a long night."

"Do you want me to go sleep in one of the guest rooms, so you can rest?"

He wrapped an arm around her waist and pulled her to him. "No. I'll fall asleep easier if you're next to me."

"I'll be quiet when I get up."

"Don't worry. I tend to sleep like the dead after a long shift."

"Well, hopefully, you won't have our daughter when you're working."

"Oh, I'll have her," he said with his eyes closed. "Fortunately, you'll be here, too."

The more he said it, the easier it was for her to imagine. Especially after hanging out with Hope last night.

"This is a pretty sick house," her BFF had said as they'd walked down the stairs to the basement. Yvette stepped carefully as she held the big bowl of popcorn she'd made with the air popper she'd found when she'd explored his gourmet kitchen. Hope carried a tin of cookies she'd brought with her along with their cans of lemonade. The cats ran ahead of them. Jerry had been friendly when Jalisco had been introduced—probably more than her cat would have preferred. Tom had sniffed him then ran off to hide, but there had been no fighting or hissing so far.

"I thought my parents' house was family friendly," Hope said as she sat down on the leather sectional. "But this puts theirs to shame."

"It is beautiful," Yvette conceded.

She looked around the giant game room. "I can see you raising a family here. The schools are great, there are plenty of luxury hotels close by if you want to go back to work full time once the kids are in school..."

"Um... I already *am* working full time, remember? That little partnership we formed called the Dragonfly Inn? The place where we just held your brother's wedding? Where I'm going to be able to raise my child while I live and work there?"

Hope waved her hand. "Taylor and Isaac could run that place in their sleep. You don't need to live on-site to do the managerial stuff. Actually, that's perfect. You can work from home, and we can alternate months going to check on things. Although we might want to consider making one or both of them a partner and hiring someone to handle reservations. I'm sure James is going to want to get a place on the water in the summer, and you're going to be too busy to go."

She stared at Hope, dumbfounded at how much thought her friend seemed to have given this. "Um, wow. That's, uh, a lot to process. But you seem to be forgetting one little thing... James and I aren't together like that."

Hope made a face. "I hate to break it to you, babe, but yeah, you are." She ticked off on her fingers. "You're currently at his house eating snacks and watching movies with your best friend while he's at work. You're sleeping in his bed. You're carrying his baby. You're still in love with him. He's in love with you and wants to marry you and have more babies..."

"How do you know he's in love with me?"

"All you have to do is look at him when he's talking to or about you. Plus, I think he mentioned it."

Yvette shook her head. "How can I trust him? He ghosted me. Straight up wiped me from his existence. What's to say he won't do that again?"

"Well, my goddaughter for one."

"I don't want him with me because he feels obligated. Nora and Pierre already taught me how that turns out."

"You said Nora and Pierre were never in love. They were just a teenage summer fling that ended up creating you."

"God, I'm living my parent's lives..."

"No. No, you're not. You and James love each other. If it wouldn't have been for Eve's ex-boyfriend not knowing who the hell he was talking to, you'd probably already be married. Stop comparing your situation to Nora's. It's nothing like Nora's—"

Yvette raised her eyebrows in silent disagreement, so Hope continued, "Other than the unplanned pregnancy. You're not Nora and James isn't Pierre."

"James said the same thing."

Hope clapped her hands together once. "Good. Now that we've got that settled, I'm thinking a small ceremony before the baby comes, then we can have a big shindig at the Dragonfly over the Fourth. Ooh, or we could do it at Steven's where it all began."

"I love how you're just volunteering your brother's place without even asking him."

"He loves us. We just gave his wife the perfect wedding, and I'm sure he's reaping the benefits on his honeymoon right now, so it's not like he's going to tell us no."

Yvette shook her head. "This is crazy. I'm not even getting married!"

"Of course, you are. Hell, you should marry him for the health insurance alone. The hospital's policy is first-rate."

Yvette rolled her eyes. "Yeah, 'cause that's a good reason."

"I'm just sayin'... if loving each other and having a child together doesn't sway you, maybe his Blue Cross plan will."

She threw a piece of popcorn at her friend. "You're impossible."

Hope picked it up and tossed it in her mouth with a grin. "I'm right though."

Yvette had a lot to think about. Lying next to the sexy man with his arm protectively around her waist with his hand on her belly while he slept was only making Hope's case stronger.

She should slip out of bed and go make breakfast. She'd have a clearer head with food in her stomach and some distance from James.

Except, she couldn't bring herself to get up. Being next to him felt too good. So, she dozed off instead with the promise to herself she'd deal with it when she got up.

****

James

He woke up in the early afternoon with a smile, having fallen asleep with Yvette in his arms. Her scent was still on the pillow next to him. He hugged it against his chest and took a deep breath, then sat up with a burst of energy, knowing she was in the house.

After a quick shower, James walked through the first floor, but there was no sign of her. Maybe she and Hope went out to lunch? The cats were nowhere to be found either.

He took the stairs to the basement. There she was looking beautiful and perfect, lying on the sectional with a blanket over her legs while she worked on her laptop. Jalisco was keeping guard between her feet while Tom and Jerry studied her from the back of the couch.

"Hey, baby. Did Hope leave?"

"Hi! Yeah, a little after breakfast. Did you sleep okay?"

"I slept great, thanks. Are you hungry?"

She grinned. "I'm six months pregnant, I'm always hungry."

"When you're ready to take a break, I'll make lunch."

Closing the lid to her laptop, she set it on the ottoman and moved the blanket aside to put her feet on the floor. "I was just getting a little work done while you were sleeping."

James stared at her while she got up. He knew he had a silly grin on his face.

She looked down at her body, then touched her face, then her hair. "What? Do I have something on me?"

He reached for her hand as he shook his head. "No. I'm just happy you're here."

"Me, too."

Whoa. Her admitting that was huge.

They reached the top of the stairs, and he asked, "What are you hungry for? I have no idea what Hope ordered for groceries. We can order takeout or go somewhere if you'd rather eat out."

"No, then I'd have to put real clothes on."

He laughed as he gave her outfit a once-over. She looked downright adorable in her black yoga pants, white T-shirt, and an unbuttoned red flannel shirt. "Those aren't pajamas."

"No, but they're lounging clothes. Not really suitable for going out in public."

"I think they're fine, but whatever you say."

"I'm kind of craving pizza."

He tapped the screen on his phone. "What do you want on it?"

After he placed the order, he put his arms around her waist and dropped a kiss on her mouth.

"Did you get a lot of work done?"

"Not a lot, but it will give me something to do when you go to work later."

"I'm sorry I have to leave you alone. I hope you don't get bored by yourself. Do you want to ask Hope to come over again?"

"It's kind of nice not having to entertain guests or supervise staff. I think I'll be able to get a lot of work done while you're gone. I might even have time to read the book you got me."

He kissed her again. "Good. Maybe that will work in my favor when I ask you to move in."

She flashed him a placating smile but didn't say anything.

James released his hold on her and reached for her hand. "Come on, I want to show you something."

He walked ahead of her up the stairs to the second floor, and she pinched his butt when she reached the landing. In turn, he grazed her nipple before directing her down the hall.

"We could have just had sex on the couch. You didn't have to make me walk up a flight of stairs..."

That made him laugh out loud. "That's not why I brought you up here."

Her face fell. The fact that she wanted him made him sprout a chub. "Oh, I'm fucking you. But after lunch. On the kitchen counter, it sounds like."

"There might be a benefit to doing it in a bed. Optimal napping afterward with minimal effort."

"You've got a point. There are two guest rooms downstairs that we can choose from."

"Just one. Hope stripped the sheets off the bed she slept in, but I haven't washed them yet."

"Leave it. I have a cleaning lady who will take care of that tomorrow."

Her shoulders slumped. "Oh, thank God. I was dreading trying to make the bed. A pregnant woman wrestling with a fitted sheet is not pretty."

"I don't want you overdoing it. Let other people take care of things, that's what I pay people for."

They stopped in front of his office door, and he pushed it open so they could step inside.

"So, I was thinking... I can move my office to the basement bedroom, and we can turn this into a nursery."

She looked up at him with her eyes filled with tears.

"It was just a suggestion! We can do whatever you want! I just thought it would be a good idea, since it's so close to the master bedroom, but if you want to do something else..."

With a sniffle, she shook her head. "No, this is perfect. I can't believe you've already thought about this."

"Well, yeah, of course. She's going to need a nursery."

Yvette stared at him for a beat. Long enough to make him shift his weight as he tried to figure out what she was thinking.

Finally, she reached for his hand. "Will you marry me?"

He blinked a few times, wondering if he'd just imagined her proposal. Her earnest expression as she waited for his answer kicked his brain into gear.

He cupped one hand around her cheek. "Fuck, yes, I will." Then he captured her mouth with his.

CHAPTER THIRTY-NINE

Yvette

Did she just ask James to marry her?

His fingers dug into her hair as his tongue explored her mouth, and she let out a soft moan.

Yeah, she did. And she didn't regret it. She loved him, and she thought he loved her. He was thoughtful and kind and going to be a great dad. Her heart was bursting with joy at the idea of having a family with him.

"I love you so fucking much," he said when they finally pulled apart, and he rested his forehead against hers.

Well, that answered that.

"I love you, too."

He grabbed her face and kissed her again. Yvette clung to the belt loops of his pants. The intensity of the emotion in the kiss made her lightheaded.

The doorbell rang, and he reluctantly pulled away. "Let's eat in the bedroom. I'll be right back."

She went into the bedroom and sat on the bed, debating if she should take her clothes off. Even though he'd assured her he thought her body was beautiful, she wasn't exactly feeling it these days. Besides, what if she dripped hot cheese or sauce on her bare skin?

"Here we go!" he announced as he came in carrying a pizza box, napkins, paper plates, and two bottles of water. After setting the items down on the small table in the sitting area in front of the slider, he turned to her and motioned to the wingback chair next to the table.

"Come on, little mama. Let's eat. I need to feed you so I can fuck you before I go to work.

"So crass," she chided with a smile.

He put his arms around her and looked down at her. "And you're going to marry me. And have my babies."

"Yes, I am. Don't make me regret asking."

Patting her butt, he released his hold on her to guide her to the chair. "On the contrary. I plan on making you thank God every day that you met me."

She lightly patted her baby bump. "Already do."

****

James

He handed her a plate with a slice of pizza, still in awe of what just happened. This beautiful woman just asked *him* to marry *her*. He'd love nothing more than to strip her naked and pleasure her all afternoon, but he wasn't going to risk her having another fainting spell, so she needed to eat first.

Pizza, then pleasuring. Still not a bad way to spend his Saturday.

He plated a slice for himself, then said, "I'd like to get married as soon as possible. I was thinking Valentine's Day, if not sooner. We could do something small at the inn, or if that's too much work, go to city hall. We'll have a big party this summer."

She cocked her head. "Have you been talking to Hope?"

"Well, yeah. Not about this, obviously. Why?"

"Because she suggested pretty much the same thing last night. Same timetable and everything."

"I wouldn't mind sooner. Like, this weekend."

"That's not a lot of time..."

He didn't want her fretting about this. The last thing she needed was stress, so he shrugged nonchalantly. "It can be lowkey. No bar or DJ, just a nice dinner afterward. No more effort than a Thanksgiving dinner."

She took a bite and chewed thoughtfully.

"We could do that. It's kind of short notice though... I'm not sure if my parents would be able to get flights this late."

Shit. He hadn't thought of that.

"Let's look and see what's available, and then we'll go from there."

"Okay, that sounds like a plan."

Now for the living arrangements. James wasn't sure how she would feel about moving to Boston, but this was the logical place to be.

"So..."

Yvette looked at him with raised brows. "So?"

"What do you think about moving in here?"

Staring out the window, it was like she was trying to think of a way to soften the blow.

You could have knocked him over with a feather when she said, "Well, it's where my husband lives, so, I guess it makes sense."

"What about the inn?"

"Taylor and Isaac can handle the day-to-day duties just fine, and I can do the administrative stuff from here."

This was turning out to be a lot easier than he expected.

"I'm sensing this was something else you and Hope talked about last night."

"Yeah." She chuckled. "She has pretty much mapped out the next three months of my life for me. She's not going to believe it when she finds out I'm going to go along with her ideas."

It was good her best friend was on his side again. Yvette tampered his enthusiasm, though, with what she said next.

"I don't think I should move in until we're married. I know we kind of did things nontraditionally," she gestured to her baby bump, "but staying at the Dragonfly until then will help me tie up loose ends."

"I'll still come on my days off, if that's okay?"

"I'd love that."

He didn't like the idea of being away from her, not even for one day. "I can take some time off. I have plenty of PTO."

She took another bite, shaking her head. "Don't you think it'd be better to save your time for when the baby comes?"

"You're probably right. I just don't want to risk you getting snowed in again and losing power. I'd be out of my mind if that happened, and I couldn't get to you."

"I agree. Although I'm glad we were snowed in together, I wouldn't want to be there alone."

The more he thought about it, the more he didn't like it. "Can we compromise? Maybe you only go to the inn when I can go with you? I'll take a few days off, that way we can stay for three or four days each week until the wedding. I have plenty of leave, I promise I'll be around when she gets here."

Yvette grabbed another slice. "Are you sure you can do that? Isn't the hospital short-staffed?"

Yeah, the hospital was short-staffed, which was why he was confident Parker wouldn't give him shit. The chief of staff wouldn't risk losing James to another hospital that was also short-staffed but willing to work with him.

"It won't be a problem. Like I said, I'm not going to leave you alone there this time of year when there's always the possibility of a snowstorm blowing through.

"If you're sure... I'd much rather have you with me when she gets here.

"I will be," he assured her. "Which reminds me, do you have ideas for her name?"

"Hope wants me to name her Faith, and I have to admit, it's been growing on me. At the very least for a middle name. Why? Do you have a name in mind?"

"My oma's name is Abigail. I'd love to honor her by naming her first grandchild after her."

"Abigail..." she said it like she was trying it out. "Abigail Faith Rudolf... I love it."

James kneeled next to her and kissed her belly. "Hey, Abigail." He felt Yvette's fingers in his hair. Her smile was tender when he looked up at her, and he was overcome with how much he loved his little family. He slid his hands from her belly to her inner thighs. Yvette spread her legs apart so subtly, he wondered if she realized she was even doing it. He stage-whispered into her belly while looking up at her with a sinful grin. "Abby, I'm about to do naughty things to your mama, so don't mind the noises she's about to make."

****

Yvette

She took his offered hand and let him help her from her chair. He kissed the back of her neck while pulling her flannel off as they clumsily made their way to the bed.

Her T-shirt was next, then her bra. By the time they reached the bed, she was left in nothing but her leggings and socks.

She tugged on his T-shirt. "I'm feeling very underdressed here."

"That's how I like you."

"Is this your take on 'barefoot and pregnant'? Your version is 'topless and pregnant'?"

James stared at her boobs as he caressed them. "Damn right."

"You're a caveman."

He leaned down, with his mouth inches from hers, and whispered, "When it comes to you? Damn right." Before taking her lips with his.

He tasted like the mint from toothpaste, and his lips were soft and warm. Their tongues dueled as he kneaded her right breast with his left hand while he slipped his right under the waistband of her yoga pants and panties. Sliding his middle finger between her folds, he slowly pushed inside her.

"You're drenched, baby."

"I know." With her raging hormones, just looking at the man turned her on, but the minute he touched her... her panties became a mess. "What are you going to do about it?"

"Fuck you, of course."

He pulled the covers back. He'd made the bed, and she made a mental note of approval before she sat on the edge.

James tugged on her pants, and she dropped to her elbows and lifted her butt when he commanded, "Off." Her pants were on the floor in one movement.

Yvette lay naked in front of him while he was still fully dressed. He pushed her legs apart and appraised her body from head to toe. He stared at her for so long she began to feel self-conscious.

Finally, he ran his finger down her slit and murmured, "Mine." Then he finger fucked her slowly. She closed her eyes and raised her hips. His voice was barely a whisper when he uttered, "So fucking beautiful."

He rubbed her clit with his other hand, and she let out a low moan. "Oh my god, that feels good."

He used both hands in unison at a leisurely pace until she was panting with need. "James..."

"What do you need, baby? Do you need to come?"

Yvette whimpered in the affirmative.

Fucking her faster, he vigorously polished her nub until her body tightened when he pushed her to the edge. She chanted, "Yes! Oh, fuck, yes!" Then her body spasmed in climax as she fell over.

He didn't stop until she clamped her knees together. "No more!"

As she lay spent on the bed with her eyes closed, she heard the rustling of clothes and the unmistakable sound of a zipper being lowered. The bed dipped, and she felt his warm, hard, naked body next to hers.

Yvette opened her eyes and looked down at his cock, jutting straight out.

"Mmm," she murmured as she stroked the smooth shaft. "Mine."

James met her eyes. "Yours."

They were still horizontal on the king-size bed, so she tapped his hip. "Why don't you get comfy."

A slow grin formed on his face. "Why?"

"So, I can fuck you, of course."

He wasted no time and moved to the middle of the bed, propping a pillow under his head to watch her with a goofy smile.

Yvette straddled his hips and rubbed the length of his cock with her pussy without penetration.

She lined his cock up at her entrance, then with a wicked grin, paused. "Maybe we should wait until we're married."

Without a word, he impaled her with his cock.

"Ooh," she murmured as she rolled her hips on his dick. "I guess that's a no."

James reached up to play with her clit. "You could say that."

****

James

His future wife was his fucking fantasy girl as she rode his dick like a siren, piling her hair on her head while she looked him dead in the eye. He rubbed her clit faster, and she leaned back on his thighs to spread her pussy wide for him.

"Are you going to come again for me, baby?"

"Yes," she hissed.

As she came undone, he held her hips and furiously bucked into her. His orgasm was not far behind hers.

Yvette rolled to his side with one leg still entwined with his.

"I could get used to this," she panted.

He kissed her forehead. "Good, wait here," he said, then went to the bathroom for a towel, stopping by his closet on the way back. In the top dresser drawer, he pulled out the black velvet box and opened it, just to be sure the ring was still there.

James returned and tended to her, then tossed the towel aside and slid beside her. She snuggled into his side and let out a contented sigh.

He flipped open the box, then put one arm around her as he brought the ring in her line of sight. She sat up like a shot, her hand to her mouth while tears filled her eyes. "How did you—?"

Taking her hand, he slid the diamond on her finger. "I was planning on asking you, but you beat me to it. Since I already said yes, there's no takebacks."

She looked at the ring on her finger, then at him.

"I don't want to take it back. I love you."

"I love you, baby." He gestured to the ring. "Do you like it?"

Yvette moved her hand, so the gem caught all the facets of the light in the room. "It's perfect."

"Hope told me what to buy," he confessed.

"I'm sure I would have loved whatever you chose, but," she glanced at the ring again, "you did a really good job."

CHAPTER FORTY

Yvette

After checking the costs of flights, then her parents' availability, they decided on January sixteenth—a Saturday— instead of February fourteenth. There was a lot to do in a short amount of time.

Even though James's hours at the hospital varied daily, they settled into a comfortable routine. When in Boston, Yvette worked remotely and spent time with Hope while he was gone, and he pampered her and made her come multiple times when he was home.

She couldn't decide if his attentiveness was his attempt to atone for ghosting her and being with other women or if that was just his nature. Hope came over for dinner one evening, and Yvette voiced her concern.

"Well, probably some of it is because you're in the honeymoon phase of your relationship. How was he before he came to San Diego?"

"It's hard to compare the two. So much of our relationship in July was over the phone, and we were in that 'getting to know each other' stage."

"Ah." Her friend got a dreamy look in her eye. "I love that stage." Then her face fell. "We're never going to have that again."

Yvette held her hand away from her body, staring at the sparkling bauble on her finger. "No, but we'll get new, different stages. Holding our babies when they're born, watching them take their first steps, holding our husbands' hands when we watch our children walk across the stage to get their diploma... those will be wonderful, too."

"Oh my God!"

Yvette cocked her head. "What?"

"You're a goner. Like, I thought maybe you were having some doubts. But you're completely gaga over James."

"So? You're gaga over Evan."

"Yeah, but I'm not talking about babies or anything."

She gestured to her belly. "Well, it's a little late for me to be having second thoughts."

Hope laughed. "That's true."

The sound of the garage door opening interrupted their conversation. A few minutes later, James walked in through the door that led to the garage.

"Hey, Hope," he called cheerfully as he set his briefcase on the floor then walked to where Yvette sat. "Hi, baby," he said with a soft smile, then gently kissed her lips.

With his lips on hers, she felt like all was right with the world

"You guys are gross."

They pulled apart laughing, and James snorted. "I'm guessing the honeymoon is over between you and Evan?"

Hope stood, picked up her plate, and walked to the sink. "Not even close. It's just gross to watch my best friend be all doe eyed."

"You aren't happy she's in love?"

"Oh, I'm thrilled. Just like I'm thrilled my parents are still so in love," she said as she put her dishes in the dishwasher. "Doesn't mean I want a front row seat to it."

James chuckled, his hand still on the back of Yvette's chair. "We'll try to tone it down around you."

"You and Evan are still planning on coming to the inn this weekend?" Yvette asked as Hope gathered her purse.

"Of course. As my mother likes to say, 'Many hands make light work,' and we've got a lot to do before the wedding."

"I know, I know. Not to mention all the stuff I need to do in the city."

"We still on for dress shopping tomorrow?"

Yvette sighed. "I guess."

"What do you mean, *you guess*?" James demanded. "Aren't women excited about that kind of thing?"

"When they aren't feeling as big as a house they probably are."

He leaned down and stared into her eyes. "I think you're beautiful. You've got our little girl growing inside you." Then he kissed her again.

Yvette sighed for an entirely different reason.

"Okay, that's my cue," Hope announced loudly and headed toward the doorway before turning around. "I'll pick you up at noon?"

"I'll be ready."

"See you then. Have a good night, lovebirds. Don't do anything I wouldn't do."

"That leaves us a lot of leeway," Yvette muttered so only James could hear.

He burst out laughing, and Hope yelled, "I heard that!" before the front door closed.

****

James

The sun shone brightly through the hospital lobby's wall of windows when he looked for his brother. Zach had called and asked James to lunch, telling him he'd meet him at the hospital. Zach appeared with a grin and a backslap, and said brightly, "There's the future groom and father-to-be!" Then squeezed James's shoulder before removing his hand. "Congratulations, man. I really am happy for you."

They walked out the sliding doors, both men in peacoats. James's was a black wool, whereas Zach's was a dark grey cashmere. Neither were that great at keeping the cold out on a blustery day, but today was one of those perfect January days when the sun was shining off the snow, making the normal bleakness of winter feel brighter.

"Mom and Dad are over the moon," Zach said as they walked toward the corner diner.

"I know, I kind of sprung a lot on them all at once."

"Well, yeah. It was probably good you led with you're getting married before explaining why."

James stopped with his hands in his pockets and looked at his brother. "I'm not marrying her because of the baby. I'd have married her if she wasn't pregnant."

Zach nodded and motioned for James to continue walking. "Yeah, but if she weren't pregnant, you probably would have never seen her again to figure out that you fucked up."

"That's true," he conceded. "You've got a point."

They ordered at the counter then found a table while they waited for their food.

"So, what the hell happened with Barbie at the reception?"

Zach closed his eyes, let out a defeated sigh, and shook his head but didn't say anything.

"I thought things were going well with you and Zoe judging by your stupid smile the whole time you were with her. I haven't seen you smile like that in a long time. Then Barbie showed up, and your grumpy expression was back in place while you seemed to forget all about Zoe."

"Didn't forget her," he grumbled as he twirled the number holder for their order. "Just shit's complicated right now."

"Aw, man. You just need to find someone and settle down. I think you'd be so much happier if you spent your time with someone you truly cared about."

He sighed and stopped fidgeting with the stainless-steel contraption. "I wish it were that easy."

"It *is* that easy. Just stop seeing these women you have no future with."

"Well, I was going to, then Barbie showed up and dropped that she's pregnant. With my kid, allegedly."

"But didn't you have—?"

"Exactly. So, while I doubt she's even pregnant, if she is, the chances that it's mine are slim to none. Especially since I always use a condom. But even I know vasectomies and rubbers aren't foolproof... things could happen, so on the off chance that she's really pregnant with my child, I'm not going to burn that bridge just yet. Which means, I need to stay away from Zoe until I know for sure."

"So... when are you asking for a DNA test?"

"Already did."

James nodded. "She was agreeable? No meltdowns?"

"No, thank God. I've already had to deal with one stripper meltdown this week. When Brandi saw me at the club when I dropped off Bambi, she came off that stage like her hair was on fire demanding to know why you weren't returning her calls. She lost it when I told her it was probably because you were getting married."

"You're such a dick."

"And you're not for ghosting her? You need a new technique, man."

"Won't be necessary. Yvette's it for me."

"Wouldn't it be funny if she ghosted you? Gave you a taste of your own medicine?"

He'd never wanted to punch his brother in the face harder. "Yeah, fucking hilarious."

The server set their sandwich baskets down in front of them and picked up the number holder. "Enjoy!"

James glowered at his pastrami on rye, and Zach burst out laughing. "I was just teasin'. She's not gonna disappear on you." His brother popped a chip in his mouth with a grin. "Even if you do deserve it."

CHAPTER FORTY-ONE

James

Zach's words hit him in the gut and seemed to settle there over the next week. He was bothered because he knew it was true—he was an asshole. Instead of manning up when he thought Yvette was in another relationship, he took the coward's way out and cut her out of his life rather than confronting her.

Hell, he'd even done that with Brandi—just blowing her off rather than dealing with the inevitable tantrum she'd throw. Although he didn't feel nearly as bad since he would bet his paycheck that he didn't even know her real name. It wasn't like they'd had anything special, but he at least owed her an explanation.

Still, it wasn't like he was just going to pop into the strip club to tell her why he'd stopped taking her calls.

The best he could do was be the husband and father Yvette deserved him to be, so that's what he was going to do.

In three days, she'd become his wife, and he'd spend the rest of his life making sure she never regretted it. Although, he hoped his working late didn't count against him because it was happening once again. Thankfully, she'd already left for the inn that morning, so she wasn't waiting for him to go.

"It's okay," she told him on the phone. "You'd probably just be in the way, anyway. We've got a lot to do before everyone arrives."

"Yeah, and I should be helping you. I'll get there as soon as I can."

"Honestly, it's okay. I don't know if you realize this, but we have some pretty amazing staff. Don't worry about it. Go home tonight, sleep, work tomorrow, and come tomorrow night. You'll still get here before everyone else does."

"You don't want me to come until tomorrow?" James tried to keep the pout of his voice.

"You're going to be exhausted when you get off work later. I don't want you driving that far."

Okay, he'd give her that. He usually was pretty tired when he got off a long shift.

"Fine, but I'm not working tomorrow. I'll be there in the morning."

"Babe. I know Parker needs you. We're good here. Besides, we shouldn't be sleeping together this close to the ceremony anyway."

"Says who?" he snarled.

"Well, everyone. It's tradition. At least the night before the ceremony, so plan on Hope being a guard dog Friday night."

"All the more reason for me to get there tomorrow morning."

"I know your job is kind of important in helping keep people alive, and you're already going to be gone until next Wednesday. Not to mention, you're about to gain a wife whose business isn't turning a profit yet, and a child who's going to need a college fund. You might want to think about working tomorrow."

Shit. She had a point.

Well, her encouraging him to work bode well for his future when his job kept him from being home. At least she understood.

Still, they were getting married this weekend. He should be helping. "I've got plenty of money, and I already started Abigail's college fund."

"I'm just saying, I'll understand if you don't make it until tomorrow night."

Looking back, he wished she'd never told him that.

*

James pulled his paper scrubs off before he walked out of the OR and looked at the time.

Two a.m. Brandi would just be finishing her shift. Zach's words still hung over him like a dark cloud. He needed to man up and tell her the truth. Then at least, he'd have closure with that.

He sat in front of his locker and debated about what to do. This was his last chance to make things right.

James: Hey, are you working?

Brandi: OMG! It's so great to hear from you! I just finished—wanna come in for a VIP drink?

He knew what that was code for. Blow job in the VIP lounge.

James: No, thanks. How about I buy you a cup of coffee? At the corner diner by the hospital.

Brandi: Coffee?

James: Yeah, I need to give you an explanation about why I stopped calling you.

She didn't answer right away, and he scanned his emails while he waited for her reply. Finally...

Brandi: Okay. I can be there in thirty.

James: I'll see you then.

He set his phone on the shelf of his locker and grabbed a quick shower. As the warm water rained down on him, he wondered if meeting her was a mistake. She was bound to make a scene. He didn't need that, being so close to the hospital, where any of his colleagues could walk in. Maybe he should have suggested somewhere farther away. Not the strip club, of course, but there had to be other twenty-four-hour diners in the city.

He got dressed, put his watch on, grabbed his phone, keys, and wallet, then pulled his coat from the hook in his locker.

This is a good thing, he told himself as he walked to the Suburban with his collar up to block the wind. *It's something I should have done weeks ago.* Now he could start his new life with his beautiful family with nothing hanging over him.

He drove the short distance to the diner and parked in their parking lot. It was bitter cold out, and he hadn't felt like walking there and back. Besides, this way, he could go straight home.

Brandi wasn't there when James arrived, which didn't surprise him—she was notoriously late every time they'd gone out.

The hostess seated him in a booth near the door when he told her he was waiting for someone. The diner was usually busy during the day but was now deserted, save for a few med students that seemed to be in the middle of a late-night study session.

James ordered a cup of decaf from the waitress and checked his watch. Brandi was ten minutes late. He decided he'd wait until he finished his coffee, and if she hadn't shown by then, he could leave with a clear conscious knowing he'd tried.

He nursed the cup as long as possible, then stood and threw some money on the table. Finally, he could close the book on this, and Zach's voice in his head could fuck off.

As he approached the Suburban, he heard, "Jamie!"

Brandi ran toward him in her ridiculously high heels and threw her arms around him. His body was stiff with his arms on her biceps to try to push her away as she tried to pull his face down for a kiss.

"I'm sorry I'm late," she purred as she wrapped her arms around his and reached for his hand.

Pulling her off him, his words came out as puffs of air he could see. "It's okay." He gestured to the diner's door. "Let's go inside and talk."

"Let's just talk in your car. I don't need coffee this time of night."

He hesitated, then, with a resigned slump in his shoulders, opened the passenger door for her before going round to the driver's side.

After starting the engine and turning the heat on, he turned to face her.

"I asked you to meet me so I could apologize to you in person. I should have never blown you off like that without an explanation. You deserve to know why I can't see you anymore."

Brandi reached over and rubbed his inner thigh. "It's okay. I forgive you."

James moved her hand away. "I'm going to be a dad. Yvette, the woman who fainted at the inn, is pregnant with my daughter, and we're getting married this weekend."

With pursed lips, she waved her hand dismissively. "You... a married man. Sorry, I can't picture it."

Well, that's because he was going through a jackass phase when he was dating her, so he could understand her skepticism.

She leaned over the center console and rubbed her hand on his dick. "One last time, for old time's sake?"

He stilled her wrist and shook his head. "I don't think so."

Brandi leaned down so her face was inches from his fly. "Come on, Jamie. You know you love my hummers."

That was true. The girl could suck a tennis ball through a garden hose. Still, he wasn't tempted.

"Sorry, darlin'. I'm a one-woman man now."

She sat up in a huff.

Shit, here comes the meltdown.

Instead, she grinned at him like the Cheshire cat. "You'll be back, begging for me to suck your cock. When your wife is fat and won't fuck you, you'll come looking for me. Mark my words."

James didn't have the heart to tell her that was never going to happen, so he let her think she'd won.

"If that happens, I'll know where to find you."

"It's not going to be cheap..."

He thought about the designer purses, shoes, and clothes she'd gotten out of him over the months he dated her. "It never was."

That made her laugh out loud. "That's true."

"Take care," he told her dismissively. Now that he'd said his piece, he just wanted her to get out of his SUV so he could go home.

With her hand on the door handle, she winked at him. "See you soon," she cooed before sliding out the door.

James let out a breath. A sense of relief washed over him. *That's done.* Putting the car in drive, he headed home to get some sleep before setting out for the Dragonfly later that morning.

****

Yvette

She faintly remembered hearing her phone ding with a text message in the middle of the night. She was too tired to reach for it, but in her subconscious, she knew it had to be James telling her he'd made it home, and he'd see her tomorrow. She rolled over and fell back asleep.

It wasn't until she'd gotten up the next morning and had breakfast that it occurred to her that she had unread texts.

Seven texts? She must have really been tired not to hear them. But they weren't from James, they were from a number she didn't recognize.

Her first thought was, *fucking spammers, texting all hours of the night! What if they would've really woken me up?* Oh, she would have been so pissed!

She clicked on the message, her finger hovering over the delete button when she read the text.

Unknown number: Do you know where your boyfriend is right now?

The picture below was James and Brandi in a car together with a timestamp of three that morning. Her first thought was to dismiss it as being old with the timestamp photoshopped and someone just trying to cause trouble. But then she realized they were sitting in the Suburban—the SUV he'd just bought a few weeks ago.

The next five texts were all photos of them touching, and the final one looked like she was giving him head.

She felt sick. Very similar to when she learned he'd taken Brandi to the animal rescue fundraiser after blocking her.

Obviously, the wedding was off. She needed to call her dad so he and Juliette didn't get on a plane later today. Same with Nora, except she wasn't leaving until tomorrow morning.

How could he have done this to her?

She stared at the pictures and recognized the thin line of his mouth. The expression he only had when he was uncomfortable. With her fingers, she enlarged the shot and realized Brandi was touching him affectionately, but he wasn't her. That wasn't like James. He couldn't keep his hands to himself when the two of them were intimate.

Maybe she was just trying to see what she wanted to see. Yvette needed Hope to talk some sense into her.

She forwarded all the photos to her BFF, who was coming to the inn later that day, with a simple text: **Got these in the middle of the night last night. Do you think there's a simple explanation for this?**

On impulse, she forwarded the messages to James, with: **I want to believe there's an explanation for this, but I think I'd just be deluding myself.**

Followed by: **Don't bother coming today. Call your guests and explain that the wedding is off.**

Hope replied first: **I'm on my way. Do NOT do anything rash!**

She chuffed out a humorless laugh, then replied: **Like what?**

Hope: I don't know. Cut your bangs. Get on a plane. Call off your wedding.

Yvette: Too late.

Her phone started ringing. It was James. She hit *decline* and a text quickly came in.

James: That is not what it looks like.

She didn't bother to reply. Could he be any more cliché?

James: Baby, I swear on Abigail's life, nothing happened.

James: Yvette, talk to me. I promise there is a perfectly good explanation.

When she still hadn't responded, he sent one more text.

James: I'm in my car. I'll be there as soon as I can. You need to hear me out.

In her gut, she believed him that nothing had happened, but it didn't explain what the hell he was doing out with Brandi when he told her he was working late.

Did she risk looking like a fool and listen to his excuses, or did she cut bait like he'd done to her?

CHAPTER FORTY-TWO

James

When he pulled in, Yvette's white Honda was still in the inn's parking lot. That was a good sign. Unfortunately, Hope's Tesla came flying in like a bat out of hell right behind him.

Hope was out of her car and marching toward the front porch before he'd even put the Suburban into park. He hopped out and jogged after her.

"You've got a lot of fucking nerve," she hissed before taking the steps two at a time. He was impressed at her ability to do so in her heels.

"It's not what it looks like."

"Yeah, well, I hope for your sake you can convince Yvette of that, otherwise, prepare for those photos to show up in your custody battle. That I will have *no trouble* financing."

"That is the least of my worries right now," he snarled as he barged past her in search of Yvette.

He started in her apartment, then the kitchen, then the rest of the house. Hope followed him around the house, each of them calling Yvette's name, but no answer. James became more frantic room by room until they came to the last room. She was nowhere to be found.

They returned to the kitchen, where he slumped down in a chair.

"Maybe she went for a walk," Hope offered. "She can't be far. Her car's still here."

"Will you call her?"

Hope pulled her phone from her back pocket and hit a few buttons. A second later, the ringtone for Tina Turner's song, "Simply the Best" rang out in the otherwise silent house. It sounded like it was coming from Yvette's apartment.

James shot Hope a look. "'Simply the Best'? Really?"

"I'm her *best* friend, get it?"

Okay, when she explained it like that, it was kind of cute.

They walked into the apartment and started looking for more than just Yvette. That's when he saw the photographs scattered on her small kitchenette table. They were hard copies of the ones she'd texted him. On top of them were her engagement ring and an envelope with his name on it.

He swallowed hard as he opened the flap and pulled out the letter inside. Scanning it quickly, he sank into the nearest chair with his head in his hands.

"I deserve this."

"What?" Hope demanded.

He lifted the letter. "She left me. She's getting back together with her boyfriend in Mexico." He huffed out a humorless laugh. "I deserve it."

"So, you did cheat on her."

He jerked his head up. "What? No, of course not. I would never do that."

Hope took the seat opposite him, lifted one of the photos to look at, then quickly tossed it aside. "Start talking. What do you mean, you *deserve it?*"

He blew out a breath.

"It all started last week when I met Zach for lunch. He took a pot shot at me and said, 'Wouldn't it be funny if Yvette ghosted me like I did her.' And then basically said I would deserve it, considering what I did to Yvette and then to Brandi. He told me I needed a new technique."

Hope nodded, her bottom lip jutting out. "Can't say I disagree with him."

James ran his fingers through his hair. He could feel it sticking straight up but didn't give a shit.

"Anyway. What he said really bothered me and I started worrying that maybe he was right. I did deserve Yvette to ghost me. It'd serve me right. I'd been a fucking asshole to not only her, but Brandi."

"And the other women you dated..." Hope pointed out.

"Maybe. Those women knew the score, so they didn't expect a phone call or another date, and they never tried to reach out to me. And although I thought Brandi knew the score too, she kept reaching out. So, I kept seeing her because it was easy. I owed her an explanation. And all I could think about was if I didn't make things right, Yvette was going to leave me."

Hope's eyes got big, and her eyebrows reached her hairline. "Whoa. That's some pretty crazy thinking there, James."

"I know. And while I tried to make things right, I ruined everything."

"This is fixable." She held her hand out. "Let me read the letter."

He gave it to her, and she started reading. Her hand came to her mouth, but she kept going. Finally, she said, "Did you even read this? We obviously need to call the police. Yvette's been kidnapped. By one of Zach's girlfriends."

****

An hour earlier...
Yvette

Looking at the pictures in her text messages again, she decided she would hear him out. If for no other reason, she owed her daughter that.

She heard a car pull up while she was in the bathroom—the story of her life. Her bladder had become Abigail's favorite pillow. Looking at her watch as she washed her hands, she furrowed her brows. Hope shouldn't be here so soon, she'd just left. Maybe James had already been in the car when she sent him those photos. Or maybe one of the staff members was early, even though she'd explicitly told everyone not to come in until the afternoon.

Perhaps it was another package from one of Hope's late-night shopping sprees. She'd gone overboard with the pink outfits.

The doorbell rang, and she smiled in spite of her mood as she walked toward the front door. She was right; Hope had struck again.

Instead of the UPS driver when she opened the door, she found Barbie standing on the doormat in her knee-high boots and fake fur coat, with her hands in her pockets.

Yvette cocked her head. "Hi?" It was a question, not a greeting.

"Oh, good. You're here." She pushed past Yvette and walked inside while Yvette grumbled, "Come on in," before closing the door.

"Are you doing okay?" the blonde girl asked. She reached for Yvette's shoulder as if offering Yvette a rigid hug was supposed to offer comfort for her. The girl was in dire need of acting lessons, because Yvette didn't buy her concern for a second.

"I'm fine. Why?"

"Didn't you get my texts?"

Yvette smelled a rat, so she played dumb. "No. When did you send them?"

"Early this morning, right after I took these." She thrust photographs into Yvette's hands. "I'm so sorry. I know what you're going through. He's just like his brother."

Yvette flipped through the pictures, then looked at Barbie. "Why are you sorry?"

"Your fiancé cheated on you! While you're pregnant with his baby! Just like Zach did to me! I know you must be in shock, but I want you to know, I'm here for you. You can come stay at my place. Screw that asshole."

Yvette handed the pictures back. "I don't think that's what happened. I need to talk to James. I'm sure there's a reasonable explanation for these."

Barbie's bad acting job had Yvette convinced now more than ever that was the case. Something was rotten in the state of Denmark, that was for sure.

Barbie pulled her hands from her coat pocket, but instead of taking the offered photos back, she produced a gun and pointed it at Yvette's stomach.

"I was really hoping we could avoid this, but you leave me no other choice." She gestured at the door with the gun then back at Yvette. "Let's go."

"Wait," Yvette said, trying to think of a way to stall, knowing Hope and James were both on their way. "I have to write James a note. He'd never believe I just left without saying goodbye."

"Pfft. Why? He did it to you."

Ouch. She hated that this woman knew her and James's dirty laundry. "But he knows *I* never would."

She narrowed her eyes and stared at Yvette, who tried to keep her face as neutral as possible. Then, after a second of considering it, she said, "Fine. But don't try anything funny. I'm going to read it."

"Of course."

They went into her apartment, and Yvette stalled by opening all the kitchen drawers, pretending she couldn't remember where she kept a pencil and paper. She paused when she opened the knife drawer but then quickly shut it. There was no way she was bringing a knife to a gunfight. Not when she had her baby to protect.

Barbie seemed to be getting agitated, so Yvette 'found' the paper and pen and sat down at the kitchenette table.

With her pen poised on the paper, she looked at her kidnapper and said, "What do you want me to say?"

"Tell him you know what he did, and that you're going back to Mexico to have your baby. Didn't you have a boyfriend there?"

Yvette nodded. "Yes, he'll believe that," she said, then started writing. When she was through, she handed it to Barbie without being asked and prayed to God that the girl with the Midwest accent didn't speak Spanish.

Barbie kept the gun in her hand, but it was pointed down as she read the letter, and Yvette briefly considered wrestling her for the weapon. But having a beachball for a belly inhibited her options.

Barbie looked up. "You have a cat?"

"Yes."

"I don't believe you. Where is it?"

Yvette reached for her phone and Barbie pointed the gun at her. "Uh-uh," she tsked.

"He's at James's house. I was just going to show you my lock screen."

She slowly held her phone up to display the cute picture she had of Jalisco on her screen.

That satisfied Barbie because she grumbled, "Dumb name for a cat." Then she kept reading. Not looking up, she snorted. "Your boyfriend's name was Herman?"

"It's a family name."

"An Irish guy living in Mexico?"

"There's a lot of Irish immigrants in Mexico. Look it up."

The younger woman didn't want to appear uneducated because she acted insulted when she handed the letter back to Yvette. "I know. I don't have to look it up."

Yvette stalled some more "looking" for an envelope to put the letter in, then again when putting on her shoes.

"As you're going to soon find out, putting shoes on when you're pregnant is no easy feat," she replied when Barbie started barking at her to hurry up.

Barbie cackled. "I'm not pregnant. What do you think I want you for?"

It was at that moment Yvette knew she was in real trouble and was suddenly in fear for her daughter's life.

CHAPTER FORTY-THREE

James

He felt his heart drop to his stomach.

"What? Kidnapped?" He snatched the letter from Hope and started to read it thoroughly. Admittedly, he'd only scanned it the first time.

Dear James,

I know all about your affair. To say I'm hurt and humiliated is an understatement. I've decided to take Herman O'Novia up on his offer to marry me and help me raise my baby. You can go back to dating whoever you want, whenever you want. Elizabeth and I will no longer be in your way.

Please take care of Ayudame. Remember, he only likes canned cat food and needs to go to the vet for his shots soon.

As Hope knows, Herman has plenty of money. Tell her that I don't need my investment back from the inn. The money is all hers. Let her know that I'll never forget her.

Thanks for breaking my heart—again—you jerk. I can't believe you would do that to me—again.

—Yvette

Hope pointed at the boyfriend's name. "She never had a boyfriend in Mexico, or San Diego, for that matter. Herman?" She traced the name. "Herman—O? *Hermano*. It means brother in Spanish. *Novia*? That's girlfriend. Her cat's name?"

"You know it's Jalisco..."

"*Ayúdame* means help me."

"Oh my God." James reached for his phone and pressed the button for 911.

While he waited for the call to be connected, Hope continued reading. "I thought you'd decided to name her Amelia? Not Elizabeth. And her 'investment' in the inn was her labor. She knows damn well I'd never accept this 'she'll never forget me,' bullshit."

"Nine-one-one, what's your emergency?"

"My pregnant fiancée has been kidnapped..."

****

Yvette

"You know the baby isn't due for another two months, right?"

"Seriously?" Barbie glanced over at Yvette in the passenger seat, then back at the road. "You're so fat."

Okay, so Yvette obviously wasn't dealing with a rocket scientist.

"Why do you want my baby, Barbie?"

The blonde slammed the palm of her hand against the steering wheel. "My name is Stacey!"

Yvette lowered her voice and kept her tone even, trying to calm her down. "I'm sorry. I didn't know. Why do you want my baby, Stacey?"

"Zach wants a DNA test. I need a baby that has his DNA."

What. The. Fuck?

"You realize that she won't have *Zach's* DNA, right?"

"Yes, it will," Stacey/Barbie argued. "James is Zach's brother. They have the same DNA."

Yvette didn't know whether to laugh or cry at how fucking stupid this chick was. She decided not to even argue with her about how DNA worked.

"I'm having a girl."

"That doesn't matter. James is her *father.* I know how DNA works, Yvette."

Yeah, obviously.

"I mean, I'm having a girl. You don't have to refer to her as 'it.' Her name is Abigail."

Maybe if she humanized Abby by telling Barbie/Stacey her name, the crazy bitch wouldn't hurt her baby.

"So, you're planning on keeping me hostage for two months?"

Yvette was quickly coming to the conclusion this wasn't the most thought-out plan.

"I'm sure there's something on Google about how to make you deliver early."

"That's not safe for the baby."

"I'm sure it wouldn't be available on Google if it wasn't safe."

Of course not.

"So, Abigail arrives. Then what?"

"I introduce her to Zach, her daddy, of course, so he can take it for a DNA test."

"Then what?"

"Then he marries me, and we raise it, then I'm set for life as Mrs. Zachary Rudolf."

Yeah, that's sounds like a legit plan.

"And, what happens to me?"

Barbie/Stacey winced. "I'm really sorry." Yvette almost believed her. "But I'm going to have kill you. I can't risk Zach finding out."

So, this whack-a-doodle was planning on killing her, and her plan of passing off Abigail as hers wasn't even going to work.

Hopefully, Barcey—as Yvette started calling her in her head—didn't have an evil lair somewhere, and Yvette had given James enough clues that the police would be able to find her in time.

CHAPTER FORTY-FOUR

James

He didn't know if "missing pregnant fiancée" was what lit a fire under the authorities' asses or that Hope's—and Steven's—dad was a federal court judge, and Hope had no problem throwing that fact out when she also called 911. Either way, the inn was quickly swarming with the Massachusetts State Police as well as the FBI.

Evan and Steven were already sitting on the lobby's couch with Hope in the wingback chair opposite them when Zach rushed in, his eyes wide.

"Tell me they've found her."

"Not yet. They're setting up surveillance on Barbie's apartment now."

Zach scrubbed a hand down his face. "You really think Barbie did this?"

He showed him a picture of the letter he'd taken with his phone.

Zach enlarged the photo and started reading. After a few beats, he looked up with a wry smile. "Herman O'Novia? Your girl's a fucking genius."

"You speak Spanish?"

"Yeah. I took it in college. What the fuck did you take to meet your foreign language requirement?"

"Sign language."

"Oh, that's right."

He looked back at the phone. "What's the cat's real name? Does she even have one?"

"Yeah, Jalisco. He lives at our house."

"If Barbie really has her, she's going to be okay. Yvette's smart, and well, Barbie isn't. Her dumb blonde act isn't an act."

"Dumb doesn't mean she isn't dangerous. She's already proven she's capable of kidnapping, for Chrissake. What could she have done to make Yvette leave?"

"I'm trying to stay positive, here."

Zach swiped the screen on James's phone, raised his eyebrows, then stepped closer to James and lowered his voice.

"What the fuck is this?"

The photos from the texts Yvette had sent were visible.

"I had coffee with Brandi last night. We think Barbie sent those to Yvette."

"Have the cops seen these?"

"Of course."

Zach shook his head in disgust. "You don't talk to anyone in law enforcement again without me—your lawyer. Do you understand? These pictures make you the prime suspect."

"They haven't treated me like one."

"Trust me, okay? I know how this shit works."

James didn't care about anything but getting Yvette back safely. Still, he'd watched enough true crime shows to know his brother was probably right.

"Okay, I won't do anything without you."

"Have they asked you about these? Like, who the girl is, and your theory about who sent them?"

"They have Yvette's phone, so they're working on tracing who sent them. And they did ask me about Brandi."

Zach nodded thoughtfully. "Okay, so they're probably already working that angle. Maybe Brandi was in on it with Barbie and will roll over quickly to save her own skin."

James remembered how she'd grinned at him before getting out the Suburban last night, like she had a secret.

He hung his head. He'd set this whole thing in motion by texting Brandi last night. Because of what fucking Zach had said.

"Is it a crime to punch your lawyer in the face?"

Zach pulled his head back. "Uh, yeah. Why?"

James ignored his question. "What about your brother?"

"That falls under domestic violence."

"Damn," he muttered.

"Why? What the fuck did I do?"

"You told me I'd deserve it if Yvette ghosted me before we got married. It fucking bothered me, so I tried to make amends with Brandi by explaining in person why I didn't want to see her anymore."

Zach chuckled. "Why the hell would you do that? You knew I had already told her why."

"You made me feel like an asshole for blowing her off without an explanation!"

"You were an asshole. But what good would giving her an explanation now do when she already knew the reason?"

"I don't fucking know! I was just trying to make amends so karma didn't bite me in the ass."

"Probably not your smartest move."

"Fuck off."

Suddenly, a man in a black suit appeared in the lobby.

"James?"

He turned around and stepped forward with Zach right behind him.

"Yes?"

"You said this woman you think has her is your brother's girlfriend?"

"Well, one of several. She just told Zach that she's pregnant with his baby. She doesn't know he's had a vasectomy."

"Is there any way you can reach your brother so we can talk to him?"

Zach stepped forward. "I'm his brother."

****

Yvette

Barcey didn't have an evil lair; she'd brought her back to her apartment, where she handcuffed Yvette to the handle of a drawer on her nightstand. One that Yvette could just pull out and carry out the door with her if she got the chance to escape.

When she got the chance. She needed to stay positive.

Her kidnapper's phone rang, and Barcey quickly answered it—her voice high like a child's.

"Hi, handsome! How's my baby daddy doing?"

Pause.

"You do?" Her voice went up two more octaves in her excitement. "Really? A car?"

Another pause.

"Yes! I'd love to!" She came into the bedroom and straight to her closet. "I can be ready in an hour."

She hung up and popped her head around the corner. "Zach wants to take me car shopping! He doesn't want his baby riding around in anything but a Mercedes." She went back in her closet, and Yvette heard the unmistakable sound of hangers moving along the rod. "See? You don't have to worry," Barcey called. "Your baby will be well taken care of. That's got to make you feel better."

The woman was clearly unhinged. Yvette had no idea how she was supposed to respond to that.

"Yes, Mercedes are known for their safety records," was all she could think to yell back.

Sitting on the floor was starting to make her uncomfortable.

"Stacey?" she called.

"Hmm?" the woman said as she walked out of the closet, pulling the hem of a bright pink, skin-tight dress down her toned thighs. Her boobs looked amazing, spilling out of the bodice. The woman was a knockout. She didn't have a flaw. There was no hiding anything in that dress. She seemed to forget she was supposed to be pregnant.

"Would it be okay if I took a pillow off the bed and sat on it?"

"Take one of the throw pillows. I don't want my sleeping pillows to be flattened."

Bitch.

Yvette smiled. "Yes, of course. Thank you."

The waiting was agony. Yvette was miserable sitting on the floor, and she was also anxious to make a break for it once Barbie/Stacey left. Finally, the younger woman came out of the bathroom with her makeup and hair flawless.

"You look beautiful," Yvette offered. "Zach is a lucky man."

"Right? I'm going to be such a MILF!"

Barcey checked the time then slipped another handcuff on Yvette's wrist. "He'll be here any minute," she said as she fastened the other end of the shackle to the nightstand's handle so that both Yvette's hands were now restrained. After disappearing into her closet again, she appeared moments later, holding the ends of a scarf in each hand.

Yvette recoiled as the blonde came closer, thinking she was about to be strangled. But instead, Barcey put the scarf in her mouth like a gag then tied it tightly at the back of Yvette's head.

"Sorry. I can't risk you yelling and drawing the neighbors' attention."

Yvette nodded in understanding. She just wanted the crazy girl to get the fuck out, so she could stand up. Her ass was asleep.

There came a sharp knock on the door.

"He's here! Wish me luck!"

She shut the bedroom door, calling, "Coming!"

Yvette heard a deep voice and tried to roll the gag out of her mouth with her shoulder, to no avail. The front door closed before she finally got it off.

She was so tired and uncomfortable. And to make things worse, she had to pee.

Tears streamed down her cheeks as she yanked on the drawer. It had the type of slides that had tabs that needed to be pressed in order to release the drawer.

Desperate, she pushed one shoe off with her heel, then the other, and tried to use her toes to push the tabs. Her round belly made the task impossible. Defeated and unable to hold her bladder any longer, she peed her pants, making sure to sit on the damn bitch's pillow while she did.

Suddenly the front door burst open, and she thought Barbie was back already, so she pushed the drawer closed. She couldn't get the gag back in her mouth, and there was no disguising her wet pants.

A deep voice she didn't recognize called, "Police! Search warrant!" and Yvette screamed, "I'm in here!"

Men in tactical SWAT gear, holding AR-15 rifles, pushed through the bedroom door and made a beeline toward her. As one man unlocked the handcuffs, another ran his gloved hand up and down her back. "It's okay, sweetheart. You're safe. We've got you."

She remembered thinking she'd never seen a more handsome man in her life, and her fiancé was James Rudolf, so that was saying something.

CHAPTER FORTY-FIVE

James

He paced back and forth across the lobby floor of the Dragonfly. Zach had agreed to help the police and lure Barbie out of her apartment so SWAT could serve a search warrant.

The FBI agent appeared, and everyone jumped up.

"They found her. She's safe."

Hope cried out, "Oh, thank God!" Then hugged Evan. Meanwhile, James sank to the floor, his legs no longer able to support his weight. He buried his head in his hands as sobs of relief wracked his body.

He remembered being helped to his feet and ushered into a government van. He vaguely recalled Hope and Evan sitting next to him on the middle bench seat as they made the trek to Boston. It felt like they were making a trip to Florida—the drive took forever.

The next thing he knew, Yvette was throwing her arms around his neck, and he was holding her tight in an embrace, refusing to let her go.

She kissed his neck and whispered, "We're okay." Only then did he loosen his hold so he could cup her face and stare into her eyes.

"I was so scared, baby."

"I know, me too. But I'm okay. The baby's fine. Everything's fine, now."

"I didn't do anything with Brandi. I swear to God."

She lifted her knuckle and ran it down his cheek. "I know that, too."

"Have you seen a doctor?"

She shook her head. "Not yet. I asked to wait until you got here. I knew you'd want to go with me."

He laid a long kiss on her forehead and closed his eyes as relief washed over him.

She was safe.

"Come on, let's get you checked out by a doctor."

"I'm sure I'm fine. She didn't hurt me."

James clenched his jaw, thinking about what he wanted to do to Barbie. Pain was definitely involved.

He looked down and realized Yvette was wearing jail-orange pants, rolled up at the ankles.

"What do you have on?"

She glanced at her feet, and he noticed a blush creep across her cheeks. "Um, she didn't let me use the bathroom."

James pulled her against him. "Oh, baby. I'm so sorry."

She shrugged. "That's the worst of it, really. Well, that and she made me sit on the floor, so my back is killing me."

He wanted to strangle the crazy bitch for causing Yvette a second of discomfort while simultaneously wanting to take all of his future wife's pain away.

"A hot shower and massage, and we'll have you fixed up in no time."

She closed her eyes. "Mmm, that sounds heavenly."

On the drive to the hospital, Hope started peppering her with questions about Barbie's motive.

They all sat in stunned silence after Yvette told them the woman's reasoning.

Hope was the first to break the silence. "Wow. Just. Wow." Then she turned toward James. "What the hell was your brother thinking, dating her for as long as he did?"

He threw up his hands. "Hey, I tried to tell him."

She glared at him. "Mmm, did ya, though? It seems like you two were partners in crime for a while there."

He sighed. There was nothing he could do but own it. "You're right. For a few months after Yvette and I broke up, I lost my mind." He squeezed her hand. "But thank God, I got her back and got my shit together. Zach has said several times he wants a woman with substance, and twice now, I've thought he was going to pursue Steven's neighbor, Zoe. But something always seems to get in the way."

"Well, hopefully, this will knock some sense into him."

James could only hope.

CHAPTER FORTY-SIX

Yvette

She and James went back to his house in Moss Hills that night. James insisted she shower then get in bed while he catered to her every whim. Feeding her. Rubbing her back. Rubbing her feet. Playing with her hair while she lay with her head in his lap. Everything but what she really wanted.

Finally, she looked up at him. "Aren't you going to make love to me?"

"No, baby. You need to rest and heal."

She sat up and pressed her tits against him. "What I need is to be as close to you as I possibly can. That means your cock inside me, in case you were wondering."

The corner of his mouth turned up, and he shook his head. "You naughty, horny girl."

Yvette put her head on his shoulder. "I just need to feel safe."

His arms came around her, and he ran his hand up and down her back like the SWAT guy had done when he found her. "And you think sex will do that?"

"I do. I always feel safe in your arms."

James lifted her chin with his knuckle. "I promise I'll do everything in my power to always keep you safe."

"I know."

He lowered his mouth to hers, and she let out a sigh when their lips touched. Yvette loved how he kissed.

A thought occurred to her, and she pulled away. "The wedding! My parents!"

"Your dad and Juliette don't arrive until tomorrow morning, and your mom and Jerry get in around noon. I've arranged for rides for both of them."

"Not together..."

He shook his head. "Not together."

"What about the wedding? Were you able to get any decorating done today?"

He chuckled and shook his head. "Baby, the inn was teaming with FBI agents and police officers. I tried sending the staff home, but they insisted on staying so they would know the minute we found out anything. Alice kept busy feeding everyone and I think the rest of them kept busy getting the guestrooms ready, although, to be honest, I'm not sure. Everything is kind of a blur." He brushed the hair on her forehead. "You still want to marry me?"

"More than anything."

She felt his cock move and smiled as she reached inside his pajama shorts to stroke his hard shaft.

"But, right now, I need you. And it feels like," she moved her hand firmly up and down his length, "you need me, too."

James moved her pajama shorts aside and pressed a finger deep inside her wet heat. "More than you know, baby. More than you know."

Yvette pulled his shorts down his thighs, and his cock sprang free.

"Such a perfect cock."

There was a glint in his eye when he growled, "The better to fuck you with, baby."

She giggled as she slid her shorts off and straddled him. Lining his dick up with her entrance, they both let out a low moan when she sank down.

Moving up and down his cock, she teased, "Are you the big bad wolf?"

James gripped her hips and thrust up hard. "Better. I'm your big bad baby daddy."

She couldn't be happier.

Epilogue

James

The pastor introduced them for the first time as Mr. and Mrs. James Rudolf, and the room erupted in clapping and cheers.

It was an intimate ceremony, with only immediate family and close friends, so after the ceremonial walk down the aisle, he and Yvette returned to talk with their guests in the salon where they'd just exchanged vows while they waited for dinner to be ready.

Zach was noticeably subdued.

"Everything okay?"

"No, not really. I think I'm having a mid-life crisis."

Yvette laughed. "Except in your case, you're going to *stop* dating women half your age?"

"And start dating ones who have a basic understanding of how DNA works?" Hope chimed in as she approached with a flute of sparkling cider in her hand.

James could see the pain in his brother's eyes as Zach whispered, "I'm so sorry, Yvette. Thank God you're okay."

His bride reached for Zach's hand. "It's not your fault. Stop beating yourself up."

"I just wish—"

She cut him off. "Not that I think you need to, but do you want to know how you can make it up to me?"

"Name it. Anything."

"Go see Zoe."

Zach scrubbed his face with his hand. "I don't think she wants to see me. Not after the way we ended things last time."

Yvette shrugged. "You never know until you try."

His brother stared at a spot on the ground for a minute, then took a deep breath in through his nose.

He lifted Yvette's hand to his lips, kissed it, then said, "You know what, *sis*?" He winked at her. "You're absolutely right."

That elicited a bright smile from his bride. "I'm glad you think so. And I love that I can call you 'bro' now."

Zach pulled James in for a hug. "Congratulations again," he said as he clapped him on the back. "But if you'll excuse me... I need to go talk to Steven about renting his beach house."

****

Wicked Bad Decisions—Zach and Zoe's story, coming May 2021. https://books2read.com/wickeddecisions

Wicked Dirty Secret—Olivia's love story, coming July 2021.

Sign up for my newsletter to get a bonus scene of James and Yvette's wedding night (when it's ready.) https://www.subscribepage.com/TessSummersNewsletter

THANK YOU

Thank you for reading *Wicked Hot Baby Daddy!*

This series is turning out to be a lot of fun. I hope you love the characters as much as I do! I'm excited to bring you Zach and Zoe's story next, followed by Olivia and her mystery man this summer. (PS—Sloane's story is also coming this summer!)

If you enjoyed the book (and even if you didn't), would you mind leaving me a review on Amazon and/or Goodreads (and Bookbub if it's not too much trouble)? Believe it or not, your review does help get my book seen by other readers, which lets me keep writing.

Don't forget to sign up for my newsletter to get free bonus content and be the first to know about cover reveals, contests, excerpts, and more!

https://www.subscribepage.com/TessSummersNewsletter

xoxo,

Tess

ACKNOWLEDGMENTS

Mr. Summers: Words cannot express how much I appreciate everything you do. Thank you for taking such good care of me.

Marla Selkow Esposito: I appreciate all the love and care you put into editing this book. Thank you for making my work better.

OliviaProDesigns: Once again, a great cover. I love it.

Anna Lena Milo: I can't thank you enough for all your help with all the things, so all I have to worry about is writing words.

The real James Rudolf: Thanks for letting me borrow your name for the hero. I hope I did you justice!

To my readers: You're the reason I get up every day and write. Thank you for letting me bring you my stories and for loving (or hating!) the characters as much as I do. I am humbled that you choose my books to read. Thank you for your support.

Other works by Tess Summers:

WICKED HOT SILVER FOX

It all started with a dirty photo in his text messages...

Yeah, Dr. Parker Preston's intentions when he gave Alexandra Collins his phone number at the animal rescue gala were more personal than professional. But he'd never expected the sassy beauty with the blue streak in her hair to send him a picture of her perfect, perky boobs as enticement to adopt the dogs she was desperately trying to find a home for.

But dang if they weren't the ideal incentive for him to offer his home to more than just the dogs. In exchange for adopting the older, bonded pair, she'd need to move in with him for a month and get the dogs acclimated. Oh, and she wouldn't be sleeping in the guest room during her stay.

The deal is only for a month though. And she insisted they weren't going to fall in love, something he readily agreed with. They had the rules in place, what could possibly go wrong in four short weeks?

Get it here! https://tesssummersauthor.com/wicked-hot-silver-fox-1

WICKED HOT DOCTOR

A single doctor and a single lawyer walk into a bar...

Dr. Steven Ericson never thought a parking ticket would change his life, but that's exactly what happened the day he goes downtown to pay his forgotten ticket for an expired meter.

As the head of Boston General's ER, he doesn't have time for relationships, or at least he's never met a woman who made him want to make time.

That all changes when he meets Whitney Hayes. The dynamo attorney in high heels entices him to imagine carving out time for more than his usual one-night stand. Imagine his dismay to find out that she, too, doesn't do relationships—they're not in her 5-year plan.

Yeah, eff that. Her plan needs rewriting, and Steven's more than willing to supply the pen and ink to help with that.

https://tesssummersauthor.com/wicked-hot-doctor-1

WICKED HOT MEDICINE

Vengeance never tasted as sweet as it did on Hope Ericson's skin.

Sleeping with his rival's wife was an opportunity Dr. Evan Lacroix couldn't refuse.

Except, it turned out, she wasn't his wife—she was his sister.

Oh, the irony. It made it that much sweeter.

Unfortunately, when Hope realized his intentions, she didn't appreciate being a pawn in his game, and the sassy spitfire turned the tables on him.

Evan never saw it coming.

And now he needs to decide which is more important—love or revenge.

This isn't a book about enemies *to* lovers. It's about enemies with benefits—until the line between enemy and lover gets blurred.

https://tesssummersauthor.com/wicked-hot-medicine

SAN DIEGO SOCIAL SCENE

Operation Sex Kitten: (Ava and Travis)
   https://books2read.com/u/3yzyG6?affiliate=off
The General's Desire: (Brenna and Ron)
   https://books2read.com/u/m2Mpek?affiliate=off
Playing Dirty: (Cassie and Luke)
   https://books2read.com/u/3RNEdj?affiliate=off
Cinderella and the Marine: (Cooper and Katie)
   https://books2read.com/u/3LYenM?affiliate=off
The Heiress and the Mechanic: (Harper and Ben)
   https://books2read.com/u/bQVEn6?affiliate=off
Burning Her Resolve: (Grace and Ryan)
   https://books2read.com/u/bzoEXz?affiliate=off
This Is It: (Paige and Grant)
   https://books2read.com/ThisIsIt?affiliate=off

AGENTS OF ENSENADA

Ignition: (Kennedy and Dante)

https://books2read.com/u/47leJa?affiliate=off

Inferno: (Kennedy and Dante)

https://books2read.com/u/bpaYGJ?affiliate=off

Combustion: (Reagan and Mason)

https://books2read.com/u/baaME6?affiliate=off

Reignited: (Taren and Jacob)

https://books2read.com/u/3ya2Jl?affiliate=off

Flashpoint: (Sophia and Ramon)

https://books2read.com/TessSummersFlashpoint?affiliate=off

ABOUT THE AUTHOR

Tess Summers is a former businesswoman and teacher who always loved writing but never seemed to have time to sit down and write a short story, let alone a novel. Now battling MS, her life changed dramatically, and she has finally slowed down enough to start writing all the stories she's been wanting to tell, including the fun and sexy ones!

Married over twenty-six years with three grown children, Tess is a former dog foster mom who ended up failing and adopting them instead. She and her husband (and their three dogs) split their time between the desert of Arizona and the lakes of Michigan, so she's always in a climate that's not too hot and not too cold, but just right!

CONTACT ME!

Sign up for my newsletter: BookHip.com/SNGBXD

Email: TessSummersAuthor@yahoo.com

Visit my website: www.TessSummersAuthor.com

Facebook: http://facebook.com/TessSummersAuthor

My FB Group: Tess Summers Sizzling Playhouse

TikTok: https://www.tiktok.com/@tesssummersauthor

Instagram: https://www.instagram.com/tesssummers/

Amazon: https://amzn.to/2MHHhdK

BookBub https://www.bookbub.com/profile/tess-summers

Goodreads - https://www.goodreads.com/TessSummers

Twitter: http://twitter.com/@mmmTessIUD

Printed in Great Britain
by Amazon